BLOOD ON THE SANDS

Action-packed thriller fiction

The Max Donovan Adventures #4

RIALL NOLAN

THE BOOK FOLKS

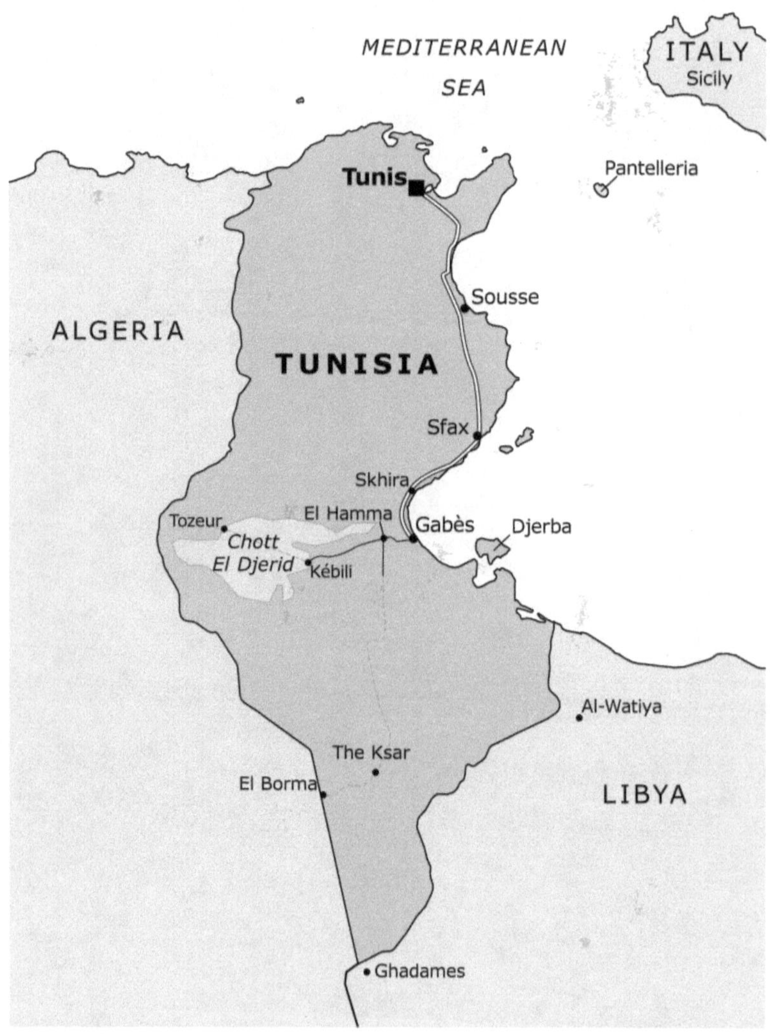

MEDITERRANEAN
SEA
ITALY
Sicily
Pantelleria
Tunis
Sousse
ALGERIA
TUNISIA
Sfax
Skhira
El Hamma
Tozeur
Chott
El Djerid
Kébili
Gabès
Djerba
Al-Watiya
The Ksar
El Borma
LIBYA
Ghadames

This is for William.

PROLOGUE

We stayed hidden down behind the low rock parapet, peeking out through gaps in the stones. Our visitors obviously knew we were up here somewhere, but they didn't yet know exactly where we were positioned. I hoped we could keep it that way as long as possible.

As we watched, one of the men carefully shot out the front right tire on our Peugeot. Then he walked slowly around the car and shot out all of the other tires, one by one. The reports of the gun were exceptionally loud in the quiet of the desert. She stirred beside me. "Oh, shit," she said in a low voice.

Oh, shit is right, I thought. The shooting of the tires basically signaled that they were intent on killing all of us and leaving the bodies here. The second man had opened our trunk now, and was busy transferring our water bottles and gas jerricans to their four-wheel drive.

The tire shooter stepped around to the front of the car and came forward a few steps. He looked up at the rock walls. He raised his pistol and waved it in our general direction.

CHAPTER ONE

I waited out in the hallway, my ear pressed against the closed door, trying to catch the conversation going on inside. I scanned the narrow corridor that led to the staircase, hoping that no one would decide to appear just now. Bali at the start of summer bakes in the heat and humidity, but the sweat pouring off me wasn't from the weather; it was nerves.

Because the next few seconds were going to be critical. I could hear voices inside the room but couldn't tell how many people were actually in there. Or even what they were talking about, since most of the conversation was in Indonesian. I can get along in a bunch of languages, but Indonesian doesn't happen to be one of them.

Still, I wished they would speak up a bit, so that I could get a general idea of how things were going inside the room. I sighed, unclipping one of the flash-bangs from my web belt. In a few seconds, I thought, it wasn't going to matter much, anyway.

If you've never experienced a flash-bang, you're in for a treat. Just don't plan on going back to work afterwards — you won't be able to hear, or perhaps even see, for some time. The G60 had been developed for the SAS in Britain in the 1970s, following a string of terrorist attacks. It's basically a non-lethal grenade, composed of magnesium and potassium perchlorate. It won't usually kill you, but it will most definitely mess you up. The intense flash will render you blind for at least five seconds. The equally impressive bang comes in at over 150 decibels, disorienting anyone in range by acting on the inner ear. I once heard a CIA guy refer to what a flash-bang does as 'subsonic deflagration.'

If you don't want to kill people, in other words – and I generally don't – the G60 is your weapon of choice. I'd bought two of them the day before for what I thought was a rather exorbitant price. But what the hell, I reasoned, I'm on an expense account, and besides, only one of them has to work.

I pulled earplugs out of my jacket pocket and fitted them in, making sure they were seated all the way. I glanced again at the hallway and the stairs that led down to the street. My driver, Budi, was waiting there in a rented Mercedes, together with the kid's parents. Denpasar is full of narrow little alleys barely wide enough for a single car. Sooner or later somebody else would come along and start honking, and in this neighborhood, that would get attention.

Time to get going. I stepped back across the hallway, all the better to kick the door in. Then I took a breath and pulled the pin on the flash-bang.

The door broke open surprisingly easily, with a sharp crack that got the attention of everyone inside. I got a quick look at four very surprised faces, a couple of ancient pistols on the table, and behind the table, the kid. Perfect, I thought, and shut my eyes tightly as I threw the flash-bang into the room. Here's hoping this works.

And work it did. The blast deafened everyone in the room instantly, and the accompanying flash took care of their vision.

No time to lose now. I charged into the room, grabbed the kid, and hauled him to his feet. His hands were tied behind him, but he could walk, after a fashion. Grabbing him by his belt buckle and the collar of his tie-dye shirt, I hustled him through the smoke, out the door, down the stairs to the street, and into the waiting car.

I pushed the kid into the middle of the back seat, got in and slammed the door. I tapped Budi, our trusty driver, on the shoulder. "Get us to the airport," I said, glancing behind to see if anyone had come out the door yet. All clear. "Fast."

The kid's mom and dad sat up front. She began to cry, while his dad grew a smile as broad as Sunday. "You got it, *pak*," murmured Budi, and we shot off down the narrow street towards Jalan Durian, on our way to safety.

* * *

That had been my exciting morning, and so far, at least, I'd seen no signs of any blowback. The kid and his parents had made it to the airport and onto the afternoon Bali Air flight to Jakarta, on their long way back to California. I stayed with them the whole time, just to make sure that no one – American or Indonesian – did anything stupid. By the time I waved goodbye at the gate, the kid was already starting to complain about being made to go home. His mother hadn't stopped crying. The kid's father shook my hand, gave me a tense smile, and handed over a large manila envelope stuffed with money.

On the way back from the airport, I opened the envelope, took out Budi's share and paid him, and then sat back and watched Asia go by, thinking about the job I'd just done. The kid had run into some bad luck, true enough, but he'd mostly brought it on himself. He'd attached himself to a small gang of European wastrels he'd met on the beach, and for a week or so, while they all sat around getting high, he apparently never shut up about how much money his mom and dad had back home in La Jolla. It's never a good idea to advertise your wealth, and although the kid probably impressed some of his newfound cronies, the smell of big money eventually reached the nostrils of some of the local *gali*, racketeers who promptly grabbed the kid up and held him for ransom.

It had taken three days for the parents to contact me, and just over a week for me to find their son. This isn't bad, as these things go. The fact that dad and mom were indeed rich as Croesus was a plus, because I could loosen tongues more easily with money than thumps on the head. Once I'd rescued him, the kid had revealed himself to be a major pain in the ass, as his conversation on our way to the airport made quite clear. I found myself marveling at how the local Indonesian *gali* had managed to put up with him for nearly two weeks without cutting his throat, and wondered whether anyone had ever translated *The Ransom of Red Chief* into Indonesian. Maybe, given a little more time, they'd have paid the parents to take him back.

No matter, I thought, as I sat in the hotel lobby later on that afternoon, relaxed and rested, a large cold bottle of Bintang at my side. I had enough money to keep me going for quite a while, and even add a bit to my retirement fund. In my line of work as a supplier, the money comes in at odd intervals and in odd ways. I make most of my living finding things – often people – and either returning them to where they belong or moving them out of harm's way. All too often, this involves getting myself into harm's way as well. It's well-paid much of the time, and risky almost all of the time. I knew very well that I was a fugitive from the law of averages, but I liked what I did, and I intended to keep on doing it until the final bell rang.

All of this lay far from my mind as I sipped my beer, relaxed, and watched a group of sweating and red-faced white guys over at the bar talking about golf. The scent of *kretek* cigarettes drifted through the room, as did elegant Indonesian ladies in colorful Imelda Marcos-type dresses with huge, puffed shoulders. Off to one side, a Filipino band was getting set up, replacing the morning's *gamelan* orchestra. Gamelan music is interesting, but not really calming to the nerves. At least, not if you've spent the morning the way I had.

"*Permisi, pak?*"

I looked up to see the hotel manager standing in front of me, hands crossed behind his back. He looked immaculate in a brightly patterned batik jacket, razor-creased white trousers, and a black velvet *kopiah* cap. Like everyone else in the country, he was smiling. "You are Mister Max Donovan?"

I smiled back, keeping a light grip on my beer bottle. "I am," I said, a little warily. If he'd come to settle scores after my recent escapade, at least I'd be able to get one good hit in.

But no. His smile broadened. "Very good." His hand came forward. Instead of the wavy *kris* dagger I might have been expecting, he held an envelope out to me.

"What's this?" I said, staring at the envelope. "Who sent it?" In my line of work, it pays to be careful. Hardly anything is what it seems, including white envelopes.

"No idea, sir," he said, holding the envelope steady. "It's a telex. The instructions were to deliver it personally, at once." He jiggled the envelope slightly and pushed it forward. "Please, sir, take it."

I put down my beer, stood up, and took the envelope from his hand. He bowed once, murmured *"terimah kasih,"* and faded back toward the reception desk.

What now? I thought, as I ripped open the envelope. Inside lay a single sheet of folded paper. The usual incomprehensible number strings and answerback codes at the top preceded the short, terse message.

'MAX,' it began.

> *BAD NEWS IMPERATIVE YOU COME*
> *IMMEDIATELY LONDON MEET ME*
> *PLATFORM NINE KINGS CROSS*
> *STATION NOON THURSDAY*
> *BONE*

Isaac Brown, known to a select few as 'Bone,' was a professor of anthropology at Berkeley and a long-time friend of mine. In addition to sharing the same general view of the world and its imperfections, we'd also shared a few adventures together. Although I supposedly live in the Bay Area, my line of work doesn't bring me back there very often, and so Bone functions as a kind of quiet and discreet business manager. Nobody's going to look too hard at a rotund, bearded academic with Buddy Holly glasses and an old briefcase stuffed with student papers.

Unless of course he happens to be wearing his trademark pig's tusks.

Bone got his nickname after he'd spent a year living up in the Western Highlands of Papua New Guinea. I was flying cargo in and out of various jungle airstrips there at the time, and brought him supplies every few weeks. He asked me once for reading material, so on my next trip to Port Moresby, I visited the Koki market and picked up a couple of crates of books for him. In Papua New Guinea, paperbacks were often used as ballast for some of the coastal trading ships, and you could buy books by the pound at the local markets. I dropped off the crates on my next run, and on the run after that, asked him what he'd particularly enjoyed reading. It turned out that we shared an appreciation for many of the same authors, as well as a taste for strong drink. And so began our friendship.

But about the bone. Professor Brown had done such a good job integrating himself into the local tribe that they made him an honorary member. I was invited, and flew in a dozen or so crates of San Miguel lager as my contribution to the day-long celebration. This featured a loud and enthusiastic *sing-sing*, together with the murder and roasting of quite a few pigs. The highlight of the day involved the good professor getting stripped naked except for a penis-sheath and some bushes covering his backside. They then decked him out with face paint and a dogs-tooth necklace. When he was pretty enough, they punched a hole through his nasal septum, and inserted a large pair of wild boar's tusks.

This hurt like hell, of course, but Bone – as he would be called from now on – was, now and forever more, a made guy, a bona fide member of the tribe. His nose swelled up to the size and color of a ripe tomato, and on my next trip up, I brought him some much-needed antibiotic ointment and a bunch of pills.

Today, Bone wears his tusks mainly while teaching, claiming that it helps to focus student attention. A few months ago, he'd informed me that for his sabbatical year, he was planning to go to Cambridge in the UK, where he hoped to confer with some of his Melanesianist cronies and explore the inner recesses of the libraries there.

I'd promised to stop by and see him on my way back to San Francisco, but I'd planned on doing that at the end of a longish swing through some of my favorite parts of Asia. I'd been hoping to spend a few more days – a week even – in Indonesia, looking around and maybe visiting some of the temples. One of the hotel receptionists had good English, a twinkle in her eye, and the coming weekend off, and she'd offered to show me around.

I sighed. Whatever Bone's 'bad news' was, it had better be good and bad, I thought.

I levered myself up out of my seat and headed for the hotel's travel desk, set back behind the fake palms at the edge of the lobby. In the other room, the Filipino band was just getting started on *Killer Joe*, a regional favorite. They'd apparently decided to see how far up they could crank their amplifiers.

I patted the telex in my pocket. Maybe, I thought, it was time to leave after all.

CHAPTER TWO

It's often a shock to come back to the Northern Hemisphere from a couple of months below the equator, and today was no exception. I'd landed at London's Heathrow Airport on a raw and wet midsummer day after a cramped and bumpy flight that ate at my soul and made my teeth rattle. England is glorious in good weather, but on this particular morning we had nothing but low grey overcast and short bursts of drizzle, which did little to improve the look of the grey industrial buildings on the bus ride into London.

King's Cross station at noon on Thursday heaved with hurrying people who avoided eye contact and didn't seem to have much interest in getting out of each other's way. Threading my way through the crowds to platform 9 was like running an obstacle course. Bone Brown waited for me at the gate, pig tusks nowhere in sight.

Bone projects substance and calm in a frame that is not particularly tall, but wide in the shoulders and somewhat portly. He possesses a full beard, shiny and black, which offsets a complete lack of hair up top. His eyes are warm, intelligent, and rather piercing; capable, I'm told, of striking terror into the hearts of underperforming students. To everyone else, he looks rather like an eccentric uncle.

I gave him a hug, catching a whiff of bay rum and tobacco smoke.

"Nice to see you, Max," he said. He looked at my shoulder bag. "Traveling light as usual, I see. Flight not too bad, I hope?"

My eyes were scratchy and my butt ached from too many hours in an aircraft seat, and I really wasn't in the mood for small talk. "About what you'd expect," I said. I looked around at the crowded platform – everyone was in motion, with a faint whiff of diesel fuel and ozone hanging over it all. "Why am I here? Your telex sounded dire."

He held up two tickets. "Let's get on the train, shall we? Departing in three minutes." He grabbed my arm and pushed me through the gate.

We walked along the concrete platform, found a half-empty carriage, and claimed two facing seats. As we settled in a moment later, a hoot from somewhere up in front of us signaled departure, and with a slight jerk the train began gliding out of the station.

Bone checked his pocket watch. "Eleven-seventeen," he announced. "Right on time. We should arrive at Cambridge station at twelve-oh-five."

"Amazing when you think of it," I murmured, as we emerged from the rail yards into the city proper. "Here, the train arrives at twelve-oh-five. In the US, the Amtrak will pull in sometime between two and four in the afternoon. And in places like Senegal, the train comes sometime on Thursday. Well, usually it does," I added.

Bone smiled. "You're back in civilization, Max," he said gently.

"I guess I am," I said, watching an endless wall of drab and identical rows of houses pass by. The train began to pick up speed now. "So, I'll ask again, what am I doing here?"

Bone had taken out his pipe and was messing with it, as he usually did before he answered an important question. "Do you remember my niece Hadley?"

"Hadley Holloway?" I dredged up a vague memory from years ago of a tall, gawky teenager with red hair, freckles, and bright, curious eyes. "What about Hadley?"

"She's gone," said Bone. "Missing. I think someone's kidnapped her."

I sat up in my seat. "She's gone missing? Where?"

"When last heard from, she was in Tunisia. As for who's done the kidnapping, I haven't a clue."

He's starting to talk like a local, I thought. "You'd better explain."

Bone sighed. "My niece Hadley is a highly intelligent but extremely independent and willful young woman. Far too clever to take advice most of the time. You haven't seen her for a few years, I know. She graduated from Stanford with a degree in history, and asked me about where to continue her studies."

He shook his head. "I feel responsible for what's happened. You see, I advised her to come to the UK for her graduate training, rather than bother with those American schools and all their silly requirements."

He frowned. "Did you know that if you're smart and hard-working, you can get a PhD in three years here? It takes twice as long, usually, in the US. Hadley had always been interested in history – another of those disciplines it's almost impossible to make money with." He smiled faintly. "Like my own."

He looked out the window, and then continued.

"Unfortunately, this time she followed my advice, and was offered a place at Cambridge. Dual degree – archaeology and history. The tuition was far less than she would have paid at home. It was a marvelous opportunity, really."

"I'm sure," I said. "And we mustn't forget the great weather and outstanding food."

Bone ignored this remark. "And she had the opportunity to work with Birdwhistle himself."

"Birdwhistle?"

"Professor Nigel Birdwhistle. One of the world's experts on Ottoman history. He's her tutor. Her advisor, as we would say. Hadley is thriving here, from everything I've heard. Loves the place, adores her tutor, and it seems she's found her passion."

"A boyfriend?"

He frowned. "No, Max. An *academic* passion. The Ottomans in Africa, to be precise. Apparently the Ottomans had their fingers on just about every part of North Africa, from Egypt to Morocco. Hadley was fascinated with that."

"And now she's missing."

Bone nodded. "She was in Tunisia, doing fieldwork for her dissertation. She'd been sending her field notes back to Birdwhistle and checking in by phone. She also called me regularly, once a week. Always at the same time. She sent a cable telling me she'd be calling with 'exciting news.' Then communications stopped; I never heard anything more from her. And that's when I sent you that telex."

I stared out the window for a moment. The city had gradually given way to the quiet rolling countryside of East Anglia. Open fields, wooded copses and the occasional town flashed by as the train sped toward Cambridge. The rain had cleared, the sun starting to push its way through the clouds. Sheep and cows grazed peacefully in the fields, and overhead, flocks of birds played tag. On a good day, I thought, this place isn't half bad. I cleared my throat. "Have you called the police yet?"

He shook his head. "No. And I really don't want to, not at this stage. I will if I have to, but I wanted to talk to you first."

"You want me to go to Tunis, don't you?"

"I'm afraid I do," he said, nodding. "I trust your instincts and abilities far more than I do the authorities."

"I can well understand that," I said.

Bone glanced over at me. "Speaking of the police, however, I don't suppose there's any reason why you can't go back there, is there?"

I shook my head, thinking back a few years to when I'd done a stint on contract in Tunisia. My job had involved flying a modified PBY Catalina at just above stall speed a hundred meters or so above the desert, dragging a magnetometer array behind me on a cable.

The PBY belonged to a Canadian prospecting company, and we were a team of six – a copilot, a mechanic, and three skinny techies to look at the readouts. They were looking for oil, of course. We flew patterns every day, crisscrossing the desert, down into the sharp corner where Tunisia meets Algeria to the west and Libya to the east. We took care not to cross national boundaries – well, more or less – and operated out of a dinky airstrip at El Borma, where we slept beside the old aircraft in a converted Nissen hut and tried to stay out of the sun when we weren't flying.

The science of all of this was a little mysterious to me, and I'm not sure they ever found anything terribly important. I didn't care. The job paid well and kept me out of sight, which was just what I needed at the time, having annoyed some of Bob Denard's mercenaries out in the Comoros a bit earlier.

I figured – rightly – that no one would think to look for me out in the middle of the desert. I passed my days reading old paperback novels, chatting with the ground crew, and working on my tan. The rest of the time I spent trying to keep the old PBY in the air. At one point we got shot at by some guys on camels, but aside from that, my time in Tunisia was about as exciting as watching grass grow.

"No," I said finally. "Nobody wants to get even with me in Tunisia."

"Good," said Bone. "Your French is still good, I'm sure. How about Arabic?"

I snorted. "I wouldn't rely on me for much in that department," I said. "I learned some stuff from the ground crew down in El Borma. Most of it is unsuitable for polite company."

Bone chuckled. "'*You taught me language; and my profit on't is, I know how to curse.*' That's from–"

"*The Tempest*," I said. "Shakespeare. I didn't just read sleazy adventure novels down there in the desert, you know?"

I looked again at the quiet, peaceful countryside slipping past the train. There were open fields, groves of trees here and there, and occasional herds of livestock scattered across the hillsides. The rain had washed everything clean, and the whole place looked as if it had been thoroughly gone over by an army of gardeners. It's like a theme park, I thought, thinking back to the woods and jungles that I felt much more at home in. This was, I decided, a very safe environment. And maybe a very boring one, too, once you'd spent a little time in it.

"So," I said finally, "if I need to be in Tunisia looking for Hadley, then what am I doing riding the train to Cambridge with you?"

"We both need more information on what Hadley was actually doing in Tunisia. And for that, Nigel Birdwhistle is the man. We're meeting him this afternoon. And we'll have another chance to talk later this evening, at High Table."

"High Table? Like in the movies, where they all wear robes and chant in Latin?"

Bone smiled. "Robes, yes. Not quite so much Latin these days. You'll find it interesting, Max, I'm sure." He checked his watch. "Arriving in five minutes or so. We'll get a cab into town and a late lunch before we meet Birdwhistle."

CHAPTER THREE

We holed up in the back room at the Eagle on Bene't Street, just off King's Parade. It was well past rush hour by now, and the place had pretty much emptied out. Bone and I were the only two occupants of an ancient wooden table wedged into a corner. As always, I sat facing the door. I'd made a note of where the doors and windows were when we came in, just in case a swift exit was called for.

Bone noticed me doing it and chuckled. "Old habits, eh, Max? Or is someone actually following you?"

I shook my head. "I very much doubt it. The folks I dealt with in Bali were strictly locals. I don't think any of them would even have the plane fare to get here. And near as I could tell, most of them didn't speak English."

"Our lucky day, then," said Bone. He glanced at the menu. "Food in this place tends to be, well, hearty. You're familiar with English cooking, I assume?"

I grinned, thinking of some past experiences. "I don't see toad-in-the-hole," I said.

"No," said Bone drily. "And they don't seem to have spotted dick, either. So perhaps I could suggest the fish and chips?"

"Safe enough," I said. We gave our orders to an earnest young man with a ring through his nose, and he hurried off to the kitchen.

That reminded me. I turned to Bone. "You, ah, wear your thing much around here?"

Bone smiled and shook his head. "England is well known for its tolerance of eccentrics, but I'm afraid that might not extend to a full set of pig's tusks. This isn't Berkeley, after all. In any case" – he sniffed – "my mustache conceals the hole in my nose, unless you look closely."

I looked around at the room. The walls, I saw, were covered with old photographs and scrawled messages. I leaned forward to get a better look. "Pilots for the most part," said Bone. "Second World War. East Anglia's airfields were where the planes took off to bomb Germany."

I nodded, looking at the lists of names, the devil-may-care messages, the photographs of young British and American boys in their crush caps and fleece jackets. As a pilot myself, I'd heard all the debates over who had the better aircraft, but in the end, it didn't seem to matter; the death rate had been shocking.

"There's said to be a lot more graffiti under the paintwork," Bone added. "I wonder how many of them made it through the war?"

I thought about old pilots and bold pilots, and about who'd beaten the odds and survived, and who had not. It must have been terrifying. I'd been up in a few of these old planes, and had taken the controls of a Fortress once for just a few minutes, courtesy of an old-timer I'd been friends with some years ago. The thing was basically put together with wire, tape and prayers, and the thought of flying it at night over enemy territory into volleys of flak while carrying thousands of kilos of high explosive wasn't at all appealing.

So I looked at the pictures of all the brash young men, and read some of their messages, and wondered, like Bone, how many of them had made it back. And how many of those might have come back here to this very room, to drink a quiet toast to their lost comrades.

"Max." Bone's voice snapped me out of it.

"Hah?"

"Our food's here." Plates of fish and chips had materialized beside us, together with two pints of warm beer. "Let's eat. And while we do, I'll fill you in on what little I know about what Hadley was doing at the time she disappeared."

The food proved to be surprisingly good. Delicious, in fact. I suddenly realized that apart from some lousy airline food, I had eaten nothing much of substance since leaving Bali. I tucked in with a vengeance as Bone talked.

"As I said, this is all my fault, really," he began. "I was the one who suggested to Hadley that she might do better getting her degree in the UK. Unlike Americans, who can't seem to remember what happened last week, people here are obsessed with history. Nowhere more so, I suppose, than places like Cambridge. For most people in this country, the Second World War was yesterday morning."

He waved his fork around the room vaguely. "Cambridge University has been a going concern for nearly eight hundred years. This pub we're in opened sometime in the 1600s. Crick and Watson used to drink here; this is where they announced to the other patrons that they'd discovered the structure of DNA. The whole place is absolutely alive with history."

He took a sip of his beer and continued. "Anyway, I thought Hadley's own interests in history might be better served in a place like this, so I encouraged her to apply. And indeed, she has thrived here. She already had pretty good French from college study abroad, but after she came here two years ago, she threw herself into studying Arabic and Turkish."

He set down his knife and fork. "Six months ago, she left for Tunis. She had a room in the dormitory at the Bourguiba Institute, and was taking advanced Arabic classes there in addition to doing her research. We set up a strict schedule for checking in, twice a week. And then she disappeared."

I swallowed the last of my fish. "Couldn't she just be, I don't know, with a boyfriend or something? People go off the radar all the time, you know?"

Bone gave me a look. "*You* do that, Max, but most other people don't. Hadley is one of the most sensible young people I know."

"Fair point," I said. I drank the last of my beer. Despite being room temperature, the beer wasn't at all bad, in fact. I was thinking of ordering another when Bone stood up.

"Time to go," he announced.

We came out of the Eagle and walked up the street, onto King's Parade. Students in droves passed by on bicycles, weaving awkwardly through the pedestrians. "Ever thought about getting one of those?" I said to Bone.

He snorted. "Unbelievably dangerous if you ask me. I walk everywhere here, it's good for the waistline."

We passed the King's College gate on our left and Great St. Mary's Church on the right, its fence posts covered with flyers for concerts, meetings, and exhibitions. "I take it you're liking your sabbatical here," I said.

"Oh, definitely," said Bone. "The food and the weather leave a bit to be desired, of course, particularly if you're coming from California, but the rest of it is quite wonderful in a way. If a bit peculiar. Cambridge isn't really one place, you see. It's a loose collection of several dozen distinct colleges, each with its own physical establishment, its own group of fellows, its own chapel, and all that. Dozens of little academic subcultures. Rather like the tribes in Highlands New Guinea, really."

"It sounds peculiar, all right. Isn't Oxford set up pretty much the same way?"

Bone shot me a withering glance. "No one here talks about Oxford, Max. Most of my colleagues simply refer to it as 'the other place.'"

We turned off onto one of the narrow side streets. Ancient brick and stone walls to either side created a corridor down which we walked, along the uneven cobblestones. "My college is just down here. Most Cambridge colleges are behind walls. In earlier times, these were basically religious seminaries, dedicated to churning out choirboys and clergy. Fellows lived inside the walls, and many still do. One's college at Cambridge determines a great deal about your experience here, and indeed, your life afterwards. As a don, it's an extraordinary way to live; quite appealing to a certain type of person. One of whom," he added, "you're about to meet."

CHAPTER FOUR

We stopped in front of the college gates. Bone produced a laminated card which he showed to the porter at the entrance, who nodded and waved us along. "In we go," said Bone.

Behind the wall, things opened up into a broad courtyard, a sort of hollow square enclosed by buildings of massive grey stone, with a wide expanse of carefully tended grass in the center. At one corner stood a chapel.

Turrets with crenellations and narrow windows stood guard at the corners, making the place look more like an ancient fortress than a modern institution of higher learning. The immaculate grass on the central green would, I thought, be the envy of many a golf course manager in the US. Small signs around the periphery, in four languages, told people not to walk on it.

Beyond the first courtyard, we went through a vaulted passage to a second, and further on, a third. "They must spend a lot of time cutting the grass and polishing the stone around here," I observed.

"They can afford it," replied Bone. "Some of these colleges have more money than they know what to do with. The better-off ones have collections – wine, paintings, silver plate, what-have-you – worth millions, and they've been at it for centuries.

"These greens," he said, indicating the manicured lawns with a sweep of his hand, "were originally designed to facilitate contemplation, deep thought, that sort of thing." He pointed to one of the signs. "But only the senior fellows are actually allowed to walk on them."

Turning into a narrow passageway at the end of the third courtyard, we began to climb a set of narrow, steep stairs. The stairs, like the building itself, looked ancient. "Yes," said Bone, as if reading my thoughts. "They built all this sometime in the early 1600s. They call it the New Annex, of course. Birdwhistle's study is up here at the top. He likes to work there in the afternoon."

The professor's lair on the third floor was tucked away down a dimly lit corridor. Neither the floor nor the walls were quite plumb. Bone knocked on a door at the end of the hallway, and when he heard a grunt from the other side, opened it.

We found Professor Nigel Birdwhistle seated at a broad table, books and papers spread out in front of him. He muttered to himself as he made notes in a spidery hand in a thick notebook. Looking up, he flashed a delighted smile as he caught sight of Bone. "Ah, Brown, how splendid, you've come just in time."

"In time for what?" asked Bone.

"In time to save me from any more of this damned drivel," he said, indicating the papers in front of him. "It's simply appalling the rubbish some of my colleagues manage to get published. And of course we've all got to read the stuff, on the off chance – the extremely *thin* off chance, may I say – that one of them actually says something intelligent."

He closed the notebook and turned to me. "And this is your friend, of course. The adventurous one you've been telling me about. Mr. Donovan, is it?"

I shook his hand. "Call me Max."

Tall and thin, Birdwhistle sported half-glasses balanced on the tip of a long nose. His large ears, partly covered by an unruly thatch of greying blond hair, reminded me of a hound dog. He wore a baggy pair of trousers and an ancient knit sweater unraveling at the cuffs and neck; it looked as if it had once been the kind of Christmas present you hid away in a drawer somewhere, or gave to the Salvation Army.

His study could have been the model for the Old Curiosity Shop. An ancient fireplace occupied most of one wall. On the mantelpiece sat a large stuffed owl, together with what looked like a very old sword. On the other wall hung a large red banner with a gold-embroidered artillery piece and the word 'Arsenal' underneath it. Every other square inch of space in the room contained books and papers, some in bookcases, others on the floor. A tiny window let in some light and air, but otherwise, we might as well have been in a mineshaft.

We sat on either side of Birdwhistle as he cleared books and papers out of the way. He peered at me over his half-glasses. "What is it that you actually do, Mr. Donovan? If you don't mind my asking, of course."

"I find things, Professor," I said in what I hoped was a confident, professional manner. "All kinds of things. Including people," I added.

He nodded. "Do you think you can find Ms. Holloway?"

"I can try," I replied, "but it would help if I had a little more information. You're Hadley's supervisor, right?"

"I am her tutor, yes. Brilliant young woman, one of the best students I've ever had." He frowned. "Aside from her tendency to, ah, speak her mind a little too freely." He smiled at us. "Although that seems to be a fairly common thing where you chaps come from, wouldn't you say?"

I decided not to bite. Instead, I asked, "What gave her the idea to go to Tunisia?"

Birdwhistle gave a quick bob of the head, his eyes bright like a bird's. "Yes, Tunisia, of course. Well, that was Hadley's own idea, really. She came to Cambridge with an interest in Ottoman history, but of course, true scholars need to have some kind of speciality." He pronounced *specialty* with an extra set of syllables. "She soon had hers picked out. She was very interested in the last days of the Ottoman Empire – the way it all came apart at the end."

He leaned forward, warming to his subject. "The Ottoman Empire had been in decline for centuries, you see. They failed in their last attempt to take Vienna in 1683, and from that point on, well, it was all downhill." His eyebrows rose. "But they'd had an extraordinary run, really; over six hundred years, dominating over a dozen countries.

"One of them was Tunisia. Tunisia was part of the Empire from the 1500s until the arrival of the French in 1881. By the time the French got there, the Beylik of Tunis had become semi-autonomous. The French allowed the Bey to remain, but not to govern."

I nodded. I wasn't sure where this was all going, but there was no stopping Birdwhistle now.

He cleared his throat and plowed on. "The last Bey of Tunis was Muhammed VIII El-Amin, otherwise known as Lamine Bey. In 1957, Habib Bourguiba, the current President of Tunisia, gave Lamine Bey his marching orders, and sent him and his family to live in a squalid apartment in the city, practically penniless and without an iota of power."

"I don't quite see—"

"Ms. Holloway became very interested in a legend that grew up during that time. In fact, I'd say she became obsessed with it. And so she went to Tunis determined to get to the bottom of the story." He paused.

I spoke. "And the story is?"

Birdwhistle stood up. "It's better if I show you," he said. He selected a folder from a pile on the desk, and opened it, taking out an 8 x 10 photograph. "Do you know what this is?"

We both peered forward to look at the photograph. "It's a brooch," said Bone at last. "A pin of some sort, quite large and gaudy. Lots of what look like diamonds and things." He shook his head. "Not really my taste, I have to say."

I agreed with him, although I didn't feel the need to say so right now.

"It's a *chelengk*," Birdwhistle said. He pronounced it *shell-enk*. "Or rather, *the* chelengk."

"The what?"

"The chelengk," said Birdwhistle, "is a Turkish military decoration. And one of the most famous pieces of jewelry in British history. It's meant to be worn on a turban. This diamond chelengk was given to Admiral Lord Nelson by Sultan Selim III of Turkey, after the Battle of the Nile." He cocked his head and peered at me. "You've heard of Lord Nelson, I presume?"

I drew myself up. "*England expects that every man will do his duty*," I intoned. And then for good measure, I added, "*Never mind the maneuvers, go straight at 'em.*"

"Yes, quite," said Birdwhistle approvingly. "The Battle of the Nile, 1798, Aboukir Bay. The Sultan had the chelengk made specially, to commemorate the occasion." He traced the outline of the jewel with a bony finger. "There are thirteen rays, studded with diamonds, to represent all the French ships lost. Nelson quite liked it and wore it on his hat."

Bone shook his head. "It just looks like an ostentatious piece of cheap jewelry to me," he said. "No doubt it's of some significance to people here. But I don't understand what on earth it's got to do with Hadley."

"Oh, the chelengk has everything to do with our Hadley, dear chap. It's what she was looking for when she went missing. And what she had apparently found. Her last message to me was 'I have found it.'"

He caught our expressions and hurried on. "The chelengk passed out of Nelson's family eventually, and became the most prized acquisition of our Maritime Museum. But in 1951, it was stolen by a thief named George Chatham – 'Taters' to his friends – and sold off to someone or other."

"Did they ever get it back?" I asked, staring at the photograph.

"Never," said Birdwhistle. "No trace of it has ever been found. Until" – he held up a finger – "a year or so ago. Ms. Holloway was interviewing Tunisian immigrants in France, collecting their memories of the handover of power, when she was told a very interesting story concerning none other than the chelengk."

He rubbed his hands together, warming to his subject. "According to the teller of this tale, the chelengk was given to the Bey of Tunis."

I blinked. "I don't understand what this chelengk has to do with the Bey of Tunis," I said. "And anyway, hadn't the Ottomans left Tunisia a long time ago?"

"Not exactly," said Birdwhistle. "Although the French declared Tunisia their 'Protectorate' in the 1880s, they allowed the Turkish Bey to remain, as a largely symbolic figurehead. If we move forward to the 1950s, however, Tunisia was headed towards independence, and Habib Bourguiba was intent on consolidating power. The Bey had to go. And go he did, in 1957, banished from his palace in Carthage. The story Ms. Holloway collected told of how a legendary piece of Ottoman jewelry had been stolen from the British, sold on several times to various people, and eventually bought back by a group of Turks, who sent it to Tunisia and presented it to Lamine Bey. This piece of jewelry, as you can guess, was none other than the chelengk.

"The Bey kept it as part of his private treasure. When he was deposed, he was suddenly penniless, with virtually nothing to his name but a small collection of family jewels. The poor man was desperate for money, simply to eat. Eventually, it was said, he sold the chelengk and the rest of the jewels to buy food for himself, his wife, and the princess."

"What happened to the chelengk after that?" asked Bone.

Birdwhistle shrugged. "No one really knows. The story goes that the jewels were sold to one of the merchants in the *souk*, in the Tunis Medina, and disappeared again. The original chelengk was said to have more than three hundred diamonds on it. The people who told this story to Hadley assumed that it had been broken up, melted down, and reworked into new jewelry."

"But maybe not," I murmured.

"Yes," said Birdwhistle. "Precisely."

We all sat silently for a moment, thinking about this. Then Bone spoke. "Three hundred diamonds, even small ones," he said, "would make this chelengk rather valuable, wouldn't it?"

Birdwhistle nodded. "Most assuredly. As a single piece of jewelry, it's certainly valuable. Broken up, it's probably worth even more. But it's much more than that to the

British. It's a symbol. And as such, it's… well, it's absolutely priceless."

"And Hadley's last message to you was 'I have found it.'" Bone spoke quietly.

"Yes. I sent a telegram of congratulations, told her I'd phone on the weekend. I called the Bourguiba Institute, was told she wasn't in her room, and no one had seen her for several days. That's when I got hold of you, Isaac."

"I also tried to get in touch with her," said Bone. "And by that time I was starting to get worried." He turned to me. "When I heard that she'd lost touch with Professor Birdwhistle, I knew something bad had happened. So that's when I contacted you."

"Then it's been almost a week since she dropped out of sight," I said. "That's not good."

"Well, that's quite obvious, isn't it?" said Birdwhistle, a bit peevishly. "The question is, what are we going to do about it?"

I took a breath. "I don't know about you two, but I'm planning to go and find her." I shot a glance at Bone. "And bring her back to you."

CHAPTER FIVE

We filed slowly into Great Hall, Birdwhistle in the lead. I watched him closely for behavioral clues. I was totally out of my element here, about to participate in something of which I had very little understanding.

It began with the robe. Or gown, as Bone referred to it. Everyone in the dark-paneled room was wearing one, including me. Birdwhistle had found a spare in his office closet, and lent it to me for the occasion. Black and made out of thick, scratchy material, the robe had long, strange sleeves ending in points. To add insult to injury, I was made to wear a borrowed necktie as well.

"I look like a crow," I complained to Bone in the vestibule, as we put them on. "Or a bat. I haven't worn something like this since I graduated from high school."

"You look exactly like everyone else," said Bone crisply as he straightened the shoulders of my gown. "And that, my dear Max, is the point. This is what the anthropologists call a ritual of inclusion. So, shut up, please, and just follow our lead. You'll be fine."

We assembled in a narrow corridor lined with portraits of ancient worthies, and walked single-file up a short flight of stairs, emerging out onto a raised dais. It reminded me of grade-school plays, and the way we'd all troop in and line up. A long wooden table, big enough to seat thirty people, dominated the dais. This must be the legendary High Table, I thought.

Just before we went through the door, Birdwhistle took my arm. "Not a word to the Master about the chelengk, dear boy," he whispered. "Or about Hadley. Let me take care of telling him."

And then we were walking out into Great Hall. Below the dais, the hall extended far back into the gloom, filled with other tables set in rows perpendicular to us. People wearing robes similar to ours were coming in from the side doors to fill the lower tables.

"Students," whispered Bone.

The walls on either side of the hall displayed large portraits of long-dead people, together with tapestries and flags, some bearing coats of arms.

This is what Dracula's castle must have looked like, I thought. I could very well imagine it two hundred years ago, oil lamps flickering in their sconces, sending strange shadows across the walls. Wolves howling in the snowy forest outside.

At the end of the hall, facing us, hung the largest portrait of them all, an aristocratic-looking gentleman dressed in billowing embroidered robes and wearing a very odd-looking hat. One hand held what appeared to be a Bible, the other clutched a sword.

"That's Sir Magnus Greatorex," said Bone. "The founder and benefactor of the college. Quite bloodthirsty in his defense of the faith, so they say. He died from eating undercooked swan." He caught my look. "Don't worry. It's not on the menu this evening."

"Good to know," I murmured, already starting to sweat in my heavy gown. "No background music, anyway. That's a plus, isn't it?"

Bone smiled – our private joke. "Yes," he said, "but if there were, I could take care of that, as you know." He took my arm. "Now come and meet the Master."

Bone steered me toward a pleasant-looking gentleman in thick spectacles, standing at the center of High Table. He smiled broadly as he caught sight of Bone.

"Professor Brown," he said, extending his hand. His gaze swiveled to take me in. "And this is your American guest, I presume?"

"This is Max Donovan, sir. I believe I spoke to you about him."

"Indeed you did." The man's eyes shone with warmth and interest. "Is it Dr. Donovan, or Professor Donovan?"

I blinked. "Just Max, actually."

He laughed. "Splendid. In that case, I'm Harry." He shook my hand, a firm warm grip, and then he turned, indicating the chair beside his own. "Why don't you sit here, Max. Isaac can sit across the table from us, and we can chat. I've another guest coming, I believe, as well. Birdwhistle, take that other chair there, will you?"

For the next few moments, we busied ourselves with getting settled. I eventually figured out how to arrange the sleeves of my gown to avoid knocking over the glasses. All the while, students and late-arriving fellows continued to file in and take their seats.

I'd just gotten sorted out when there was a bell and a loud gong, and everyone stood up. I struggled to my feet, bowing my head with the others as someone in the room intoned an elaborate Latin grace in a deep and rolling voice. There was a pause, and then the entire company – except me – gave the response "*deo gratias.*"

Finally, we were seated again. The Master sat on my left, Bone sat directly across from me, and to his right, another gentleman, just arrived, had taken the chair next to Birdwhistle. He sat down with a murmured apology. He looked tanned and fit, with a short Van Dyck beard and tinted eyeglasses. After a moment, I realized that he was almost certainly an Arab.

My guess was confirmed as Birdwhistle made the introductions. "Max, this is Ali Akbar Al-Trabelsi, one of my former students" – he beamed – "who has done very well for himself, if I may say."

"You're most kind." Al-Trabelsi had a rich, deep voice. We shook hands across the table. "It's a pleasure to come back to college after so long." He waved a hand around the room. "So many memories."

"Well, yes," said the Master. "And it's always a pleasure for us to have such a distinguished guest." He turned to me. "Mr. Trabelsi is the economic attaché with the Libyan embassy in London." He smiled. "And in recognition of his high status, we all agreed to relax our dress code for him this evening."

I looked again at Al-Trabelsi. He wore the same academic gown as everyone else, but without a necktie. Instead, his formal shirt was collarless, and buttoned at the neck. Al-Trabelsi smiled. "Our people," he said, "don't care much for neckties. It's really a symbol of the Crusades."

I nodded in sympathy. My own necktie was killing me, and I pulled at it to loosen things up a bit. "Weren't the Crusades almost a thousand years ago, Mr. Trabelsi?"

His smile broadened, although I noticed that the good cheer didn't go as far up as his eyes. "Not even last week for many of us, Mr. Donovan. Do you remember what your writer Faulkner said?"

I did indeed remember. *"The past is never dead,"* I quoted. *"It's not even past."*

"Well said," said the Master, lightening the moment. Servers had appeared by now, setting plates of roast beef and boiled vegetables in front of us. Wine was passed and poured. Al-Trabelsi asked for, and was given, sparkling water.

After a moment, the Master turned to me. "And what brings you to college tonight, Mr. Donovan? Are you a Cambridge alumnus, by any chance?"

I was in the process of composing an answer when Bone spoke up. "Max and I are old friends. Max is, ah, an international negotiator."

The Master beamed. "You don't say. I did a bit of international work myself, prior to coming back to Cambridge. We should chat sometime."

Al-Trabelsi smiled at me. "Are you teaching here now, Mr. Donovan?"

I shook my head, wondering how much to say to these people. Again, Bone saved me. "Max is just visiting," he said. "He's about to go on holiday."

"Holiday? How nice," said the Master. "Where, may I ask?"

"Tunisia," I said brightly. I've learned over the years that if you're going to lie to people, then try to tell at least a bit of the truth. "I'm, ah, going to Tunis."

Al-Trabelsi glanced up from the fig pudding he was wrestling with. "Tunis, how interesting. Right next door to us. What attracts you there?"

"They say it's cheap this time of year," I said offhandedly. "There are ancient ruins. And the beaches are supposed to be nice." I couldn't help but add, "Better weather, too."

Everyone laughed uneasily. Finally, Al-Trabelsi spoke. "We have better ruins and beaches in Libya, Mr. Donovan. Unfortunately, it's rather difficult for people like you to go there just at present." He smiled nicely as he spoke.

"So I've heard," I said evenly. "Perhaps, things will change."

"Things always change, don't they, if you wait long enough?" said the Master jovially. "Well, jolly good. I hope you have a splendid time."

Birdwhistle had lost interest in us during this exchange, and was just getting to the punch line of a joke he was telling to the man on his other side. "…so then she said, *'I've told that girl a thousand times not to put her feet on the furniture!'*" Hearty chuckles erupted down at his end of the table.

A few moments later the gong sounded again. We stood as another lengthy benediction was pronounced in Latin. We said our goodbyes, and as we made our way out of the hall, I murmured to Bone, "Tell me you don't have to do this every night?"

I looked behind to see Birdwhistle shuffling slowly along, locked in conversation with Al-Trabelsi as they moved toward the door.

Bone chuckled. "It's not as bad as it might seem. Most of the fellows are quite interesting, and a few of them are eccentric. It makes for good entertainment most of the time."

We said goodnight to the porter and walked out through the gate onto Sidney Street. It was very pleasant, I thought, to be here on a warm summer evening in the company of an old friend, strolling down a cobbled street in the dark, past buildings hundreds of years old. Here and there, lights shone in some of the windows, and through them I could see books piled on desks, laboratory benches with odd bits of equipment, and once in a while, someone bent over a contraption of some sort.

"It's rather remarkable, really," Bone was saying. "This entire place is ancient, but down in some of these basement labs, people are working on things that most of us can't even imagine."

"You mean like time travel, or interstellar flight?"

"You probably meant that as a joke, but yes, I wouldn't be at all surprised if someone here came up with something like that." He puffed his pipe. "And then, there are the ghosts. Cambridge is reputed to be full of them. And not just ghosts, either – actual bodies. Did you know that Cromwell's skull is supposed to be buried under one of the college courtyards?"

A pair of students clattered by on their bicycles, taillights winking on and off as they disappeared into the murk. Just then I sensed headlights approaching from behind us, and turned to see a car coming fast down the narrow street. "Let's step off to the side," I said to Bone. "I don't think this guy can see us."

"Yes, I think we'd better."

The car bore straight down the road toward us. It almost seemed to be accelerating as it got closer.

It was indeed accelerating, I realized. The motor roared loudly as it headed straight for us. I grabbed Bone, pushing him hard into a doorway, just as the car flew by. Its side mirror slapped my arm, hard, and then it was gone.

But not before I'd gotten the plate number, clearly illuminated as it flashed by. As the big car sped out of sight, I'd started repeating it to myself. "Paper. Pencil," I hissed to Bone, repeating the number sequence over and over, before I could forget it.

He passed them to me, and I scribbled the numbers and letters in his notebook.

My breathing steadied. "Bastard tried to run us down," I said finally.

"So it would appear," said Bone. "We had a narrow escape just now. Thank you, Max. Quick thinking."

"We're not done yet," I muttered. "Tomorrow, you need to call the police, report this, and find out whose car that is. Will you do that?"

"Most assuredly."

Our little drama over, we walked on. After a moment, I said. "Did I say too much in there? About Tunisia, I mean?"

Bone shook his head. "No, not at all. Plenty of people around here go to Tunisia on holiday. None of them need to know why you're going. With any luck, you can find Hadley and get her back before people realize she's missing. It'll all be much easier that way."

"Well, I can try," I said. "But shouldn't somebody at least tell the university she's gone?"

"Ordinarily, yes," said Bone. "And I suppose we'll have to, quite soon now. But I want you to try to find her yourself first. There'll be an awful fuss if she's officially listed as missing, and right now, we've no real proof that she *is* actually missing. All we're sure of is that no one knows where she is."

"That might be what you academics call a distinction without a difference," I said drily.

"I suppose so," said Bone. "But the sooner you find her, the better. And if I wanted to find someone, I can't think of a better person to call on than you."

I thought for a moment. "So, the only people who know about the chelengk, and about Hadley, are you, me, and Birdwhistle; is that right?"

Bone nodded.

"We'll give it until the end of the week, then," I said. "If I haven't found her by that time, you really have to call the authorities."

"I suppose so," said Bone grudgingly. "But God, what a mess that will be. For everyone."

I smiled at him. "Then let's just do our best in the meantime, shall we?"

We carried on slowly down the street, our gowns rustling in the soft darkness. It had sprinkled a bit during dinner, and the cobblestones gleamed, reflecting the streetlamps above. I spoke again. "That dinner was pretty, ah, strange, don't you think?"

Bone smiled. "It's a ritual, Max. I told you that. And like all rituals, it serves a very important purpose."

"Dressing up in gowns and speaking Latin?"

"Max, this is the way the UK trains its ruling class. It's not an accident that almost all of the important political figures in this country come from either Oxford or Cambridge. The High Table rituals are a bonding event. The future rulers get to know one another, they are introduced to older, more powerful members of the establishment, and they are schooled in the language and lore of power. By the time they graduate, they are ready."

I thought about that for a few moments as we walked along. "So, it's kind of an incubator for the elite," I said after a moment. "But it's really just a closed-in world. How much do these folks really know or care about what's going on outside the walls? In other countries, other places?"

Bone gave a short laugh. "More than you might think. Don't forget, Max, that until quite recently, these people were actually running many of those other countries."

We came through the Lion Yard onto St. Andrew's Street and stopped in front of the taxi rank. "Time we were heading home," Bone said. "You have a big day tomorrow."

"I do indeed," I said as we climbed into the cab.

CHAPTER SIX

The Air France Airbus did a slow turn over the coastline and lined itself up for the approach, flaps rumbling down and engines changing pitch as the big plane hung in the air for a moment before starting to fall slowly earthward.

Below us lay the Lac de Tunis, the narrow arms of La Goulette, and beyond, the broad Mediterranean, blue and sparkly in the afternoon sun. I tore my eyes away from the window and looked around me at the business-class cabin. Bone had somehow wangled me an upgraded seat, which was fine with me. I love flying, but only if I'm in the pilot's seat. The rest of the time it's either boring or uncomfortable, usually both. Here, I at least had room to stretch.

Bone and I had gotten up at sparrowfart, hopped on the train, and gone to Luton airport, where he wished me good luck and handed me tickets and some cash. I caught the first plane to Paris, and then, with twenty minutes to spare, the flight to Tunis. It helped that I'd brought nothing with me but my shoulder bag. It's the way I generally like to travel, with little more than a change of clothes, passport and money, some shaving stuff, and a few other odds and ends. Anything else I'm likely to need, in my experience, I can either buy, borrow or steal once I get to where I'm going.

I'd enjoyed a comfortable seat and good weather, as well as time for a good long morning snooze before they started the lunch service. The meal they'd given me turned out to be surprisingly decent. Most of my fellow travelers on the plane, to judge from their looks, were Tunisian businessmen. They mainly wore dark suits, but I could see a few embroidered kaftans, and here and there, a red felt *chechia* hat. The steerage section in the back of the plane seemed to consist mainly of European tourists, roughly equal numbers of Brits, Germans and French, most of whom would be on some kind of package holiday. They'd shoot straight through Tunis on one of the tourist buses, heading for the resort hotels further down the coast. Or possibly the island of Djerba, in which case they'd connect with another flight here for the short hop down.

As I ate my lunch, I wondered if I hadn't made a mistake, agreeing to do this for Bone. As a very self-employed person, I know that I always need to be making clear and smart decisions about where to be, what to do, and who to get involved with. It's not always about the money, of course. In this case, with Bone's niece Hadley and her strange piece of jewelry, it certainly wasn't about the money. Quite the contrary – Bone and I were spending our hard-earned cash on this little venture, with absolutely no hope of a financial return.

No, in this case, it was much simpler – we were hoping to save a life. And that alone made it worthwhile. Kidnapping is one of the very worst things that one human being can do to another, right up there with rape and murder. Statistically, kidnap victims don't do well at all, which is why I needed to get to Tunis and start trying to find the trail. Because with every hour that went by, my chances of success went down. Maybe this would turn out to be a fool's errand. I had no leads, no idea where to start.

But that didn't mean I didn't have a plan, I thought as I sipped the last of my coffee. A day in Cambridge could give you the mistaken notion that the world was an orderly and predictable place. And perhaps if you stayed inside the walls of the college, it was. Bone and his colleagues lived according to schedules and lists, and the unsurprising march of the academic calendar. They knew more or less what they were going to do on a given day, from the time they got up in the morning. Some folks are lucky that way.

I hadn't had that luxury in quite a while. I don't work from schedules or lists. Instead, I scout territory, like a hunter. At the outset of a job, I have very little idea of what's actually inside the woods, so to speak. And the only way for me to find out is to go inside. I check all my equipment, cinch up my belt, and then I step out the door, into the woods, beyond the circle of the firelight, past the wire. Into the dark unknown.

From that point on, things generally happen pretty quickly, and whether I get what I'm looking for depends largely on how I respond to what comes at me. That might not sound like much of a strategy, but it had worked for me many times before. The problem of finding Hadley wasn't going to be much different, as far as I could see.

I'd be doing most of it in French, of course. French and Arabic were the two languages in use here, and although I was pretty good with one, I couldn't say the same for my abilities in Arabic. Flying around down in the desert, I'd learned the odd word or two, and I did actually teach myself the alphabet at one point. I thought it might be a good idea to understand what was stenciled on the fuel drums, so that I didn't refuel with diesel instead of avgas.

So that was the plan, such as it was, I thought, as the stewardess cleared my tray, and the seat belt signs went on for landing. Get into town and just start poking around.

I'm ready, I told myself. Or at least as ready as I can be.

* * *

With a bump and a squeal, we kissed the tarmac at Tunis-Carthage. A moment later, the brakes went on and the engines reversed thrust, slowing us as we approached the terminal building. I peered out the window. No jetways, same as the last time I'd been here.

Walking across the tarmac toward the terminal, I noticed a cluster of vehicles off to the side, parked around a 727. They seemed to be police vehicles, and in among them, I noted a couple of what looked to me like armored personnel carriers. Squinting, I managed to pick out the lettering on the side of the plane. 'Libyan Arab Airlines.' Don't see too many of those around, I thought.

Some of the other passengers had noticed, too. "Ooh, look at that," said one of the French tourists. "That's Colonel Gaddafi's plane. And are those women soldiers, guarding the plane?"

I looked again, more closely this time. Indeed, they were. A dozen of them in camouflage battledress and red berets, assault rifles at port arms, ringed the aircraft. All women. What on earth, I thought, was Col. Gaddafi doing here? I stopped and stared at the women until one of the Tunisian policemen gestured at me impatiently. "Keep going, keep going, nothing to see here. *Allez, continuez.*"

Nodding, I picked up my feet and hurried toward the arrivals door and into the customs and immigration hall. There, I faced a scene of barely controlled chaos. A phalanx of grey-uniformed officials barked at us to form a line for immigration procedures. Along the wall, I noted other uniforms, Garde Nationale fatigues this time, worn by hard-looking guys sporting fierce mustaches and assault rifles, whose eyes scanned the crowd looking for troublemakers.

"They, ah, seem to take security seriously here," an English tourist beside me said in a quiet voice.

"Apparently so," I replied. "It's probably because of that plane we saw outside. If Gaddafi is here, something's up. Plenty of opportunity to make mischief, for those so inclined." I gave him a nudge. "Go on up, the passport guy's waving to you."

When my turn came, I stepped smartly up to the grilled guichet, put on my most charming face, and handed my passport across, photo page open. The official behind the grill grunted once, stamped the passport with a flourish, and slid it back. "*Bienvenue à Tunis, Monsieur.* Welcome."

"*Merci, chef,*" I murmured, and was on my way.

Baggage claim involved even more security, but I breezed through. I had nothing but my shoulder bag, and it held nothing of any interest to the inspectors. Years ago, I'd learned the hard way not to bring anything into a country that you wouldn't want featured on the cover of one of the supermarket checkout tabloids. My shoulder bag contained some spare clothes, my money, and a few French paperbacks I'd picked up at the airport in Paris. And, of course, my battered but trusty Zippo lighter.

The customs inspector was quick, thorough and quite humorless, so while he worked I stood still, hands at my sides, exhibiting good posture and a sunny demeanor. This was clearly a class operation – the baggage guys had throat microphones into which they would mutter stuff from time to time, so I assumed that everybody in the place was either one of the watched, or a watcher. They're worried about something, I thought. And I'll bet it's got to do with that Libyan plane outside.

Then it was out the door and into the main terminal hall itself, crowded with people of all descriptions. Paris-suited businessmen rubbed shoulders with men in traditional *jebbas*, women draped modestly in white *safsaris*, and – of course – tourists in shorts and T-shirts. Porters pushed dilapidated baggage trolleys through the crowd, barking at people to make way.

I looked around and finally spotted a man in a rumpled black suit and a red *chechia* holding a cardboard sign with 'TAXI – VILLE DE TUNIS' scrawled on it. I walked up to him and mustered what I could remember of my Tunisian Arabic. "*Aslemma,*" I said. "*Shnuwa issmik, inti?*"

The man looked me up and down, grunted and answered me in French. "What's my name? It's Mansour. Why?"

Since I'd just used up a sizeable percentage of my local language, I switched to French as well. "I just like to know who I'm doing business with," I said. "Well, Mansour, can you take me to town?"

"Of course," he replied with a matter-of-fact stare. "I'm a taxi, monsieur. That's what the sign says, doesn't it?"

"Indeed it does," I murmured. It was nice to be back. "Let's go."

"*Behi*," grunted Mansour, and we trotted off toward the parking lot.

* * *

Mansour drove an old and very comfortable Peugeot 404 station wagon. He pulled out and got us rolling, past the suburb of Charguia on the left and down towards El Menzah. The traffic was thick and chaotic, the cops directing us off onto side streets, slowing us down. "It's Abu Shafshoufa," grumbled Mansour. "That idiot. All his fault."

"Who's Abu Shafshoufa?" I wanted to know.

"Why, Muammar Gaddafi, of course. That's what we all call him. Didn't you see his airplane when you landed? He's come to see the president."

"President Bourguiba?"

"Of course, *monsieur*. We've only got one president, *n'est-ce pas*? The two of them are up in the palace in Carthage right now, blowing hot air at each other. And while they talk, the police and soldiers block all the roads, damn them." He blasted his horn at a slow-moving van in front of us.

Mansour detoured down Avenue Charles Nicolle and then took side streets through Mutuelville and around the Belvedere Park until finally, on the right, we spotted the Hilton International, atop a modest hill overlooking the city. A winding drive led up to the portico, where an attendant dressed like a Ruritanian cavalry officer opened the rear door and let me out.

I paid Mansour with some French francs I'd found in my shoulder bag, and thanked him. He gave me a brief nod and headed back down the driveway, his car belching black smoke.

I took a look around. The Hilton was large and quite modern, with a wide hilltop view of the city. Beyond the low, white-topped roofs of the city's offices and villas lay the Lac de Tunis, and beyond that, the bay and the airy slopes of Jebel Boukornine on the other side. On the hotel lawn a group of workers struggled to set up a very large tent, the kind of thing you might see being prepared for either a small circus or a Christian revival meeting. Somehow, I didn't think this was going to be either.

Inside, I found a large and pleasant reception area, flanked on one side by a bar, and on the other by a dining room. The desk clerk took my credit card and name, and then looked down at his papers, frowning. Finally I said, "Is there a problem?"

He shook his head. "No problem, monsieur. Not really. I'm just moving you to a higher floor." He looked up at me and smiled. "An upgrade, actually; a suite. We need to move everyone off the lower floors."

"Why?"

He lowered his voice. "It's the Colonel. That's his tent outside. And his security guards have taken the first two floors inside the hotel."

I looked back out the window at the tent going up. "Colonel Gaddafi's staying here? In a tent on the lawn?"

"He takes the tent with him everywhere he goes. It's said to be bulletproof. He claims that he wants to stay close to his desert roots." He paused, and then added, "But it's really because the Great Leader seems to be deathly afraid of heights."

Hell, I thought, this is going to complicate things. "How long is he staying?"

The clerk rolled his eyes. "Who knows? They come when they want; they leave when they want." He shot a quick glance to either side. "And sometimes, they don't pay their bills."

"That won't be a problem with me," I said, tapping my credit card. "Have you got somewhere close by where I can rent a car?"

He pointed to a desk at the end of the lobby. "Right over there, monsieur." He handed me a key. "Enjoy your time in Tunis, Mr. Donovan."

* * *

Five minutes later, I sat on my bed and picked up the phone. After some negotiation with the hotel's switchboard operator, the call went through. A moment later, it was picked up.

"American Embassy."

I crossed my fingers and spoke. "Karl Quackenbush, please."

Silence, and then: "That'll be communications. Putting you through now."

Two rings later, a familiar rasp came down the phone. "Yeah. Quackenbush."

"Boomer, it's Max, Max Donovan."

Deep silence on the other end of the line. Then a loud bray of laughter. "Donovan! Where the hell are you calling from?"

"I'm in town, Boomer, at the Hilton." I paused. "Can we meet?"

His voice suddenly grew wary. "Shit, boy. What kind of trouble are you in now?"

"No trouble, Boomer. Not yet, anyway. But I'd like to get caught up on things. Been a few years since I was here."

There was a moment of silence. Boomer knew better than anyone what you should and shouldn't be talking about on the phone. Especially an embassy phone. "I guess that'd be all right, then," he said at last. "I'm due off in an hour. We could have a drink if you like."

"Perfect," I said. "Where?"

"Meet me at the Café des Nattes out in Sidi Bou Said at four o'clock. That work for you?"

"I'll be there," I said.

I hung up the phone, picked up my shoulder bag, and went downstairs to collect my rental car.

CHAPTER SEVEN

I slid into a chair next to Boomer Quackenbush at the Café des Nattes at just past four o'clock. Wearing baggy shorts and a Grateful Dead T-shirt, Boomer put down the *shisha* he'd been smoking, blew out an enormous cloud of fruit-scented tobacco smoke, and wrapped me in a bear hug.

"You old bastard," he said with a wide, toothy grin. "How the hell are you? In trouble again?"

I disengaged myself, stepped back and smiled. "No more than usual, Boomer. Not yet, anyway."

Boomer hadn't changed very much. A great hulk of a man, he carried his weight well. With his spade beard and shaggy hair, he looked like an overweight Midwestern hippie turned farmer, but underneath the bulk lay pure muscle. He could move like a striking snake when he needed to, and behind his wide blue eyes, now brimming with mischief and delight at seeing me again, lurked a keen intelligence that didn't miss very much at all.

Boomer worked as an embassy communicator. Communicators form a group apart in most embassies that I've observed. The upper-level diplomats, ambassadors, deputies, and so on are all polished, slick and very careful about what they do and say, and particularly about how they look to others. The people working under them, the administrative staffers, tend to be relatively faceless, their jobs not much different from what people would be doing in Washington, Miami, or Cat Scratch, North Dakota.

But the communicators are a bit special. These people are the eyes and ears of the embassy. They know everything that goes out or comes in, because they're in charge of telecommunications, the encryption machines, the code books, everything connecting the mission with the outside world. The roof of a typical US embassy is a forest of antennae of various sorts, and it's the job of the communicators to keep all of that humming along. In case the you-know-what hits the fan, they will be the ones disabling the equipment, burning the paper, and pulling every plug they can to make sure that nothing falls into the wrong hands.

You'd think these guys would be very buttoned-up and straight-arrow, but the reverse is usually true. They're mavericks, outsiders to the staid diplomatic community. You'll see them at the diplomatic parties in small groups, usually apart from the others, drinking beer out of the bottle and laughing a little too loudly. They don't much care what they look like, or what other people think of them.

It's hard to find good communicators, I'm told, because it requires an unusual combination of skills and attitudes. Smart ex-military people with a signals background who're used to working on their own are usually the best bets.

People, in other words, like Boomer.

The waiter appeared. I cocked my finger at Boomer. "You're still a beer guy, right?"

He nodded. "They've only got non-alcoholic stuff here, but you know what they say, there's no such thing as bad beer."

"*Zooz birra, iyaishik,*" I said to the waiter, holding up two fingers.

"*Behi.*" The waiter moved off.

Boomer chuckled. "Impressive, for somebody who's been away. You were always good at picking up the local lingo. Did pretty well with us that time out in Somalia, as I recall. You were out on the sand yakking away to the locals like anything." He paused, and then said thoughtfully, "Didn't stop 'em trying to kill us both in the end, though, did it?"

I grimaced, remembering back. "No, it surely did not."

Boomer and I met for the first time in Nairobi, both of us independently hired to find a load of missing NGO money. We bonded on the Somali Airlines flight into Mogadishu, where we were served boiled goat over spaghetti, with warm Fanta. Boomer leaned over and explained, "That's the Somali national dish, Donovan. Better get used to it." Boomer had been on one previous outing in Somalia and just about everything he told me turned out to be true.

We took a low pass over the Mogadishu airport before landing, and the place looked like a wrecking yard. Indeed, that proved to be exactly what it was. The sides of the single runway contained a litter of crashed planes, the sight of which brought back a few unpleasant memories from other times and places. Among the wrecks, I spotted a 707, an ancient Ford Trimotor, and a couple of Soviet MiG-15s from God knows where.

Boomer and I had spent the next couple of weeks snuffling around the town, checking out leads and finding that most of them led nowhere. We sheltered from the late afternoon heat in the bar at the Croce del Sud, where, if you stuck around for dinner, you could usually get something other than spaghetti and boiled goat to eat.

Our enquiries eventually led us upcountry. Things finally came to a head in a local warlord's camp outside of Bardera near the Juba River. There, Boomer and I had a brief but highly unpleasant encounter with the warlord himself and his double-barreled 12-gauge shotgun. It was over in minutes, but it took us a bit longer to blow the safe where he'd stashed the stolen aid money. We had a rather narrow escape, finally putting enough distance between us and the junior warlords so that when the last good tire on our car finally blew, we figured we were probably safe for a while. We'd been driving through the bush instead of using the dreadful so-called road, and as a result, our tires looked like porcupines.

Eventually, we stumbled across a couple of boys herding goats. An hour or so later, we were each perched on the back of a dirt bike, holding on for dear life as we roared and bounced along a complex set of trails, in the general direction of the Kenyan border. They let us off a kilometer or so from the crossing, gratefully accepted our gift of the double-barreled shotgun, and we walked across, heading toward the town of Wajir Bor some fifty kilometers distant. We eventually got a ride, and from there, hitched to Dadaab and down into Nairobi.

The NGO got most of its money back, minus our expenses, overhead, and a general aggravation fee, but they seemed pleased. Boomer and I took our proceeds and headed for Paris. We parted company a week later, he to Bangui to chase up a hot lead, and me back to my small apartment in Berkeley.

We kept in touch sporadically, and eventually, he told me he'd "gone inside" as an embassy communicator for the State Department. I wished him well and thought no more about it. Until, of course, I arrived in Tunis.

Now, as the heat of the day began to fade, a cool breeze crept up the street from the sea, several blocks away. Sidi Bou Said is a pleasant town, much of it up on hills with spectacular views. Just about every building in town is painted white, with blue trim on the windows and the doors. The Café des Nattes has a nice porch up above a set of whitewashed steps leading down to the street, and you can sit up there and survey the street below.

From our perch, I gazed down at the small shops and cafés, their chairs filling up slowly now as people finished their day. Newspaper sellers strolled through the crowds, hawking afternoon editions of *Le Monde* and *France-Soir*.

Children eating large sticky pastries walked alongside their mothers, their cheeks stuffed like chipmunks. In the cafés, small groups of men earnestly discussed the affairs of the world hunched over their cups of Turkish coffee.

I spotted an old man coming along carrying a round flat tray of *machmoum* jasmine bouquets. I called him over and bought one. I inhaled its perfume deeply, sighed, and stuck it behind my ear.

Boomer chuckled. "Gone local already? You've only been here what, a couple hours?"

"Don't forget, I used to work here," I said. "I love the smell of this stuff." I pulled the bouquet from behind my ear and sniffed it again. "I don't think they have this kind of jasmine anywhere else in the world."

Our beers came, and Boomer, as was his wont, got straight to business. He drank half his beer, and took a pull on his *shisha*. Then he belched, blew out a cloud of fragrant smoke, and opened the meeting.

"So, what brings you to our fair town, Max? I'm assuming you're not here for the sunshine."

There it was.

"The sunshine's nice," I replied, "but no, that's not what brought me to your door. I'm looking for someone." During the next five minutes, I explained about Hadley, the chelengk, and Hadley's cry for help.

Boomer grimaced. "Kidnapped. Not great, Max. But hey, you probably know that better than anyone." He paused. "How much danger do you think she's in?"

"Hard to say. From what the folks at Cambridge told me, I'd guess she's being held for information. She seems to have found this chelengk thing, and they're holding her hostage until she tells them where it is. She's alive because they hope she'll lead them to it."

Boomer nodded slowly. "And when she does—"

"Then they'll probably kill her," I said. "You can see why I'm in a bit of hurry here."

Boomer drank the rest of his beer, thought for a moment, and belched again. Finally, he said, "And what do you think I can do for you?"

"I'm not really sure. I assume Hadley's not a person of interest for the embassy?"

"I've got a super-high security clearance," he began, "and I'm not supposed to tell people like you shit about shit." He shook his head. "But there's nothing to tell. I don't recall seeing her name on any cables or reports. None that have come our way, at any rate."

His eyes narrowed. "There's always the cowbirds downstairs, of course. They tend to keep their own information close, but I'd be surprised if they knew anything. If they did, you can bet your ass they'd have cabled it back to Washington by now, and I'd have seen it."

"Cowbirds?" I said.

"You know, the Intelligence dudes," he explained. "Just about every diplomatic mission has at least one undercover person. I call 'em cowbirds. Cowbirds lay their eggs in other birds' nests, so their young grow up among the other hatchlings, hopefully unnoticed." He snorted. "Or not. Out in places like this, cowbirds are generally dead easy to spot. They're usually the only folks in the mission who actually speak the local language." He shook his head. "No, I doubt very much that they'll know anything useful."

He sat back. "Like I said, if there'd been any discussion about her through the regular channels, I'd have heard about it." He grimaced. "People are supposed to register with the embassy when they travel here. Helps us find them in case something goes wrong. Most people don't, of course, including your girl whatsis."

"Hadley," I said. "And she's not a girl. She's a doctoral student, and twenty-five years old."

"Well, pardon me all to hell," said Boomer with an aw-shucks grin. After a moment, he said, "Am I right in assuming you don't want the embassy brought into this?"

"Not right now," I said. "If we tell the Americans, then in effect, we've told everybody. The Brits, obviously, will have to get involved. So will the Tunisians. And for all I know, the Turks will take an interest."

"And that'll be a goat rodeo for sure. So, I'll ask again: what can I do for you?"

"Give me some context, to start with," I said. "What's going on in the country these days? What's keeping you guys up at night?"

He sighed. "Where to start? If you're gonna be poking around here, you'd better be damned careful. We live in a bad neighborhood, don't forget. We're wedged right in between Algeria and Libya, two big countries run by outlier governments. France has a continuing interest here, of course. The Islamist militants do as well." He pointed up the street. "Did you know that a couple of years ago, the PLO set up its office only a few kilometers away from here? This town's full of spies, and everybody's on the earie, as they say." He paused. "Course these days, most of the trouble's coming from our crazy neighbor to the east."

"Gaddafi? I spotted his plane at the airport this morning. My taxi driver called him 'Abu Shafshoufa.'"

Boomer snorted derisively. "Means 'Old Fuzzhead.' Good name for the fool. Oh, yeah, we know about Gaddafi's plane. But we don't know what he came for, to tell the truth. He just kinda showed up. We try to monitor things over there pretty closely, but we don't really have any good way of keeping tabs on him these days. We pulled out of our embassy in Tripoli in '79 and labeled Libya a 'state sponsor of terrorism.' We shut down their embassy in Washington a little while later. And then there was that Gulf of Sidra mess back a while ago."

"When the planes got shot down?"

"Yep. We had some F-14 Tomcats off the carrier *Nimitz* out patrolling the Gulf. They ran into two Libyan fighters, and when our pilots heard them say on their radio that they were ready to fire, we brought 'em down. Caused a hell of a rumpus around here, let me tell you."

"Our pilots heard them on the radio?" I said. "Boomer, I know the Marines are all super-smart and capable, but I didn't know many of them spoke Arabic. That's impressive."

Boomer grinned. "Most jarheads can't even speak English properly, Max, as you well know. No, those pilots were speaking in English."

"Then—"

"Their pilots weren't Libyan. We think they were either Cubans, Russians, or North Koreans. He's got military advisers from all three countries in there right now."

We were both quiet for a moment. Then Boomer said, "In spite of all that, it's really not bad at all, living here. The people are friendly once you get to know them, the weather is decent, and the beaches are great. I took up scuba diving last year — there are wrecks off the coast, and even a few sunken Roman towns. Bought myself a sixteen-foot Zodiac, me and some of the boys go out diving on the weekends." He gave me a grin. "I figure if the deal ever goes down here, I might be able to take off out of here in the Zodiac."

"Better than a motorbike through the desert," I said.

He chuckled. "Been there, done that." He stared into his empty beer glass. "So, what's your next move?"

I shrugged. "What I usually do. Go out on the street, ask a lot of questions, and see who bites. That usually works."

Boomer grunted. "Yeah, except that sometimes, you get bit."

"It would help," I said, "if I had a name or two to start with. Any ideas?"

"I take it you don't want the local cops involved?"

I shook my head.

"Wise decision," he said. "I'd imagine the last folks you'd want in on this are the Tunisian police. The bureaucracy in this country was set up by the Romans,

Italians, Ottomans and French. Each one layered on top of the other. You can imagine how well it works."

He thought for a moment. "Okay," he said finally. "Go see Basli the jeweler. He might be a place to start. Down in the Medina. Nosy old bastard; knows everybody and everything. If this piece of jewelry passed through the market at any point, he'd almost certainly know about it. Might even have sold it on. He operates as a fence, in addition to his legit business. Here." He pulled a ballpoint pen from his baggy shorts and scribbled a name and address on the back of a paper napkin. He passed it across the table. "Samir Abdelmajid Basli. Nice guy, so don't go pissing him off. He's got this place down near the mosque. Ask the shopkeepers around there; they'll direct you. Mention my name so he won't get jumpy."

Boomer leaned forward. "And listen, Max, you need to be careful. I don't know much about the historical relics crowd, but like I said, this town has some tough people in it. Some days I think just about everybody's working a double game. The Libyans are the worst. Gaddafi's arrival this morning isn't good news."

"What do your folks at the embassy think he's up to?"

"Damned if we know. He does this every once in a while – takes the plane and shows up here and there. Our cable chatter says it's an informal visit to discuss cooperation ties with President Bourguiba. Maybe so, but Bourguiba himself thinks Gaddafi's a dangerous fool, and besides, he funds other dangerous fools like himself all around the world. Bourguiba's pretty much obliged to receive him if he chooses to visit, but he's trying to keep his distance. He won't put the delegation up in the palace out in Carthage. I hear they've got Gaddafi and his people down in the Hilton, in town. Word is, he pitched his tent out on the lawn."

"Yes, he did," I said. "That's where I'm staying, in fact. Not in the tent – in a suite on the top floor."

Boomer chuckled. "Well, that'll be fun, then. Hopefully they've got his guards confined to one or two of the other floors, but you're going to see a lot of armed security around there for the next few days. Don't plan on misbehaving."

"So, you've got no idea at all why he's here?"

Boomer shook his head. "Not really. There's a couple of folks in the embassy who think he's not here for discussions at all, but as cover for something else."

"And what something else would that be?"

Boomer shook his head. "Dunno, Max. Nobody knows. But here's the thing: you bring an official delegation into a country, there's gonna be baggage, right? Lots of it. Every one of those folks on the plane has a bunch of suitcases. The guards have their kit, too, right? Sometimes they bring it all in crated up, just like we do. There's a lot you can hide in a crate, and none of it is subject to inspection – diplomatic rules." He snorted. "They could bring pretty near anything they wanted into the country that way. Happens all the time, and not just here." He winked. "We've been known to do it ourselves from time to time."

"Or," I said after a moment, "they might be planning on taking something out."

Boomer nodded, his face thoughtful. "Yeah, I suppose they could, at that. But what?"

I sighed. "Anybody's guess. And maybe none of our business, in the end."

I checked my watch. Nearly five o'clock. If I was going to pay a visit to Mr. Basli today, I'd better hurry. I stood up and put some money on the table. "Nice to have seen you, Boomer. Let's not leave it so long next time."

Boomer chuckled. "If I know you, Max Donovan, we'll be seeing each other again sooner than you think."

"How do you figure?"

"You're gonna get yourself in the shit," Boomer said matter-of-factly. "You nearly always do. And when you step in it, you're gonna want your friends to come in and pull you out, aren't you?" He slapped me on the back.

I smiled, thinking back. "Seems like the last time, it was *me* who dragged *your* sorry ass across the border, out of Somalia. Or have you forgotten?"

He looked at me, his face gone suddenly serious. "No, I haven't forgotten, Max," he said quietly. "I owe you for that one. If the time comes when you need help here, you know how to reach out." His stare hardened. "But for Christ's sake, be careful, will you? Folks around here play hard, and they play to win."

"Yeah, well, so do I," I said. We shook hands, and I went off to find my car.

CHAPTER EIGHT

I stopped first at the Institut Bourguiba, a no-nonsense grey stone building on Avenue de la Liberté just past the Rue de l'Inde. The massive metal doors were thankfully open, and inside, I was able to quickly locate the woman who'd been *de service* on the night Hadley disappeared.

"*Oui, monsieur,*" she said, bobbing her head with assurance. Her nametag read Aziza Benattiya. "It was definitely Mademoiselle Holloway that I saw. She got into a white van."

"A white van?"

"Yes, I saw it very clearly. The kind with doors in the back, you know, the kind that stores use for deliveries. It had a damaged bumper, I noticed that when they pulled up. I thought that a bit strange. One man held the door, the other man helped her inside."

I wasn't at all sure about the 'helping' part, but I didn't want to get bogged down. "Did you recognize either of the two men?"

Aziza sniffed. "American women, in my experience, are far too casual around men. They talk to whomever they like, they go out with them by themselves, they do whatever they like." She paused. "I'd never seen these two before. They didn't look all that suitable to me, but it's none of my business now, is it?"

I could see I wasn't going to get much further, so I thanked Aziza and went back to my car. Now for Basli the jeweler. I drove all the way down Liberté until I got to Avenue de France, in the center of town. There, miraculously, I found a parking space. Five minutes walk brought me to the Bab el-Bahr, the entrance to the Medina.

I started up the narrow street, and with each step, walked back into an alternate reality. Most of Tunis is a modern city, predominantly French in overall flavor, its buildings reflecting its multinational and multicultural heritage. Inside the Medina, however, it's a different world altogether, a mysterious labyrinth where the past and the present come together in strange and fascinating ways.

To the tourist, it probably looks like something out of *The Arabian Nights*, and the word 'exotic' undoubtedly comes to mind. But this is Tunis's shopping district, the mall, so to speak, for the thousands of people who crowd its precincts. The economic beating heart of the city. Almost anything you can think of is for sale here, tucked away inside narrow shops lining the equally narrow passages that wind here and there. Much of the Medina is covered over, adding to the feeling of being in Ali Baba's cave, and wherever you go, scents of perfume, incense, spice, coffee and tobacco follow you. In addition to the hundreds of shops, there are restaurants, mosques and even schools hidden inside.

I walked past shop after shop selling textiles in a dizzying variety of colors and fabrics, merchants calling out to me as I passed. Other shops were filled with pots, pans and utensils, while from the inner recesses came the sound of a small army of apprentice metalworkers hammering away. Here was a shop selling nothing but elegant wire-filagree birdcages, and next to it, a display of leaded-glass hanging lamps in various colors. Colorful tilework lined the walls of the narrower passages. Here and there between the shops, ornate and ancient wooden doors lay half-open, offering glimpses into mysterious private courtyards from which came snatches of children's laughter, Arab music, and low conversation.

I threaded my way past groups of women bargaining for cloth, and dodged children running hoops along the cobbled pavement. Here and there, groups of men in *chechias* sat together at tiny wooden tables sipping small cups of strong coffee and drawing on their *shishas*. In and around the throngs of people, market cats on the lookout for food or prey dodged the legs of shoppers.

Vibrant, strange, and beautiful it certainly is, but finding your way through it is another story altogether. Waving the scrap of paper Boomer had given me, I walked slowly in the direction of the Ez-Zitouna Mosque. I had to ask for directions three or four times before finally winding up where I thought I ought to be.

And by that time, I'd become aware of someone following me.

A narrow maze of small streets branching off from the mosque's main square led in the general direction of the Rue des Andalous, and it was on one of these alleyways that I eventually found Basli's jewelry shop. I gave it a quick glance and walked on by.

I thought about what to do about my shadow. I'd debated trying to lose him, but curiosity got the better of me. Strangers in any country are going to attract a certain amount of attention, but this doesn't usually extend to following them through the streets. Not unless there's a good reason. I was interested in what that reason might be.

Whoever he was, my tail wasn't very good at his job. As I strolled along, I stopped at several stalls, pretending to inspect the merchandise, chatting with the owners. Each time, my man stopped and hung back, pretending – like me – to be fascinated with something on the display table. I kept this up for ten minutes or so, and then made a series of turns into side streets, just to see what he'd do. He followed. In the narrow passageways, it was virtually impossible for him to hide himself, but with dogged determination, he kept trailing me.

Not only was he inexperienced and inept, I thought, he was almost certainly alone. I had become very curious about this person, but I set it aside as I came back up toward Basli's shop again. The shop looked like most of the others – a narrow front with a long room extending back, every square inch covered with merchandise of some sort. Basli sold more than jewels, it appeared – he had rugs, ornaments, and a wide variety of expensive-looking knick-knacks on display.

None of which was of the slightest interest to me, of course.

Samir Abdelmajid Basli turned out to be a round, solid man in his late fifties. He wore a nicely embroidered *jebba* and a faded *chechia* over a bristling Zapata moustache that contrasted with his kind, intelligent eyes. These eyes took me in as I stepped into the shop and shook hands.

"*Aslemma.*" I gave him the standard greeting.

His eyebrows went up as he gave me the standard reply. Tourists probably didn't greet him that way. "Who are you?" he said in the local vernacular.

I switched to French. "I am a friend of Boomer Quackenbush," I said quietly. "He thought that you might help me."

Basli nodded and smiled. "Ah. You are looking for fine jewelry? I have nothing but the best."

"Not jewelry," I said. "Information."

The eyes changed then, focusing closely on mine. Windows to the soul, that's what everyone says the Arabs think about the eyes. He peered through mine, examined my soul for a moment, made an assessment, and then nodded abruptly. "Come," he said. "We'll talk back here."

He led me to the back of the narrow shop. "Toufik," he called over his shoulder, "take care of the customers."

We sat comfortably at the back of the store, drinking Turkish coffee from small cups with the traditional glass of water on the side. Basli began to explain to me the peculiar history of Nelson's chelengk, and what he knew – and didn't know – about it.

Sunset was approaching, dusk creeping into the alleyways of the Medina, and lights began to blink on in the shops. From the Ez-Zitouna Mosque nearby, the *maghrib* call to prayer drifted out.

Basli made a dismissive gesture. "I'll pray a bit later," he said. "More coffee?"

"Why not?" I accepted a small refill.

He continued his story. "*Alors*, the Bey was deposed, stripped of his power and his riches, and sent to live in a wretched apartment somewhere over in La Goulette, near the port. I was just a young man at the time, but it was all that the adults talked about, for weeks."

"And he had the jewels at the time," I said.

He nodded. "Yes. He had the chelengk, together with a small collection of jewelry. That, apart from some clothing and a few bits of furniture, was all the old man had left."

"How did he come to possess the chelengk? It had been stolen in England, after all."

Basli shook his head. "A mystery, *n'est-ce pas*? It is said that he was given it by a group of Turkish supporters. The story is that they bought – or stole – it from whoever stole it from the British. By that time, of course, Turkey itself had completely abolished the Ottoman Sultanate. But rather than give the chelengk to the Turkish civilian government, they gave it as a gesture of respect to the last remaining member of the old Ottoman order. They did this in 1955, just before Tunisian independence."

He took a small sip of coffee and set his cup down carefully. "But eventually, the Bey sold his jewels, simply to buy food in order to eat and survive. Sometimes when a rich man dies, his valuable possessions are scattered, either among his surviving relatives, or into the hands of a large number of individual buyers. In that sense, the treasure disappears, like dust grains on the wind."

"But not in this case?"

"No one really knew what had happened to the Bey's jewelry, not for over twenty years. We're not talking about a large quantity of jewelry – a dozen small pieces at most. The collection may have been hoarded somewhere, or stashed away and forgotten. But eventually, the jewels resurfaced.

"They came to me two years ago." His eyes met mine. "I won't tell you how, so don't ask." He sighed. "A collection like that presents a simple jeweler like myself with a problem. There's simply no place to start. No way to assign a clear value. No way to determine their legal standing. I put the jewels in my safe, out of sight, and waited.

"These were not things that a tourist should buy; everyone understood that. Everyone in the Medina also knew that I, Samir Abdelmajid, had them under lock and key, waiting for the right person to appear."

"And eventually one did."

"Yes, last year. *Bon moment, bon endroit.* Right place, right time. I needed money, and he had quite a bit of it. We negotiated for several days, and finally settled on a price. He paid me, took the jewels, and disappeared." He looked up. "And that, monsieur, is all I know."

We'll see about that, I thought. "How much did he pay you?"

Basli gave me a Mona Lisa smile. If eyes were supposed to be windows, then his shades had suddenly come down. "I'm not going to tell you that either, of course."

"Did you get a name?"

He shrugged. "He gave me a name, but of course it turned out not to be his real one. He showed me a Tunisian *carte d'identité*, but I could see right away that it was a forgery, and not a very good one at that."

I sighed. "So you have no idea who he was?"

"None. He spoke excellent Arabic, but with an accent I couldn't quite place, with a few odd words here and there." He gestured vaguely. "The borders in this part of the world are largely conceptual, Monsieur Donovan. Imaginary. People move around quite freely. It's our history; in our blood. He might have been Tunisian, but he could also have been Libyan, or Algerian." He paused. "In fact, there is a story that he was actually one of Lamine Bey's distant cousins, trying to recoup the family's heritage." He gave another shrug. "No one knows, monsieur. Certainly not I."

I tried another tack. From my shoulder bag I pulled the picture of Hadley that Bone had given me and pushed it across to Basli. "Have you ever seen her?"

He smiled. "Oh, yes. Indeed I have. The American woman. Student at some university in England, she told me. She, too, was interested in Lamine Bey and his chelengk. I told her just what I have told you. She was quite charming, actually. Excellent French, and her Arabic was very good, too."

"Do you know where she is now?"

"I last saw her more than two months ago, monsieur. I have not seen her since. I have no idea where she is."

I thought about that for a moment. Then I asked another question. "And the man who bought the chelengk. How would I go about finding him?"

Basli laughed. "Not possible. He took the jewels and went south. It is said that he bought a camel in Sousse and went into the desert. That was almost a year ago. Since then, no one has seen or heard from him."

"Why would he go into the desert?" I asked.

He shrugged. "He was clearly on his way to somewhere. If you go far enough south, you come to the borders of Libya and Algeria."

"Is that where you think he was headed? Why?"

"Who knows? Only one thing is certain. He was very smart to buy a camel. It's the best way to travel in the desert, and an excellent way to remain unremarkable, particularly to the authorities." He held up a finger. "On the other hand, if you attract unwelcome attention, a camel is hardly a very good *voiture de fuite*. What I believe you call a 'getaway car' in English.

"He went south to disappear, in my opinion. And, again my opinion, you would be very foolish to try and find him. A year is a long time; wherever he is, his trail is very cold by now. You will not find him. As I said, Monsieur Donovan, simply not possible."

I was starting to think that Basli might be right. Then his son spoke, from the front of the shop. "*Baba.*"

We both turned.

"*Baba*, there's a man outside."

"A customer?"

"No. He's been watching the shop for twenty minutes now. He's spying on us, *baba*. And he's giving me the creeps."

I stood up. Time I dealt with this. "He's looking for me," I said. "He's been following me."

Basli frowned. "Do you want me to call the police?"

I gave him one of my best smiles. "That won't be necessary. I'll deal with this myself." I looked around. "Do you have a back door?"

He shook his head. "No. But we do have a ladder up to the roof."

"Perfect," I said.

* * *

Ten minutes later, I stepped carefully across the arched tiles of the roof covering the narrow street, headed toward what I hoped was a ladder down. I'd put a couple of hundred meters between me and whoever was watching for me outside Basli's shop, and I figured that ought to be enough for what I had in mind. Prayers had come and gone, and it was almost fully dark now. I knew that they locked up most parts of the Medina at night and patrolled with dogs to deter potential thieves, all of which fit into the plan now forming in my mind.

I reached what I assumed was another rooftop access ladder, behind a closed metal door. Mercifully, it wasn't locked. A moment later, I was smiling and bowing to a very confused rug merchant, as I exited his shop and stepped back out into the narrow street with a confident stride.

Three doors up, I found what I was looking for; a shop selling hardware. I picked out three meters of stout braided rope, and then spotted a packet of long plastic cable ties, the kind used by electricians. Perfect. I paid, stuffed my purchases into my shoulder bag, and exited the shop, smiling.

Now for the fiddly part, I thought, starting back down the narrow passageway toward where I hoped my watcher would still be.

And sure enough, he was. He lurked in a narrow doorway across from the jewelry shop, looking in exactly the wrong direction as he waited patiently for me to reappear. Well, here I am, laddie, I thought. I crept up behind him, clapped one hand over his mouth, and dragged him back by the collar of his leather coat, through the door and into a nearly-dark vestibule.

Before he had a chance to fully react, I had him in a sleeper hold. You have to be careful if you're going to do this. The idea with a sleeper hold is to cut off the brain's blood supply by constricting the carotid arteries. This will cause your opponent to pass out, but for it to work, you have to constrict the blood vessels on both sides of someone's neck. It can be hard to do with someone who's an experienced fighter and who knows – or suspects – what you're up to.

Do it wrong, and it turns into a choke hold, which can easily kill someone in very little time. I had no intention of killing my watcher, whoever he was. I just wanted to discourage him.

Fortunately for me, my guy wasn't much of a fighter. I'd taken him completely by surprise, and now, in the near darkness of the vestibule, I let go of his mouth and quickly wrapped my arm around his neck. With my other arm, I pushed his head down toward his chest. My forearm was pressing on one side of his neck, my bicep on the other. I spread my legs and leaned back, applying as much pressure as I could. I was in a hurry, but I didn't want to hurt this guy unless I had to.

He obliged me by passing out quickly. He went limp in my arms, transforming into deadweight. I eased him to the ground, rummaged in my shoulder bag, and drew out a couple of the plastic cable ties. These I used to bind his arms and his legs. I found his pistol stuck into his trousers at the small of his back, a Soviet Makarov 9mm, the kind of weapon that turns up just about everywhere. I stuck it in my shoulder bag.

Then I felt in the pockets of his leather jacket, extracting a wallet containing a laminated ID card and a wad of Tunisian dinars. The dinars also went into my shoulder bag, a contribution to the Find Hadley Holloway Fund. The ID card I put in my shirt pocket, to look at later. I also found a dirty handkerchief, which I balled up and stuck into his mouth, using a length of the rope I'd bought to secure it in place. Bound and gagged, he now began to regain consciousness, not at all pleased with his new circumstances.

He'd begun to struggle a little at this point, but I clipped him smartly across the ear with the flat of my hand to get his attention, and then spoke softly to him in French. "I don't know if you can understand me, and frankly, I don't care all that much. You're alive, which is the main thing. And with any luck, you'll be alive tomorrow morning. But if I see you again after that, you've got no guarantees. You understand?" He nodded, his eyes wide and bulging.

"Excellent," I said. "Then I think we're done here." I dragged him into a corner and tied him to the metal stair banister with the rest of my rope. Somebody might come through the door in the next five minutes, or – as I hoped – not until the next morning. In either case, I'd be gone. I patted his cheek. *"Bislemma,"* I said, easing myself out the door and into the street.

It was going dark across the Medina, the shops dousing their lights and pulling down their metal shutters. I made my way up the Rue Jamaa Ez-Zitouna toward the Bab, out onto the Avenue de France and my parked rental car.

I sat for a moment behind the wheel and pulled my thoughts together. It had been a long, strange day. I snapped the interior light on and peered at the ID card I'd taken from my watcher. It was indeed his, to judge from the photograph, but since everything else on it was in Arabic, I had no idea who he actually was or where he came from. One thing for certain, he wasn't Tunisian. Tunisia uses both French and Arabic as national languages, and this was in Arabic only.

I put the card away and started the engine. Time later to figure all that out. I was dead tired, and the last actual meal I'd eaten had been on the Air France flight coming in. It seemed like days ago. I pulled the car out, turned up the Avenue de la Liberté, towards Parc Belvedere and eventually, my hotel.

A nice quiet dinner and then a phone call to Bone Brown. After that, I thought, some much-needed sleep.

CHAPTER NINE

It's often hard to describe to someone else why I like the kind of life I lead. In fact, it's sometimes hard to explain it to myself.

But here's how I've come to think about it. Civilization is like a huge board game with lots of complicated rules. The rules, like civilization itself, are unevenly distributed. Cities, of course, are where the civilization stuff is the most concentrated and the most intense. Hence, cities tend to have the most rules. Walk here, don't walk there. No right turn on red. This is safe, this is not safe. One way. No entry. No shoes, no shirt, no service. Stuff like that.

It's not that hard to learn to live in civilization, because it's basically all set up for you in advance. The rules are everywhere, and if you get confused, there are people all around you who will be more than happy to tell you exactly what to do. Where to go, how to live, and how to think.

Out where I spend most of my time, however, civilization tends to be spread a little more unevenly. There are far fewer rules in some places, and almost none in others. And not much agreement, much of the time, about what the rules actually are. As a newcomer, you're often not good at reading the rules right away, which can lead to major problems on occasion.

In places like that, you're pretty much on your own in terms of figuring out what to do and how to do it. And when you get it wrong, you take the consequences of your decisions. This makes daily life quite a bit more interesting. It also keeps you in a mild state of constant alert, which I find is good for my mental health. I decided a long time ago that I kind of liked being in these sorts of places and living in that way.

And so I do, every chance I get.

* * *

I got back to the hotel at just after eight. I parked the car, went upstairs, and stashed the Makarov under my mattress. I quickly counted the dinars I'd taken off my watcher. Over three hundred. That'll buy a few nice meals, I thought, thinking about the dining room downstairs. I took another look at the ID card as well. The Arabic hadn't gotten any more understandable, but the colors and the emblem gave it away as decidedly Libyan.

I stuck the ID back in my pocket and wandered downstairs, where the dining room was still open. I needed food, and some quiet time to think about the events of the day, what the events meant, and where things went from here. Perhaps the next steps would reveal themselves to me on a full stomach.

The dining room was nearly empty, and I had my choice of tables. I settled in at a table beside a large picture window, giving me a very nice view of the city lights spread out below me. Probably the best view in town. I opened my napkin, placed it carefully across my lap, and looked around for a waiter.

Instead, I saw four women in military camouflage uniforms approaching my table. Their green shoulder boards and red berets identified them as members of the same group I'd seen earlier in the morning, at the airport. These were Gaddafi's female bodyguards. As they approached, I also noticed that all of them wore sidearms and long, wicked-looking daggers.

The leader, tall, and broad-shouldered, wore her long hair in a ponytail and sported an honest-to-God black eyepatch. She strode straight up to me and stopped just inside my zone of comfort. For North Americans, this is anywhere between eighteen and twenty-four inches away.

Get inside this zone, and you are likely to be either an enemy or a lover.

She wasn't anyone I remembered dating recently. Her nameplate was in Arabic, and as she stood staring at me, I was able to spell it out – El-Sharif. If the emblems of rank displayed on her shoulder boards were similar to the Tunisian ones, then she was a *ra'id*, or major.

Major El-Sharif pointed at me, and then at the door. "*Okruj.*"

As I've said, my Arabic isn't very good, but among the useful phrases I've learned, this was one I understood very well. *Get out.*

The other women had lined up behind her. Their expressions were impassive, but their body language said otherwise.

I decided to play it dumb. "I, ah, beg your pardon?"

The major glared at me. "No Arabic?" she said. "English, then. *Get out! Now!*" This time she raised her voice.

I stood up slowly and pushed my chair back. "Now, just a second," I said in my most reasonable tone of voice. "I'm just about to have dinner here."

One of the other women stepped forward. Unlike her colleague, who was staring daggers at me, this one's eyes were sympathetic, almost kind. When she spoke, her English was fluent, almost accentless. "You're not having dinner anymore," she said quietly. "Not here. You need to leave, right now. We require the dining room."

Her nameplate said El-Khoury, and she had the three gold stars of a *naqib*, or captain. "The Colonel and his party are coming for dinner soon," she continued. "They like the view here. We need everyone else out. Now. It's a security matter." Her eyes were the color of Baltic amber. I wondered what she looked like when she was smiling.

She wasn't smiling now. I looked at her, and then back at the major, who'd stepped back, still glaring at me. When in doubt, I thought, go to the top. I took a step towards her.

The captain put her hand on my arm. "Don't do anything stupid," she whispered. "Just walk away. Better for everyone."

Something inside me shifted. It had been a very long and tiring day, and this was just the last straw. "To hell with that," I said, batting away her hand. "You people are way out of line here, and–"

I never got to finish the sentence. The captain stepped back out of the way, and without warning, the major with the eyepatch launched herself at me. I barely had time to react. She did something with her hands and feet, very fast, and suddenly I was upside down. I landed with a loud and painful thump on the floor, and lay there stunned, trying to catch my breath.

The eyepatch major stepped back, her hands up in front of her in a combat stance, daring me to fight.

I'll fight when I have to, but this, I thought, might not be the time. I levered myself up on one elbow. The captain with the amber eyes leaned over me, her lips close to my ear. "I warned you, Mr. Donovan," she breathed. "Now leave quietly. Otherwise Major El-Sharif will have you taken outside, and you can continue your discussion with her there. You'll have some difficulty walking afterwards, I would imagine." She paused. "Your choice."

I thought for a moment. Fight another day, I decided. "I'll leave."

She smiled then. Yes, I thought through my pain. She's actually quite striking. She pulled me to my feet with one smooth, powerful motion. Around us, several waiters hovered, casting fearful, anxious glances our way.

I shrugged myself back into shape, testing arms and legs for damage. I was shaky, but able to move on my own. I collected what dignity I could, picked up my shoulder bag, and headed slowly for the door. *"Pas de problème,"* I muttered, brushing aside one of the waiters on my way out.

In the lobby, the manager came rushing up. "Monsieur Donovan, I'm so sorry. I had no idea—"

"Never mind," I said with a weak grin. "All I've lost is my pride. I'm still hungry, though. Do you have room service?"

"Yes, of course. Order whatever you like. It's on the house."

I thanked him and walked, just a little stiffly, toward the elevators.

* * *

An hour later, I was starting to feel better after two beers – real ones this time – a *steak-frites* and some chocolate mousse. I dragged myself up onto the bed, picked up the phone, and made an international call to Bone Brown. He answered on the second ring.

We skipped the pleasantries as I told him about my day. In particular, about my watcher in the Medina, and my humiliation in the dining room at the hands of a female paratroop major. "It's been a very strange day, Bone," I concluded. "The strangest thing of all is that the captain, the one who spoke good English, actually knew my name."

"Well, here's something equally strange," said Bone. "You remember how we almost got hit by a car coming back from college the other night?"

"I remember it well," I said. "Any luck with the number plate?"

"Actually, yes," said Bone. "You may not believe this, but the car is registered to the Libyan embassy in London. In the name of our friend Ali Akbar Al-Trabelsi."

I gave a low whistle. "The economic attaché. The guy we met at dinner."

"The same," said Bone.

"Does this make any sense to you?"

"At first, no, it did not," said Bone. "But then I met Professor Birdwhistle this afternoon. Over coffee, he let slip that earlier in the day, he'd actually told Al-Trabelsi about Hadley, the chelengk, and why you were going to Tunis. So there's the connection. The damned fool couldn't keep his mouth shut." Bone was silent for a moment, and then he said, "Are you worried, Max?"

"A little," I admitted. "There's some sort of Libyan connection to all of this, but I can't yet see what it is. And until I have that figured out, I'm still walking around in the dark. And in the dark," I added, "you can sometimes bump into sharp and dangerous things."

"Do you want to stop? Perhaps it's time to turn this over to the authorities."

"Not yet," I said. "There's something here. I can't quite see it yet, but I'll bet if I poke some more, something will happen."

"Something will happen, all right," said Bone. "You've been lucky so far, you know?"

There was silence on the line for a moment. "One more day," I said. "Just one more day. If things aren't clearer by then, I'll turn it all over to the embassy and the police."

* * *

After I'd hung up, I got out of my clothes and into a pair of boxer shorts and an oversize T-shirt. I got the Makarov pistol out from under my mattress, racked the slide to make sure there was a bullet in the chamber, and stuck it under my pillow. Then I slipped into bed. I was exhausted, and badly in need of sleep.

It did not come right away. Nearly getting hit by a car on a Cambridge back street was one thing, but being tailed by a man with a gun through the back alleys of Tunis was another. And then, of course, there was the fiasco at dinnertime, where a strange woman had set me on my butt with almost no effort. I stayed awake, eyes wide open in the dark, thinking about all those things and what they might mean. What bothered me particularly was the paratrooper with the lovely amber eyes. The one who'd spoken to me as I lay on the floor. How did she come to know my name?

The *what* of it all was fairly clear: I was a target for the Libyans. The *why* wasn't at all clear. I lay in the darkness and ran it all through my mind.

Generally speaking, there are only a limited number of reasons why someone turns into a target, and over the years, I'd seen examples of most of them. One is because of who you happen to be. Your nationality, your ethnicity, your religion, your profession, your affiliations – any and all of these can make you a target for someone. Another reason people become targets is because of things they possess. The obvious example is money, but there are many other things capable of attracting unwelcome attention. And then, of course, you could become a target because of what you know.

I wasn't aware that the Libyans were particularly interested in people like me, so that would seem to eliminate the first reason. Nor did I have anything that anyone else might want. And as far as I could tell, I didn't know anything of much use to anyone else.

That left the final reason folks get targeted: because of something they've done. I stared at the dark ceiling and thought about what I'd been doing. And here, the answer was crystal-clear: I'd been looking for Hadley Holloway. And that, it seems, had triggered a great deal of interest among the Libyans.

Occam's Razor. In other words, the simplest explanation was usually the right one. Or as Bone Brown put it to me once, *"Entia non sunt multiplicanda praeter necessitatem,"* which basically means "Don't overthink things."

Bone thinks I don't understand Latin, but I do, the result of several terrifying years spent in Miss Evans' class in a missionary school overseas.

The outline of things was becoming just a bit clearer now. Al-Trabelsi had picked up on my interest in Hadley from Birdwhistle and from our conversation at High Table back in Cambridge. He had then tried to run me over. When that didn't work, he got on the phone and alerted his North African cronies. It wasn't yet clear that they wanted to actually kill me, but they obviously wanted to stop me from trying to find Hadley. At least, that's what it looked like, from the available evidence. And everybody seemed to be in on it, from street thugs to officers in the Libyan armed forces.

It wasn't even nine o'clock in the evening, but the sandman was calling. I wasn't going to get any further with this right now, so I decided to call it a night. I felt under my pillow and patted the pistol. Then I turned on my side, shut my eyes, and drifted off to sleep.

CHAPTER TEN

Just after three in the morning, I snapped awake. Lying perfectly still, I listened to the darkness. Somebody – or something – was scratching at my door.

Although I'm generally a deep sleeper, I'm can also come awake instantly. This is a holdover from my early years in Thailand, where even in the city, you could get unwanted creatures coming into your bedroom. Later, of course, it had been a professional necessity to be able to wake up quickly, without sound or movement.

Whoever – or whatever – was outside my door was being pretty quiet, too. But not quiet enough. I opened my mouth slightly to improve my hearing, and listened some more. After a few seconds, I understood what was going on.

Somebody was picking the lock to my door.

Well, shit, I thought. The perfect end to a rather annoying day. And perfectly in line with the emerging pattern. I'd contemplated changing hotels tomorrow morning to get away from the Colonel and his crowd, but it looked now as if I'd left things a bit too late.

Or perhaps not.

I'd been quietly kicking myself for not having interrogated the guy who'd followed me in the Medina. I had his ID card, but I couldn't read it, and besides, what I'd really needed to do was talk to him.

Maybe, I thought, I can talk to this one.

I slid my hand under the pillow, grabbed the pistol, and ever so quietly, rose from the bed. Once on my feet, I tiptoed across the room to the door, positioning myself to one side so that I'd be behind it when it opened.

I know quite a bit about picking locks, and apparently whoever was on the other side of my door did too, because a few seconds after I'd gotten myself into position, there was a click, and the door swung slowly open. The night lights in the hallway illuminated the interior of my room somewhat, but since my bed was actually around the corner, whoever had just opened the door would have to fully enter the room in order to see if I was there.

Which they were now in the process of doing.

A single person, carrying a small duffle bag, began stepping very quietly into my room. I waited until they'd come fully inside. Then I kicked the door shut, grabbed the intruder around the neck with one arm, and jammed my pistol hard into the small of their back.

The duffle bag hit the floor, and then three things became immediately apparent to me. The first was that I had my arm around the neck of a woman. Both her hands came up, and I learned the second thing: that she wasn't carrying a weapon. The third and final realization, following very quickly on from the second, was that I was badly outmatched. She bent forward and grabbed me. A split second later I flew through the air and landed on my back with a hard thud, thinking as I did so that this was getting to be a familiar position.

Fortunately, I'd managed to keep hold of the pistol. I raised it now and croaked, "Enough."

To my great surprise, she complied immediately, stepping back and raising her arms as I got to my feet. Keeping the pistol trained on her, I moved to the wall and snapped on the room light. I blinked in surprise as I recognized my intruder. Standing in front of me was the paratrooper captain. The one with the amber eyes and the nice smile. The one who'd spoken to me in English in the dining room, just before I'd been thrown to the floor by her buddy with the eyepatch.

"Huh," was all I could think to say. Then I added, "I hope you haven't come back for a rematch. I'm not really in the mood."

She shook her head. "I'm not here to fight with you, Mr. Donovan. And I apologize for what happened earlier. I want to talk to you." She spoke flawless English.

I took a closer look at her. The eyes were what you noticed first, I thought, but the rest of her face was attractive as well. I'm a sucker for noses, and hers was great, just the right size and shape over a wide mouth and full lips. Her thick black hair was pulled back into a sensible ponytail. If you undid it, it would probably go halfway down her back.

If I'm not going to have to fight with you, I thought, I would love to talk with you. "We can talk," I said. "Are we doing this in English?"

She gave me a brief smile. "English is fine. Or French. Or Arabic. Take your pick."

"English it is, then," I said. I kept my pistol on her, staying far enough away so that she couldn't aim a kick my way. "Breaking into someone's hotel room at—" I consulted my watch "—three o'clock in the morning is a strange way to begin a conversation."

"It was the only way I could think of," she said. "We're watched all the time."

"We?"

"My sisters and I. The guards. The Colonel has security people everywhere, watching. Even watching us."

She still had her uniform on. Blue camouflage battle dress, together with a web belt holding her service pistol and what looked like a combat knife. Big and sharp.

"Take off your web belt," I said. "And throw it over in the corner there, behind me."

"I'm not going to hurt you, Mr. Donovan," she said as she took off her belt and pitched it underhand into the corner.

"We're just making sure of that," I said. "Okay, let's talk. Who are you?"

"My name is Nadia. Nadia El-Khoury. I— I'm a captain in the *Ar-rahibat ath-thawriyyat.*"

"In the *what*?"

She grimaced. "In English, it translates as 'The Revolutionary Nuns.' It's a stupid name, I know. Western journalists like to call us 'the Amazons.' We're Gaddafi's personal bodyguards."

Most of the nuns I'd met in my life had been anything but revolutionary. Nor did they dress in military camouflage. "Well, sister," I said after a moment, "why are you here? What did you come looking for?"

"You, Mr. Donovan," she replied steadily. "I came looking for you. I need to talk to you."

"How do you know my name? You called me by name in the dining room."

"We all know your name, Mr. Donovan. Our informants identified you at the airport. We monitor all persons of interest coming to Tunis, you know."

"Did you send that guy to follow me this afternoon, down in the *souk*?"

She cocked her head slightly. "No. No, we didn't. He was probably with the *mukhabarat*. We don't have responsibility for that sort of thing. You say you were followed?"

I walked over to where I'd draped my shirt over a chair and pulled out the ID I'd taken from the man outside Basli's shop. I tossed it to her. "Followed by this man. Do you know him?"

She scanned the laminated card quickly, and then looked up at me. "I don't know who he is, but that's a *mukhabarat* ID. The intelligence agency."

"You people have intelligence agents here in Tunis?"

She gave me an exasperated look. "Of course we do," she said. "Just as your government does. And every other major European country. The Colonel likes to know what is going on with his neighbors. It's normal, wouldn't you say?"

"Nothing around here's been normal so far," I said. "Why is the *mukhabarat* interested in me?"

"They're not particularly interested in you. They're interested in the person you're looking for. The American woman. And also that thing she claims to have found."

"The chelengk? They're after the chelengk?"

"Is that what you call it? All we were told is that it's supposed to be a piece of old jewelry."

"That's one way of putting it," I said. "Do you know where it is?"

"No, of course not. But the *mukhabarat* think that the American woman does."

"And this for some strange reason has brought you to my door," I said. "But I still don't understand why."

"It's very simple, Mr. Donovan. I know where the American woman is."

I blinked. "You know where Hadley is?"

"Hadley?"

"That's her name. The one who found the chelengk."

"So yes, I know where Hadley is. And I have come to tell you that." She took a breath. "Before I do, could you possibly put the gun down? It's making me very nervous. I'm not going to hurt you. I swear it by God."

I thought about that for a moment. She didn't seem as if she wanted trouble, and she wasn't armed anymore. On the other hand, she was strong and well-trained, as I knew all too well. I'm strong, too, but I'm not keen on fighting. I rely more on deception, cunning and my big fat mouth, and none of them were going to do me much good in the here and now.

I looked her up and down. In street clothes, she'd be a very attractive woman. I shrugged inwardly. Then I put the gun down.

"Okay, Captain Khoury," I said. "Tell me where she is."

Her eyes came up and met mine. They really were quite beautiful, I thought. "There is," she said, "one other thing."

I sighed. "There's always one other thing, isn't there? Whatever can it be?"

"You have to get me out of here."

I stared at her. "Get you out of where?"

"Out of the country. I want to desert. To defect. To escape. Whatever you want to call it."

"And go where?"

"Anywhere I can be safe. I don't care. But you need to help me." Her eyes bored into me, radiating intensity. "I'll tell you where the woman is, but you must help me in return. The *mukhabarat* say that you're clever, dangerous and resourceful. I need someone exactly like that to help me get away from here."

I took a breath. "Let me get this straight. You're going to desert from the Libyan army, and you want me to get you out of the country. And in exchange for that, you'll tell me where Hadley is."

Her head came up. "I'll do better than that, Mr. Donovan. I'll help you rescue her."

I thought for a moment. I had no idea how I was going to get this woman out of the country, but I'd solved bigger problems before, and in any case, you take things one step at a time. Getting Hadley away from whoever was holding her here was the first priority.

"Well?" she said.

"I'm thinking," I replied. I could use an ally, I thought. I had no real idea whether I could trust Captain Nadia El-Khoury, but there was only one way to find out. "Okay, one more question." I pointed to the duffle bag. "What's in there?"

"Passport, some money, a change of clothing." She paused. "And extra ammunition for my service pistol."

"Ready to go, eh?"

She nodded. "Very ready. Do we have a deal, Mr. Donovan?"

I gave her a half-smile. "If we're going to be partners, call me Max."

She smiled back. "I'm Nadia, then." She looked at her wristwatch. "And we should get started."

"Started on what?"

"Rescuing your Hadley. Right now. You see, they're planning to take her to Tripoli later today. On Gaddafi's plane."

CHAPTER ELEVEN

"Park it here," said Nadia. "Just pull off to the side."

I did as she asked, pulling over the side of the road and killing my lights. We were outside the city, just down the road from the American War Cemetery in Carthage. Past the cemetery, bare fields opened up on either side of us. Overhead, the stars shone sharp and bright. I rolled down the window and felt the warm night breeze hit my face.

"We should talk here before we go in to get her," she said. "People rarely come this way. And if they do, they won't take any notice of us." She moved closer to me on the seat. "They'll think we're lovers. This is where Tunisian girls come to make out with their boyfriends." She paused. "To watch the submarine races."

I stared at her. "Submarine races? How on earth do you know about submarine races?"

She gave a soft chuckle. "Because I used to come here myself," she said. "For the races," she added.

"But you're not even from here," I said. "Or are you?"

"No," she said, smiling now, "I'm not. But I lived here for a while. I suppose I should tell you a little about myself."

"Yes, Captain," I said. "I think you had better."

"Okay, first of all, it's no longer 'Captain.' That went away the moment I came into your hotel room. I'm Nadia now, remember? Nadia El-Khoury."

"So – Lebanese?"

She nodded. "Originally, yes."

"That's why you know French," I said. "But where did you learn your English? It's perfect."

"I have an honors degree from the American University of Beirut. Dual major in English and History. All our instruction was in English. When I graduated, everyone said I had a bright future." Her face clouded. "And then my life changed."

"How so?"

"I came here. On vacation." She paused. "And while I was here, I fell in love with a Libyan boy. His name was Tariq, and he was from Tripoli. He was handsome, he was smart, and he was a revolutionary."

"Ah."

She nodded. "You can probably guess the rest. We stayed together in Tunis for a few months. Then I went to Tripoli with him, and I joined the *jamahiriya* – Gaddafi's revolution. For a while, I believed in it – all of it."

She turned to look at me. "People need to feel they're a part of something bigger. They need to feel that they're helping to change the world. Did you never feel that way, Max?"

I nodded. "Oh, yes," I said. "I've felt that way from time to time." Along with many thousands of others, I thought. For some, it's the priesthood; for others, it's teaching, or a political cause. And for some like me, it was a war in a faraway country which turned out to be not at all what any of us had imagined.

"At first," Nadia continued, "it was exhilarating. It was everything I'd dreamed of. To be part of a national revolution. To join with others for the common good. The Colonel's speeches were inspiring – magical, almost. Tariq joined the army, and so did I, two young revolutionaries together on an adventure. We trained together, and it turned out that I was a much better soldier than he was. He was impulsive, and headstrong, and would talk back to his superiors. He never took the training seriously, the way I did. Finally, he said the wrong things to one of the officers, and they posted him to Chad. He was killed two weeks later, in the fighting around Faya-Largeau."

She shook her head. "Tariq was never meant to be a soldier. I realized that afterwards. He was a big talker, a dreamer." She paused, and her expression darkened. "But he was also a liar. When they brought his body back from Chad, I found out that he'd been married for two years."

I considered all of that for a moment while I let the night breeze cool my face. "But there's more to this story, isn't there?"

She nodded. "Oh yes, there's more. When I heard about Tariq, I was devastated. I was in shock. Then when I found out about his wife, my shock turned to anger, and to disgust with myself for having been so stupid."

"It happens," I said, thinking of several incidents in my own highly uneven past. "It wasn't really your fault."

She shrugged. "In the end, it didn't matter. At just about that time, the Colonel decided to put together the so-called Revolutionary Nuns. I was invited to join." She paused. "And I did." She gave a short bark of a laugh. "You could almost say the Colonel caught me on the rebound. Isn't that what you say in English?"

I thought back to the women I had seen on the airstrip, the same ones who'd thrown me out of the dining room. They were the Revolutionary Nuns, and here I was talking to one of them. It had been only hours before, but it seemed like days ago now.

"So, you joined the Nuns."

"I did. All women, and very tough indeed. We got sent for specialized training in the Soviet Union, believe it or not. A place called Perevalne in Crimea, near the Black Sea. I learned to parachute. I also learned small arms, communications, and sambo."

"Sambo?"

"*Samozashchita bez oruzhiya,*" she said. "Sambo. It's a kind of martial art system the Russians teach their soldiers. It's what Fawzia used on you in the dining room. And me, too, up in your room just a little while ago."

"And so all the women in your, ah, paratroop detachment learned this sambo thing?"

She nodded. "They made it part of our required training. Probably the most useful thing they taught us. You might have noticed that in this part of the world, men often don't listen to women."

"Not just here," I said.

"No doubt. Well, here for sure. We've found that it's just a good way of getting male attention on occasion. It also saves time, if you see what I mean."

I nodded, thinking back to how hard I'd hit the floor in the hotel dining room. "Two for one," I said. "Nice. But why women? As bodyguards, I mean?"

She tossed her hair. "Oh, that was just one of Gaddafi's stupid ideas. He used to tell people that Arabs would never fire on a woman. So as long as he kept himself surrounded by women, he thought he'd be safe." She grimaced. "It was actually a lot simpler than that. He just liked being surrounded by women."

"And now you want to get out."

She gave me a look. "I *am* out, Max. I'm a deserter. If they find me now, they'll kill me. As for why I decided to do that, it's simple: I woke up and came to my senses. When I went to Tripoli I was just a young, idealistic woman. I thought I was in love. Maybe I was, but Tariq got blown away by some tribesman in Chad before we'd had much of a chance to be together. So, I turned to the revolution. It took longer, but eventually, that got blown away, too. Don't get me wrong, Gaddafi did some good things for the people – education, healthcare, things like that. But the rest of it was a mess.

"After a while I started to see how crazy it all was. Gaddafi talked big, but the so-called Green Revolution didn't change much of anything. His stupid war in Chad killed thousands of his so-called followers. He sent money and arms to the IRA. To Uganda. Anywhere he could make trouble. He poked the Americans, the Europeans, and even some of the other Arabs, and for what? And sometimes, they poked back."

I nodded, thinking back to what Boomer Quackenbush had told me about the Marine pilots from the Nimitz shooting down the Libyan fighters over the Gulf of Sirte.

"But that wasn't the main thing, Max. I finally realized that the man is crazy. Literally crazy. People wouldn't believe some of the stuff that happens with him. The bulletproof tent. The weird suits. The women – oh, God, the women. It was hard to watch. And sooner or later, I thought, it's going to be me going into that tent with him. I could see the way he looked at me sometimes.

"So Tunis was my chance. He wanted to come and talk to Bourguiba about something or other – any excuse to make a big show. But we were briefed on the secondary mission, which was to get this woman Hadley and bring her back to Tripoli. They wanted to find out about this chelengk thing she is supposed to have found."

"Why the interest in the chelengk?" I asked. "Does Gaddafi think it's really that valuable?"

"It's not about money, Max. This is Gaddafi's ego, his pride. Gaddafi sees this chelengk thing as a symbol of imperialism and oppression. Libya was once part of the Ottoman Empire, you know. Ataturk himself fought for the Turks in Tripoli. And the British, well, are the British. He'd love to poke both of them in the eye."

"So naturally Gaddafi wants the chelengk."

She nodded. "He's dying to get his hands on it. They showed us a picture of this thing at our briefing before we flew out here. It's exactly the kind of gaudy decoration that Gaddafi would love to wear on his turban. I can just see him inviting the Turkish and British ambassadors to his desert tent, in order to parade it in front of them."

"And they think that bringing Hadley to Tripoli is going to help them?"

"They do. According to our briefing earlier today, she hasn't yet told them where the chelengk is. If they bring her to Libya, they can use, ah, more persuasive methods to question her."

"Won't it be hard to get her out of the country without anyone noticing?"

She shook her head. "Not at all. Don't forget, we're a diplomatic mission. Nobody has the right to inspect what we bring in or take out. You could bring a camel in if you wanted. Or out. No, Hadley will be drugged and put into a crate or a large mailbag. That's the plan."

"And when is this supposed to happen?"

"Today. The plane leaves at noon. That's why I was in such a hurry."

We sat side by side in silence for a few moments. The stars burned bright overhead, the night air felt cool on my face. Everything around us was silent. Just the night for a submarine race.

I spoke at last. "So, this is where you came to make out, huh?"

She laughed softly and moved a little away from me. "Don't get any ideas."

I shifted on my seat. "Are you kidding? You threw me to the floor just a little while ago."

I checked my wristwatch. It was almost four in the morning. If the Libyan delegation was leaving today, we had very little time left. I started the car. "Time to go."

She put her hand on my shoulder. "Wait," she said. "You meant it, right? About helping me get out of the country?"

I put my hand over hers. It felt warm, but not at all soft – I'd hate to get hit with it. "I'll get you out," I said. "I'm not sure how yet, but I'm pretty good at this kind of thing. We'll figure it out once we have Hadley. Trust me."

She squeezed my hand. "I trust you, Max."

"Good," I said, and put the car in gear. "Then, let's go get her."

CHAPTER TWELVE

"There," said Nadia. "That house, there. Number 511."

We drove at a crawl down the Rue des Palmiers in La Marsa. I had the window open, catching the fresh salty breeze coming in from the beach just over the hill behind us.

The house, going slowly by on our right, resembled a hundred others in the neighborhood. White, two-storied, with windows and doors trimmed with blue. It was hard to see very much else, thanks to the five-foot wall running all around the lot. Bougainvillea and grapevines spilled over the wall from the garden to the inside. In the open carport, I spotted a white delivery van with a crumpled fender.

"Do you want to go around again, get another look?"

I shook my head. This was a residential neighborhood, and although no one was on the street at this time of night, I had no doubt that anyone looking out the window would eventually notice a strange car driving repeatedly past the house.

I turned up the side street, found a parking spot, and pulled over. From where we were parked, we could just see over the wall to the back of the house. There was a wide balcony off one of the bedrooms. The windows on either side had heavy metal shutters, closed tight now. There was a light on in one of the upstairs rooms. I rolled down the window again and listened, but heard no sounds coming from the house. No voices, no music.

According to Nadia's briefing, Hadley was inside the house. And the van confirmed that this was indeed the house in question. But neither of us knew any more than that. We had no idea about the layout inside, and we didn't know how many people there might be in residence. Nor how well they were armed.

On the other hand, we knew precisely how well we were armed. We each had a Makarov pistol. Which is to say, not very well armed at all.

Nadia spoke quietly. "What are we going to do?"

I let my breath out. "Let's think for a moment," I said. "That balcony's too high to reach without a ladder. The ground-floor windows are all covered with iron grills. To approach the house, we'd have to get over the wall first."

"And somebody might see us."

"Exactly," I said. "Someone on the street might see us, and somebody inside the house is even more likely to see us, if they're staying alert."

"Those are all the things that won't work. What will?"

I thought about that line of Lord Nelson's I'd quoted to Birdwhistle: *never mind the maneuvers, go straight at 'em.* "We'll go in the front door."

Beside me, I heard a sharp intake of breath. "How, exactly?"

"Simple," I said. "You're still in uniform. You walk straight up to the door and ring the bell. They'll look out and see a Libyan army officer. All you have to do is get them to open up."

I learned across her and rummaged in the glove compartment, pulling out the car rental agreement in its cardboard folder. I took the cardboard folder, tore it in half, and handed the torn half to her.

"And when they do, stick this in the door latch on your way in, to keep it from closing all the way. Once you get inside, you need to create a fuss. I don't know, maybe you could start yelling at them about their treatment of their prisoner. Or why isn't anybody walking the perimeter? Or why haven't they shaved today?"

"That's ridiculous," she began. "They don't–"

I put my finger to her lips. "What I'm saying is, it doesn't matter what kind of commotion you create. It just needs to be loud, and urgent. And it needs to get everybody there into the room with you, and focused on you. Got it?"

"Loud and urgent. Get them all together. Focus them on me." She was starting to smile now, getting into it.

"Ten seconds later, I'll be inside, too. It's important to get all of them together, because there are only two of us. If there are people in different parts of the house coming at us from all directions, we're screwed. Well, maybe not screwed, but there's likely to be gunfire, and we really don't want that."

"Okay," she said. "Assume this works. What happens then?"

I opened my shoulder bag to show her the spare cable ties I'd bought that afternoon in the Medina. "We tie them up with these, grab Hadley, and take off."

I paused. "That's the plan so far, anyway. Of course, no battle plan survives first contact with the enemy. Field Marshal von Moltke said that."

She sighed. "Well, whoever he is, let's hope he's wrong."

I took her hand again and looked straight at her. "We'll make it work, Nadia. We have to – we don't have any other options. Remember," I said, "desperation is the *real* mother of invention." I caught her look. "And no, von Moltke didn't say that. I did."

* * *

We stood in front of the gate now, Nadia in plain sight, me back at the side, behind the wall. She pulled off her nameplate and handed it to me. "Get inside," I whispered. "Pull your gun if you have to; I'll be right behind you."

She looked at me. "If this doesn't work—"

I put my hand up. "I know." I took out my pistol and racked the slide. "We're probably dead. Now go and do it."

She strode up the walkway to the door of the house and rang the bell. I took a deep breath. The next sixty seconds would decide this thing, one way or the other.

After a moment, the outside light went on. From inside, I heard someone bark out "*Shkuun?* Who is it?"

Nadia had a brief and staccato exchange with someone behind the door, and then it opened and she walked in. As it began to close again, I pushed through the gate and ran up the walk to the house.

I waited ten seconds, and then gave the door a push. It opened silently, just as shouting erupted from somewhere upstairs. I pushed the door all the way and went inside, my pistol in a two-handed combat grip.

There was no one in the entryway. Upstairs, I heard Nadia yelling at people, and people yelling back.

I was in a darkened building with an unknown layout and about to face an unknown number of hostile individuals. I glanced quickly right and left, seeing nothing. The lights from upstairs were enough to show me a salon to my left and a small dining room, together with what looked like an entrance to the kitchen. That would be where the back door was. I took five big steps and stuck my head through the kitchen doorway. Empty, and the door to the outside was locked.

Then, another round of shouting came from upstairs. Someone up there had finally figured out that there was somebody else in the house now. Time to get going. I took the stairs three at a time, wishing I had one of the flash-bangs. I got to the top of the stairs and looked right, into a big room where Nadia, pistol steady in her hand, had four guys backed up against the wall.

"Downstairs is clear," I announced.

"About time you got here," Nadia muttered. "Tie them up."

One by one, I beckoned the men forward, turned them around, and zip-tied their wrists together.

"*Kess ommik*," one of them hissed at me, telling me to do something not at all nice to my mother.

I grinned and pulled his ear, hard. "Same to you, friend."

The second guy was equally unhappy. He glared at Nadia and said in a low and deadly voice, "*Ya sharmouta*." I decided things had gone far enough. I slapped the side of his head soundly with my open palm, bouncing him hard against the wall.

"Don't talk about my sister that way," I said as I hauled him upright again.

Nadia gave me a wink. "Thanks, bro."

In a few moments, it was done. I turned to Mr. Sharmouta. "Where is she?" I said in French.

He shook his head.

Nadia sighed and kicked him in the shins, hard. "Where's the woman?" she repeated, in Arabic.

He spit at our feet and shook his head defiantly, but not before I saw two of the others look sideways at the closed door at the end of the hallway. I hefted my pistol. "Sis, why don't you secure these idiots to the radiators," I said, handing her the rest of the cable ties. "Keep them well apart from one another. I'll go see what's in the other room."

The locked door yielded easily to my boot. Inside, a young red-haired woman sat gagged and tied to a wooden chair, her eyes wide with terror. I snapped the light on, stuck my pistol in my belt, and smiled. "You're Hadley, right?"

She nodded frantically.

"I'm Max Donovan," I said as I took off her gag and cut her bonds. "I'm a friend of your Uncle Isaac's, and here to get you out of this place. He'll be glad to see you again."

I took her hand and brought her to her feet. Hadley Holloway was tall and skinny, with freckles and short red hair, looking a little like a cross between Katharine Hepburn and Dorothy of Oz. Her green eyes flashed as she looked around the room. "What did you do with the four assholes?" were the first words out of her mouth.

"All taken care of," I said.

Nadia poked her head around the door. "Everything okay, here?"

I nodded. "This is Nadia, my partner. Nadia, Hadley." The two women nodded at each other. I turned to Hadley and winked. "Don't let the uniform fool you, she's on our team. Now go find your stuff. We're getting the hell out of here."

* * *

Ten minutes later, we were parked back at the American Cemetery, just as before. Hadley sat in the back, Nadia up front with me. "We need to get out of here," Nadia said. "Those idiots won't stay tied up forever."

"You're right," I said. "But let's take a moment and figure out our next moves." I checked my watch. Nearly 5 a.m. now. I felt like I'd been up for days. "We'll go to the airport. That's probably the safest place for us right now. Catch the first flight out in the morning."

Nadia looked at me. "To where, exactly?"

"Anywhere off the African continent would do at this point, I think. Let's try for France – there's sure to be an early flight we can get on."

Nadia put her hand on my arm. "That won't work, Max. My Libyan documents are no good, and even with my Lebanese passport, I need a visa to get into most countries." She thought for a moment, and then brightened. "Except maybe Turkey. That should be okay."

I nodded. "Turkey it is, then. We'll all go together. Once we get there, I'll take Hadley on to London with me."

"You know I'm right here behind you, right?" Hadley's voice piped up from the back seat.

I started the car and put it in gear. "Don't worry, Hadley. We've got plenty of money for tickets. We'll be safe at the airport, and we—"

"No, Max. Stop." Hadley's voice was louder now. "We can't leave yet."

I put the car back in neutral and turned around. "Hadley, in a couple of hours, we'll have a dozen people searching for us. By noon, two dozen more. We need to leave. Now."

"What about the chelengk? The thing I came for? Surely Uncle Isaac told you about that."

I nodded. "He told me all about it, actually. You found it, right?" She nodded. "And you know where it is?" She nodded again. "Then it's simple. We get out of here this morning, and you and I can come back in a week or two when things have calmed down and collect this chelengk thing from wherever you stashed it."

Hadley leaned forward, grabbing my shoulder. Her fingers were surprisingly strong. "You think I'm just a piece of luggage, don't you? Well, think again, mister. This is my professional life on the line here. I've spent almost a year looking for this damned thing. And I finally found it. I found it, and I hid it again in a safe place. One that only I know about. And I am damned if I'm going back to Cambridge without it."

"Hadley, I–"

"No! We have to get it *right now*, Max."

"Wait. What's the big hurry?" Nadia's voice was calm in the darkness.

Hadley drew a breath. "Because– because I already told them where it is."

"*What?*" Nadia and I spoke at the same time.

"The guys back at the house – the assholes. I already told them where it is."

I couldn't believe what I was hearing. "And you told them this why?"

"They were going to take me out of the country, for God's sake," she said, her voice tight with anger. "So earlier this evening I told them, not an hour before you two showed up. They phoned somebody, cancelled their plans to get me on that plane. Instead, they were planning to take me to where I'd hidden it." Her grip on my shoulder tightened. "They know where it is now, Max, don't you see? We've got to get down there first, before they do."

"Down where, exactly?" Nadia sounded like she really didn't want to know the answer. Strangely enough, neither did I.

"South," said Hadley. "Way south." She paused. "Down in the desert."

Well shit, I thought, as I put the car into gear and eased back onto the road. Von Moltke would be laughing his ass off right now if he could hear this.

CHAPTER THIRTEEN

"Max, wake up." Somebody's hand was shaking me.

I opened my eyes and sat up, looking out the window of our car from the back seat, where I'd been sleeping. Morning had arrived, and we seemed to be in a parking lot filled with large trucks.

Nadia leaned over from the front seat, handing me a paper cup of hot coffee. I took it gratefully, and swilled some around in my mouth to cut the scum. Then she held out a fresh bread roll, covered with some sort of jam. "Breakfast time," she said.

I took it and bit off the end, chewing thoughtfully. Figs, I decided, and delicious. She'd also somehow managed to change out of her camouflage fatigues and into loose trousers and a cotton shirt. Much easier on the eyes.

As I chewed, I looked around at our surroundings. Nadia had pulled our car back, behind a row of big Berliet and Mercedes trucks, nicely hidden and out of sight from the road. That was smart, I thought. There were few people in evidence, but any one of them could be on the Libyan payroll, and the presence of a young red-haired foreigner would be instantly noticed.

Paranoid? Perhaps. But it didn't mean they still weren't after us.

"Where are we?" I said at last.

"In a truck stop, just outside Sfax. It's nearly half past eight."

"Um." I swallowed the last of the bread roll, thinking back over the night's events. We'd left La Marsa with Hadley's abductors gagged and zip-tied to the radiators in the house. I drove us to an all-night Total station in town, near Bab Suika. After filling the car, I gratefully accepted Nadia's offer to drive. Then I crawled into the back seat and fell asleep almost immediately.

Now we were in Sfax, nearly three hundred kilometers south of Tunis. I looked around. "Where's Hadley?"

"Coming now," said Nadia, pointing to Hadley, who was walking across the pavement from the small convenience store with more coffee, several big bottles of *gazouza*, and a pile of flat Arab bread.

She handed it all to me through the back window, and plopped into the front seat beside Nadia. "That's all the stuff they had in there," she said. "It'll do for a while, but we need more supplies if we're going south. We'll have to go shopping in town first before we get on the road again."

I rubbed my face, feeling two days' worth of stubble. "And we're going where again?" I asked.

"It's a *ksar*," she said. "About four hundred kilometers south of here, as the crow flies."

"What's a *ksar*?" I asked. The strange word was awkward on my lips.

"An old Berber fort," she said. "*Ksar* is the singular, *ksour* is plural. You'll hear both. They say the word is very old, possibly from the Latin word for the walled encampments the Roman legions used to build."

"*Castra*," I said, thinking back to Miss Evans' Latin class, many years ago.

"That's it. There are dozens of *ksour* out in the countryside. Many of them deep in the desert. This particular one happens to be abandoned. It's where I found the chelengk."

I brushed breadcrumbs off my shirt. I didn't know anything about Berber forts, and less about the desert.

"Where exactly is this *ksar*?" I said. "How do we get there?"

"You know where Gabès is?" Hadley asked.

I cast my mind back to when I'd used maps of Tunisia to fly with. "Um, more or less," I said. "South of here, isn't it? On the coast, almost to Djerba."

"That's right. Well, where we're going is inland, south of Gabès." She paused "Quite a bit south of Gabès, actually."

"And there's a road?"

Hadley gave me a shrug and a smile. "In a manner of speaking," she said as she pulled a map out of her bag and unfolded it. "Here."

I leaned forward to see where she was pointing. "Show me the way down."

"Sure." She ran her finger south along the coastal highway, from Sfax to Gabès. "It's about a hundred and thirty kilometers from here to Gabès," she said. "After that, we'll cut west, and go down the C211." She drew her finger a long way down the map. "The *ksar* is near here," she said. "It won't be marked on any map. It's abandoned, just off the sand track." She caught my look. "But don't worry," she said brightly. "I know exactly where it is. I could find it with my eyes shut."

I looked again at the map. Out of Sfax heading south, the road was a thick red line, which meant that it was wide and paved. After that, however, the road changed from thick red to the thin dotted yellow line she was tracing with her finger. I wasn't entirely sure what a dotted yellow line signified, but I knew it wasn't good.

"This C211," I said. "What's it like?"

Hadley gave me the kind of look people give you when they don't really want to tell you the bad news. "Well," she said finally, "it's a real road, and some of it is paved. But a lot of it is sand, and the sand gets blown around by the wind, so you have to be careful."

"But you know where this *ksar* place is?" I said.

She gave me an exasperated look. "I said so, didn't I? I spent weeks driving around down in that area. Desert driving isn't difficult, once you get the hang of it."

"What were you driving?"

"The Bourguiba Institute's Land Rover," she said. "Why?"

"This will probably be a little different," I said. "We don't have a Land Rover. This tiny little car is some French thing."

"It's a Peugeot," Nadia said helpfully. "A Peugeot 304, to be exact. Quite a nice car, really."

"It's French, as I said. And not really designed for the desert."

"Oh, shut up, Max," Nadia said in a friendly tone of voice. "It might not be ideal, but it's what we have. So we're just going to have to make the best of it."

I nodded. She was right, I thought; we had what we had. I glanced out the window again. Across the road, the sun was already high up over the Gulf, a gorgeous red-orange ball hanging over the sea. Nice, I thought, and then I began thinking about what that same sun was going to feel like a few hours later, when we would be moving through the desert.

"It's almost nine o'clock," I said. "Time we were on our way."

"Not so fast," said Hadley. "Like I said, shopping first. We'll need a few things for the desert."

I glanced at my watch. "Well, the lads back in La Marsa have probably gotten themselves untied by now, and if they have, then the alarm's gone out. So let's get what we need and be on our way."

CHAPTER FOURTEEN

We drove into Sfax, found a large Monoprix store near the market, and spent the next hour shopping. "We're going to need proper equipment," explained Hadley. "Neither of you look as if you'd last a day in the desert."

"I really didn't plan on being there even that long," I said. "It's going to take us a few hours at most, right? Go down, find your chelengk, come back."

"Maybe," said Hadley, rummaging through a bin of cheap sunglasses. "Maybe not. But if you go into the desert with that attitude, you're asking for trouble. Here. Try these on."

I put on the sunglasses, thinking that Hadley was probably right. My on-the-ground experience with deserts had been mostly drives from Los Angeles to Las Vegas. But as a pilot I was very familiar with the idea of a total environment. When you're in the air, you play by the air's rules. The air doesn't care a bit whether you are there or not, and if you disrespect it, it will mess you up in an instant, without a second thought.

I imagined that the desert would work that way, too.

We followed Hadley around as she picked out things and put them in our shopping cart. Three shovels – two big and one small. Four jerricans – two for water, two for fuel. Flashlights and extra batteries. Long-sleeved shirts and khaki trousers for her and Nadia, and some cheap woolen blankets.

She looked at my shoes. "Those look okay," she said approvingly. "And Nadia's got her combat boots. But I need something better than these stupid sandal things." She took Nadia by the hand and pulled her toward the shoe section. "Help me pick something out." They left me contemplating a rack of electric couscous makers.

Ten minutes later they were back, Hadley clutching what looked like a pair of Doc Martens knockoffs. She looked pleased.

Then we bought food. Mainly fruit and dates. Lots of dates. "Why so many dates?" I asked. "And do you really think we're going to need forty liters of water for only one day?"

"Let's hope we don't," Hadley said. "But we have to plan for a breakdown. Who knows how reliable that rental car of yours is? If we do break down, we could be there for three or four days. It would be nice to have something to eat and drink, if that happens."

"Three or four days?"

"It's the desert, Max. People don't come that way very often. There aren't any stores, garages, or even telephones. If we get stuck out there, we just have to wait it out until someone shows up. And we'll be glad that someone had the foresight to bring water and food."

On our way to the checkout, Hadley stopped. "Oh, one more thing."

"What now?"

"Probably the most important thing," she said, turning to what looked like a bin full of large, checked dishcloths. "Each of us needs a *shemagh*."

"A what?"

"You know, that thing the Arabs wrap around their head in the desert. A *shemagh*. People also call it a *keffiyeh*. Come here," she said to me, pulling one of the scarves out of the bin. "I'll show you how to wrap it."

I stood still and let her drape the cloth over my shoulders and around my head. I put my sunglasses on and turned to look at myself in one of the store mirrors. "Donovan of the Desert," I breathed.

"Don't laugh," she said. "Take it from me, the *shemagh* will keep your brains from boiling when you're out in the sun."

Nadia looked me over with a critical eye. "Not bad at all," she said approvingly. She turned to Hadley. "And you've even tied it properly. You're probably more of an Arab than I am."

Hadley blushed and smiled.

I tapped my watch. "If you two have enjoyed the fashion show, why don't you each pick out a *shemagh*, and let's get going."

We paid for our things, using the dinars I'd taken off the Libyan *mukhabarat* agent in the Medina. There was a Total station one hundred meters from the Monoprix, and we filled up again on gas and water.

As I rearranged the jerricans in the trunk of our rental car, I took mental inventory. We had food, water and gasoline, as well as some desert-suitable clothing. We had money. Each of us had our passport. Nadia and I each had a pistol. And, of course, I had my trusty Zippo lighter.

We were set; we were on our way. We were driving a crappy French car down into a remote part of the desert, with almost no real idea of what we were doing.

What could possibly go wrong?

CHAPTER FIFTEEN

"What happens afterwards?"

Nadia spoke quietly, as Hadley dozed in the back seat. She'd stretched out once we were through Sfax, and was almost instantly asleep. Outside the car, the Tunisian steppe went by at a steady pace of sixty kilometers an hour, a concession to both the state of the road and the various groups and individuals, human and otherwise, that were sharing it with us.

"You mean after we find the chelengk?" I said.

She nodded.

"We leave," I said. "As quickly and as quietly as possible."

"I hope you can come up with a very good plan for that," she said. "Because I can't."

I thought about how best to respond to that. The easiest and quickest way to leave a country is usually to get on a plane. But that might not be the best way, not if the *mukhabarat* were looking for you. They'd be staking out major airports and seaports, and we'd never know who the watchers were.

Getting across land borders is usually pretty easy, but not so much in our case. Libya to the east was the very place we'd been trying to stay away from. To the west lay Algeria, not exactly a user-friendly country in its own right. I had no doubt that I could get us inside. I just didn't know how long it would be before we all got arrested.

Honesty, I thought, was probably the best policy here. "I don't have a plan yet," I said after a moment. "But I will, when the time comes. You know what they say."

"No, what do they say?"

I smiled. "When the student is ready, the master will appear."

Nadia gave a small snort of disbelief. "I certainly hope so." She gave me a look. "You're kind of full of it sometimes, aren't you?"

We rode on in silence for a while.

From Sfax to Gabès the road had been good, although Tunisian drivers themselves sometimes left something to be desired. It was a bit less than a hundred and fifty kilometers, and we made it easily just before noon. After Gabès, the road turned west, toward El Hamma, thirty-five kilometers away, and from that point on, things began to slowly but surely deteriorate. The pavement narrowed, and rough patches and potholes began to appear.

Hadley woke up a few kilometers outside El Hamma, and we stopped at a gas station. "This is it," said Hadley, opening the car door. She pointed to a road branching off, heading south. "That's the C221, our route south. This place here doesn't have a name. But it's our last chance for gas, food, water, and the opportunity to actually pee inside."

While Hadley and Nadia headed to the *toilettes*, I gassed up the car once again and checked our oil and water. All okay. Despite my generally low opinion of French manufactured items, the Peugeot was proving to be a sturdy little car, and with luck, we'd be okay. Or not. It's like that with flying: you keep your equipment in shape, you check everything before you take off, and then you hope for the best. As Pasteur said, chance favors the prepared mind.

The women came back and switched seats. Nadia climbed in the back to catch some sleep, while Hadley sat up front with me. The C221, although not great, was still good. The countryside around us was flat, with low hills here and there, and I enjoyed the rise and fall of the road as we gradually moved south. The soil was rocky more than sandy, and I was grateful that so far we were still on a real road.

Hadley must have sensed my thoughts. "Enjoy it while you can, Max," she said. "Eventually, the paving will stop."

"Eventually?"

She grinned. "Pretty soon, actually. Maybe another fifty kilometers."

I grunted. "And what's it going to be like then?"

"Better than you might expect," she said. "They keep the track in pretty good shape, because of the trucks going down to the oil fields. And for the pipeline. The problem is the sand. The wind blows it across the road, and sometimes it piles up pretty good. Enough to bog you down if you're not careful."

"There's a pipeline?"

She nodded. "It runs more or less parallel to the road in places, although you don't often see it. There are a dozen or so oil rigs all over the desert down here. Some are operating, some aren't. There are none anywhere near where we're going – they're mostly further south, along the Algerian and Libyan borders."

I nodded. "I know some of those. A few years ago, I used to fly supplies and equipment out of El Borma, over to the west. Ever been there?"

She shook her head. "I hear it's not much. Well, if you've flown around this area, you know how big it is. And how empty."

"I do. It would be pretty easy to get lost down here, I'd imagine. How'd you manage, all by yourself?"

She gave me a look. "How'd *you* manage, all by your little old self up in that great big airplane?"

I laughed. "Touché," I said. "Sorry. I just meant–"

"I'm just teasing you, Max," she said. "It's true, you can get into trouble in the desert if you don't know what you're doing. I'm told they lose a couple of tourists every year like that. But if you're careful and have the right equipment, you'll probably be okay."

"Yeah," I said, "That's certainly been my experience with airplanes."

Being careful, and having the right gear was important, but as I've learned the hard way on more than one occasion, it was being smart that really got you through, because fools can find trouble almost anywhere. Even in the state forest at home, you can go for a perfectly lovely afternoon hike and come back with your eyes sparkling, a spring in your step, and tales to tell. Or, you can make some dumb decisions, find yourself off the trail and at the bottom of a ravine, your leg broken and sharing your lunch with a bear.

Look on the bright side, I told myself. We're three smart people, with two Makarov 9mm pistols and extra ammunition, thanks to the Libyan government and the generosity of the Soviet Union. Nadia has military training, and both she and Hadley speak Arabic. All of that ought to count for something, shouldn't it?

We'll be fine, I told myself. This was a simple recovery mission, in and out. And once we lay hands on the chelengk, we'll figure out some way to get out of the country without attracting the attention of either the Libyan *mukhabarat* or the paratroop guard, on our way to greener pastures.

Speaking of which, I'd noticed that there wasn't a lot of green left in the countryside now. The landscape had turned more sandy and steppe-like, with stretches of tiny humps looking like sandy snow moguls, each one topped with some kind of scrubby sage-like plant. The bigger bushes had thorns, and the only trees in sight seemed to be the occasional scrubby acacia. It looked, I thought with a shiver, a lot like Somalia. Off in the distance, I could see a line of six camels plodding west, their human companions nowhere in sight.

We were approaching the desert.

We'd passed the last small collection of low buildings fifteen minutes ago, and I hadn't seen anyone, riding or walking, for at least that long. The road in front of us ran nearly straight south toward a distant dun-colored horizon, the sky above immense and limitless, a washed-out blue without a cloud in sight. The temperature had been climbing, slowly but steadily, ever since we'd left the coast at Gabès, and I could feel dampness on my back.

"Not much around here, is there?" I said to Hadley, mainly to make conversation.

She nodded. "No, not much. But there are some strange things down here in the desert, if you take the time to look for them."

"Like what?"

"Abandoned oil camps. Wrecked trucks. And dozens of old airstrips, from the Second World War. The oil guys still use some of them when they go out prospecting. And then there are the *ksour*. They're really fortified towns, built mainly out of stone and mud-brick. The houses are all run together, surrounded by a wall."

"And they did this for defense?"

"Partly. But the *ksour* were also granaries – places to store crops. A lot of them were situated on the old caravan trade routes. Kind of like truck stops."

I nodded, thinking about the small towns I'd seen in parts of the Midwest consisting mainly of a grain elevator, a biscuits-and-gravy restaurant, and maybe one or two small churches. I looked out at the bleak landscape going by. "But you said most of the *ksour* are abandoned now. Why did people leave? What happened?"

Hadley shrugged. "The twentieth century happened, Max. It wasn't just one thing. Trade routes shifted or disappeared. The environment changed, got drier and harsher. The Berbers started abandoning nomadism and drifted to the towns."

We drove for a while in silence. As predicted, the road had now turned into little more than a sandy track. I was still feeling confident. We were fully gassed up, with spare water and fuel in the trunk, along with shovels, blankets, flashlights and all the other junk that Hadley had insisted was essential on any trip into the desert.

We all had our headscarves and dark glasses on, looking a lot like a crew that knew what it was doing, but of course I knew that our actual competence was probably more appearance than reality. Hadley was the only one who really knew this territory.

We edged into the hottest part of the day. There was virtually no traffic on the road now. Here and there, lizards scampered across the track, and once in a while we could see strings of camels out on the sand. The tiny settlements we passed at increasingly longer intervals all seemed shrunken and beaten down by the sun, their white walls a poor defense against the heat.

Hadley, however, seemed to be in her element as we moved further into the desert. "Did you know," she said to me, "that there are people not far from here who live underground?"

"In caves?" I asked.

"No, but sort of. They excavate a big round hole, maybe seven or eight meters deep and ten meters wide. Then they dig rooms into the sides. That's where they live. It provides protection from the heat, and it's easier to heat in the winter."

I tried to imagine it. "Sounds like something you'd see in a science fiction movie."

She looked at me oddly for a moment, and then she chuckled. "Doesn't it? Like I said, lots of strange things around here."

The land was now mainly varieties of ochre sand and gravel. A few small sage-like bushes remained, poking up out of the sand here and there, but otherwise the landscape was almost entirely barren. The good news was that if anyone were chasing us, we'd be able to see them coming from a long way away. The bad news, of course, was that there was nowhere to hide if that happened.

The road had deteriorated quite a bit, and driving required total concentration now. It wasn't flat but more like a series of rills, a constant up and down. Although it couldn't rain down here more than a hundred millimeters a year, and probably less than that, the occasional cloudbursts had carved channels across the roadway here and there, practically impossible to see until you were on top of them. Hitting one of those at top speed would probably break something, I decided, so I slowed things down a little.

Deep sand had also blown across the road in spots, and we had already stopped twice to dig out. The shovels that Hadley had made us buy were lifesavers here. When we got stuck for the third time, Hadley took over the driving. "No offense, Max," she said, "but I did this for months. There's kind of an art to it."

I was happy to turn the driving over to someone else; keeping an eye on a treacherous road while maintaining your speed is wearing. I sat back, pulled my *shemagh* down over my eyes, and tried to relax. "How much longer?" I asked.

"About forty klicks," Hadley said, shifting down fast to plow through a patch of sand. "We'll be there in less than an hour."

Unless something happens, I thought.

CHAPTER SIXTEEN

The outside temperature had to be close to one hundred degrees. Out in the open, without shade, the sun would suck you dry in an hour. Already the dashboard of the Peugeot was too hot to touch.

The track was still decent, but even in the parts that had no drifting sand, the washboard ridges – that I knew so well from West Africa – were a problem. Hadley knew the trick to driving on that type of surface, for she kept the Peugeot steady at about seventy kilometers an hour, just fast enough to plane the car over the top. You had to keep your eyes on the road, however, in order to slow down for ruts and channels, and the occasional large rock.

The landscape outside the windshield now looked a bit like the surface of the moon. We'd seen our last human being over an hour ago, and there was nothing on the horizon except sand moguls and the occasional scrubby bush. "Does anybody live this far down here?" I raised my voice to make myself heard over the noise of the engine and the road.

"A few people did in the old days," said Hadley. "The French once had a fort over there, a few kilometers to the east. It used to be called Borj Bourguiba."

"Bourguiba after the president? You mean he comes from around here?"

She laughed. "Oh, cripes, no. *Borj* means a castle or a fort. This one was actually a prison, where Bourguiba was kept for a while before independence. At that time, it was called Borj Leboeuf. They changed it once the French left." She waved at the desert. "There are a few little settlements left here and there, but they're hard to spot. You need to know where they are. Most of them are abandoned."

"And the one we're headed to? This *ksar*?"

She shook her head. "Been deserted for years."

On the horizon, I saw a small dust devil form, skitter across the landscape for a few hundred meters, and dissolve into nothing. I wouldn't want to encounter a bigger one of those, I thought. "How'd you find this place? I mean, it's not exactly calling to people, is it?"

"It was a combination of research and blind luck. I'd been poking around in Tunis and some of the other smaller cities down the coast, trying to trace the survivors of the Bey's family. I managed to locate a few, and when I interviewed them, one of them mentioned the missing jewels. This got me very curious, so I started following the threads, and eventually, I heard the story of Ali Bey, one of the cousins. One of the jewel merchants in the Medina claimed to have sold him the chelengk."

"Samir Abdulmajid Basli," I said.

Her head came around. "You know him?"

"He and I have talked," I said. "Go on with your story."

"Well, Ali Bey was traveling in disguise, headed for the Libyan border. He probably thought that he and the jewels would be safer there, although God knows why." She paused, biting her lip as she steered us around a tiny mountain of sand that had accumulated on the track.

"And what happened to this Ali Bey?" I asked.

"He got killed," she said simply. "At least I think that's what happened. It's the most likely explanation, since he's never turned up anywhere. Killed by whom and for what is probably always going to be a mystery. It might have been for the chelengk, or it might simply have been for whatever was in his pockets. Simple robbery is what I think, most likely by one of the bands of desert nomads that come through here."

"Nomads?"

"Berbers, Tuaregs, Bedouins – all nomads. People get them confused, but it doesn't really matter much in the end; they're all desert tribesmen. Ali Bey met someone – or a group of someones – on his way south to the border. They robbed him and they killed him. End of story."

"But they didn't get the jewels."

She nodded. "Well, I wondered about that. I went back to the jewel merchants in Tunis and asked if they'd heard anything. None of them had. So, I decided to go south into the desert and try and retrace his steps. To look for myself."

"You came down here by yourself. Alone. In the desert."

She snorted. "I thought we'd been through this already, Max. I'm not a kid. I grew up in Vermont, with tractors and four-wheel drives. If you can maneuver through snow and mud, you can drive in sand. And heck, I've been climbing and camping since I was ten years old. I can handle myself in the wilderness."

"I stand corrected once again," I said with a grin. "Okay, so let's get back to the story. How'd you find the jewels?"

"It took me nearly two weeks. The last anyone had seen of Ali Bey was in that place we stopped. Al-Hammah, just outside of Gabès. If you keep going west, you get to the Chott el Djerid. You know what a *chott* is?"

I nodded. "I've never been there, but I know what it is. A big dry salt lake. We used to use it as a landmark when we were flying plots over the desert."

"Well, there's a whole lot of nothing in the *chott*, and if you keep going across it and heading west, you get to the Algerian border. But from everything I'd heard, Ali Bey was headed to Libya, not Algeria. So, I figured he must have turned south." She downshifted again, plowing through a patch of soft sand and out the other side.

"I went further south, too, checking out every single place I could think of where he might have stopped. One or two people remembered a lone traveler on a camel, but that's not at all unusual out here. I looked for villages or ruins, or anywhere someone might spend the night."

"I don't see any villages around here," I said. "I haven't seen any for quite some time."

"And you won't," she said. "There are a couple of small settlements back off the road. We passed one an hour ago. No, what you have out here is nothing but the remains of a few old Berber settlements from back during colonial times. All abandoned now."

"But you found it nonetheless," I said.

She smiled happily. "I surely did. I'd just about run out of hope. And gas, and water. And I'd gotten really sick of desert camping and the crappy food that I had to eat while I was out here. Then I found this place, and somehow, I knew it was the right one. I parked the truck at the bottom and hiked up. I had about an hour of daylight left, and I spent it poking around, making a slow scan of the area. I found the remains of a campfire. I found an old rusty can of sardines. And finally, wedged into a crevice, I found a headscarf – you know, like the ones we bought."

"And so you concluded that Ali Bey had stopped there," I said.

"I was sure of it. By that time, it was nearly dark, so I got out my tent and my bedroll, unwrapped the last of my bread and sardines, and settled down for the night. In the morning, I started looking for hiding places among the ruins. I tried to imagine what had happened to him. The *ksar* is up maybe a hundred meters above the rest of the desert – they built them on rises so that they could see people coming."

"Makes sense," I said.

"So Ali Bey probably saw them coming, whoever killed him. I looked for tire tracks or footprints, but of course the sand would have erased any traces within days, if not hours. And even if the robbers came in a car or truck, Ali Bey would have had time to hide things."

"How long did it take you to find the jewels?"

"Almost the whole day," she said. "Archaeologists are trained to work slowly and very carefully when they go over a site. I cut a few corners, but I was methodical. I figured that he'd have picked a place to hide them that was ready-made; he wouldn't have had the time to dig out a hiding place himself. It had to be right there. At around three o'clock, I started working on one of the walls, and all of a sudden, there it was. At the base of the wall there was a flat stone covering what must have been an old water cistern. I moved it aside, and there, down at the bottom, was a leather bag. And in the bag were the Bey's jewels. Including the chelengk."

Nadia had woken up by this time, and her voice floated up from the back seat. "And what did you do then?" She spoke in a quiet voice, but I knew she was on the same track as me.

"I was super excited, of course." Hadley paused. "But I was kind of scared to take the chelengk. Partly because it was so valuable, and partly, well, I guess I was scared to be carrying the thing around all by myself out here in the desert."

"You were probably right to be," I said. "Did you go straight back to Tunis? Did you tell anyone what you'd found?"

She frowned. "I'm not stupid, Max," she said. "I knew I had to be careful. So I put it back, exactly where I'd found it, and drove back to Tunis. I figured I'd wait a few days and get a couple of the guys to come back down here with me, just so we'd be a group. In case of any trouble, you see."

"Smart," I said.

"But I just had to tell someone. So when I got back to the Institute, I sent a cable to Professor Birdwhistle, telling him what I'd found. Then I sent another cable to Uncle Isaac, telling him I'd be telephoning the next day. It's expensive to phone overseas from Tunisia, but I figured it was worth it, given the news."

"Yes, Bone and Birdwhistle both got your cables," I said.

"The next day, two men came to the office where I do my documentary research. It's just a little closet thing off the main library. They said they were from the university, with an invitation to meet the Dean of the social science department. I thought this was a bit strange, but they were pleasant, and quite convincing. They asked if I was free to have lunch with the Dean. They had a van waiting outside."

I sighed. "And you got in the car with them."

"I knew it was a mistake the minute I did it," she said. "But by then, it was too late. They tied me up, took me out to that house in La Marsa, and started asking me questions. I was scared out of my mind."

"I'm sure you were," said Nadia. "Did they– well, did they–"

She shook her head. "No, not at all. They were perfect gentlemen, if I can use that word about a bunch of kidnappers. Only one of them spoke English, and not very well. My Arabic's okay for everyday, but they were

Libyans, and the dialect isn't quite the same. There were four of them. One of them spoke pretty good French, so we used that most of the time."

She paused, collecting her thoughts. "All they wanted was for me to tell them where the chelengk was. They didn't even seem all that interested in the rest of the jewels. Just the chelengk. I didn't really understand it. I have no idea how they even knew about it."

Nadia leaned forward, putting her hand on Hadley's shoulder. "They probably had a tap on your phone, Hadley. You and hundreds of other people in the city."

Hadley frowned. "Okay, a phone tap. But of all those hundreds of people, why pick me?"

"If you'd been asking around in the Medina about this chelengk thing, then somebody in the *mukhabarat* found out about it. And there's a reason why they're interested in your chelengk. The Colonel wants it."

"Yes, that's what they said. But I don't understand – what's Gaddafi's interest in some old piece of jewelry?" asked Hadley.

"It's his latest obsession, apparently," said Nadia. "It was an Ottoman symbol at the beginning, pinned to the Sultan's own turban. Then it was given to a British admiral, and became a national treasure, a symbol of another sort. The mighty British Empire, ruler of the seas. You know all this, of course. But Gaddafi sees it differently. He considers the chelengk as the ultimate imperialist emblem. Owning it would be a poke in the eye for the Turks and the British. Both of whom," she added darkly, "he hates."

Hadley frowned. "And you know all this how, exactly?"

"We were briefed on it," Nadia said simply. "Before our detachment left Tripoli. It wasn't our job to recover the chelengk – we were protecting the Leader, after all – but we were told all about the effort to recover the jewel, and the absolute need to bring it back with us to Tripoli."

Hadley nodded. "That makes sense, I guess. He'd see getting his hands on the chelengk as a victory over the forces of reaction, blah, blah, blah."

"Exactly," said Nadia. "And now the *mukhabarat* knows where it is."

Hadley's face was grim as she wrestled the car along the sand track. "Yeah, well, I didn't have too much of a choice about telling them, you know," she said. "I held out for as long as I could. I was in that house nearly a fucking week. It took me about thirty seconds to figure out that I was only valuable to them for what I knew, and that once I'd told them, they were under no obligation to keep me alive. So I kept my mouth shut for as long as possible."

"What changed your mind in the end, then?" I asked.

"They were going to take me to Libya, that's why," she said. "If you hadn't found me, I'd be on my way there now. What you've just told me makes sense of things now. They said that Gaddafi was visiting Tunis, and that when he left, they were going to stick me in some sort of diplomatic shipment, get me out of the country without anyone knowing." She paused. "And then I'd be in Tripoli, with the Colonel himself as my interrogator." She grimaced. "I didn't think that would be such a great situation to be in."

"Well, you were certainly right about that," said Nadia.

CHAPTER SEVENTEEN

We pulled off the rough track and powered the car another hundred meters through the sand, tires spinning, up the gentle hill toward the *ksar*, perched on top. The *ksar* itself didn't look like much; a low wall of crumbling stone and mud, with an occasional tower or blocky structure here and there.

But it was just what Hadley had said it was – a fortress. From the top, it would be easy to spot approaching attackers, and easy, too, to rain misery down upon them as they struggled up the hill. As for where these people had gotten their water and food, I had no idea. In any case, they were all gone now. The place sat baking in the late afternoon sun, silent, keeping its secrets to itself.

Except for one secret, which was why we were here. If Hadley was right, the chelengk was hidden somewhere inside those walls, and the sooner we recovered it, the sooner we could get the hell out. The place was already beginning to give me the creeps. The heat didn't help.

The car looked to be good where it was. We probably weren't going to be able to move it any further up the hill. I picked up my shoulder bag, grabbed a shovel from the trunk, and turned to the others. "Ready?" There were nods all around. "Then let's get this done."

Single file, we trudged up the hill toward the ruined walls of the *ksar*, a hundred meters away. The wind had picked up again in the past hour or so, and I held my hand in front of my face against the stinging grains of sand.

"Use your *shemagh*," said Hadley. "Look – like this." She pulled the fabric down to cover her face, leaving only her eyes exposed, but protected behind dark glasses.

I nodded, adjusted my covering, and trudged on.

It was still wickedly hot. The wind was no relief, since it was just blowing hot air at us. I'll be really glad to get out of here, I thought. Once we've found what we came for.

* * *

On top, I took a few moments to climb one of the rock walls, catch my breath and take in the view. What there was of it, that is. The *ksar* sat about a hundred meters above the desert floor, and the view before me stretched out unobstructed in all directions. Apart from the track we'd come down on, nothing man-made appeared anywhere that I could see, all the way to the horizon. The desert at this point was a series of low hills, with a few stunted bushes here and there. But it was mostly fine sand, as far as one could see. I marveled again at the strength and skill of the people who'd lived here, not so long ago. I hoped that wherever they'd finally wound up, they were well-fed and watered now, and slept in peace on soft beds at night.

Unfortunately, it didn't look as if we'd be able to enjoy any of those things as long as we stayed here. My watch said four o'clock now. The heat, in any normal environment, ought to be dissipating, but here it didn't seem to be. I watched a rock lizard dart out from behind a crevice, look me over for a few seconds as it did a series of quick pushups, and then disappear over the edge of the wall with a flick of its tail. High overhead, half a dozen buzzards circled slowly, keeping a hopeful eye on us. I wondered idly where they went at night.

I climbed down and joined the others. "We should get on with it," I said to Hadley. "Do you remember where this chelengk is?"

She nodded, pointing to one of the walls further inside the compound. "It should be in there," she said. "Right where I left it." She paused. "Unless someone's come by and taken it."

Nadia looked at her sharply. "You didn't tell those *mukhabarat* guys exactly where it was, did you?"

Hadley shook her head. "I only told them where the *ksar* was located," she said. "I figured they might keep me alive a little longer that way."

"They were planning to take you to Tripoli," Nadia said. "And who knows what would have happened to you there."

"Instead," I said, "here we are." I slapped dust from my trousers. "Go get it, then. We'll watch the road."

Hadley nodded and walked back into one of the narrow passageways between the buildings. In a moment, she was out of sight. "Hurry up," I called after her. "The sooner we're out of here, the safer we'll be."

When she was out of earshot, Nadia turned to me. "Do you really think we're in danger here?"

"We've been in danger ever since we left that house in La Marsa," I said. "We know two things. One, the Libyans have the location of the *ksar*, because Hadley told them. Two, they're hell-bent on recovering it. What we don't know is what resources they have at their disposal. So far, it's only been a few guys more or less off the street. But if Boomer is to be believed, the city is crawling with Libyan agents, some of whom presumably know what they're doing."

Nadia nodded. "And they could be on their way here now."

"Exactly."

There was a shout from behind me, and we turned to see Hadley holding up a small leather bag. "I've got it!" she yelled. "It was right where I'd hidden it. Want to see?"

She brought the bag over, set it on a low wall, and emptied it. There were a dozen or so rings and pendants, but none of us paid any attention to them. All eyes were on the chelengk.

It was bigger than I'd imagined, but otherwise, just as Birdwhistle had described it. The core was a kind of complex flower, out of which sprouted thirteen long diamond-studded rays or petals. I picked it up, and it more than filled my hand.

"Each of those rays or stalks represents a ship captured by Nelson," said Hadley, touching them gently. "If you turn it over, you'll see the clockwork mechanism. You're supposed to be able to wind it up and make the petals vibrate. It's spectacular, don't you think?"

Nadia shook her head. "I think it's gaudy, to tell you the truth. The sort of thing you see in the flea markets.

Leave it to the Turks to come up with something like this."

"Well, whatever it is," I said, staring at it, "it must be a powerful symbol, if Gaddafi is so intent on finding it."

I poked the chelengk experimentally with my finger. "Not something I'd choose to stick on my own hat, though." I paused. "Just saying, that's all."

Hadley smiled. "Lord Nelson obviously felt differently. He wore it on almost every possible occasion." She put it and the other jewels carefully back in the leather pouch, and stuck the pouch into her shoulder bag.

We all sat there on the rock wall for a few minutes, staring out at the limitless sand, the sun on our foreheads and the breeze blowing through our hair. "I've decided," I said after a moment, "that I rather like the desert."

"Really," murmured Nadia, mopping her forehead with her *shamagh*. "And why is that?"

"It's what T. E. Lawrence said. It's clean."

She smiled. "Most people think he never actually said that, Max."

"Maybe," I said after a moment, still staring out at the sand. "But it's pretty to think so, isn't it?"

She gave me a soft dig in the ribs. "I didn't take you for a reader, Max. First Lawrence of Arabia, now Hemingway."

I grinned back at her. "And I never thought an Arab girl soldier would know about either of those guys," I said.

She gave me a harder dig. "First of all, I'm not a girl. Second, the American University of Beirut happens to provide a first-rate education. And by way, did you know that Lawrence learned his Arabic in Byblos? That's about ten kilometers from where I grew up."

I cocked my head and stayed very still, staring out at the sand.

"Max, are you even listening to me?"

"Heads up," I murmured.

She turned. "What is it?"

I pointed northward, to the plume of dust I'd seen on the horizon. Nadia followed my pointing finger and nodded.

"Party's over, folks," I said. "I think we're about to have visitors."

CHAPTER EIGHTEEN

"Go and get your gun," I said quietly to Nadia. She nodded and moved off. I turned to Hadley. "Sorry to break up the party," I said, "but we're about to have company."

She peered at the dust plume, moving closer now. Behind me, I heard a *snick* as Nadia checked the magazine on her pistol. I felt in my bag for mine, got it out, and did the same.

"Do you think it's them?" Nadia spoke quietly.

I shrugged. "We're about to find out," I said.

"Shouldn't we be getting in the car and taking off?" asked Hadley. "After all, we've got what we came for."

"Too late for that," I said. "There's only one road. If we go south, there's nothing but desert for a long, long way, and then you get to the Libya-Algeria border. Not a place we want to be. Head north, back the way we came, and we have to go through these guys. It's possible that they have backup, further along up the road."

"So we stay here?"

I cinched up the straps on my backpack. "We're in a fort, on the high ground. It's too late to just try and drive away. Maybe we can talk to them."

The fear was starting to show in Hadley's eyes. She'd just spent nearly a week with some of these people, and she clearly wasn't looking forward to a second round. "And if we can't?"

I gave her what I hoped was a reassuring grin. "Then we'll just have to try and bamboozle them, won't we?"

We could see the car now, some sort of biggish four-wheel drive with one of those elevated intake snorkels used for desert driving. It was coming along at a pretty good clip, fishtailing slightly through the patches of sand. They'd be here in about two minutes, I reckoned.

Not a lot of time to get ready. I turned to Nadia, pointing to her pistol. "I'm hoping you actually know how to use that thing," I said.

She gave me a not-very-nice smile. "We got excellent training in the Soviet Union."

"Good to hear," I said. "Let's hope it pays off."

The car was almost to us now. I turned to Hadley. "Stash that bag with the jewels out of sight somewhere. Let's not make it easy for them. And when you're done, move back over here beside me."

She nodded, and faded back among the rocks, further back inside the *ksar*.

The car stopped below us, ten meters away from where we'd left the Peugeot. I could see now that our visitors were driving an old Toyota Land Cruiser, somewhat the worse for wear. The two men inside got out slowly, their guns drawn, and looked around them. Their shoes and clothing marked them as city guys.

One of the men reached back inside the Land Cruiser and pulled something out. For a moment I thought he was holding a hand grenade, but it turned out to be a microphone. He began speaking into it, stopping from time to time to listen to the response.

Shit, I thought, he's got a damned radio, and he's telling the rest of them where we are. I looked over at Nadia. "Stay close," I said, "and stay under cover. Ever shot anyone before?"

"Not yet," she replied evenly.

"Do you think you can?"

"I think so," she said quietly.

"Good," I said. "Because I think you might have to in the next few minutes."

CHAPTER NINETEEN

We stayed hidden down behind the low rock parapet, peeking out through gaps in the stones. Hadley crouched next to me, Nadia next to her. Our visitors obviously knew we were up here somewhere, but they didn't yet know exactly where we were positioned. I hoped we could keep it that way for as long as possible.

I watched the two men walk slowly around our car, looking everything over, both of them holding their pistols loosely in their hands. The pistols made things a little complicated. Subduing people who have guns can be difficult and dangerous, particularly when they're trying to hurt you and you're not really trying to hurt them quite as much. It makes for a very uneven playing field and almost always ends in tears for someone.

I had a vague sort of plan for the next little while. If we could get these two guys under control, I thought, we could truss them up with the plastic cable ties we had left over from our night-time caper back in La Marsa. The ties were somewhere in the back of our car, along with our extra bottles of water and cans of gasoline. So it would be simple to tie them up, disable their vehicle, and leave them in the *ksar* with enough water for a couple of days. With luck, someone would be along eventually. And in the meantime, we would be safe and sound in Tunis. Or, better yet, a thousand kilometers away from Tunis, in a

European city where the lights were bright and nobody knew our names.

It was the first part of my plan that worried me, though. Kind of like preparing alligator stew, where the recipe begins 'first, kill your alligator.'

I didn't want to kill anyone, and I was hoping against hope these guys would go away nicely, but that was apparently not to be. As we watched, one of the men carefully shot out the front right tire on our Peugeot. Then he walked slowly around the car and shot out all of the other tires, one by one. The reports of the gun were exceptionally loud in the quiet of the desert. Hadley stirred beside me. "Oh, shit," she said in a low voice.

Oh, shit is right, I thought. The shooting of the tires basically signaled that they were intent on killing all of us and leaving the bodies here. The second man had opened our trunk now, and was busy transferring our water bottles and gas jerricans to their four-wheel drive.

The tire shooter stepped around to the front of the car and came forward a few steps. He looked up at the rock walls. He raised his pistol and waved it in our general direction. Then he shouted something.

I looked at Nadia. "*Istislam?*" I whispered. "What does that mean?"

"Your pronunciation is terrible," she said. "He's telling us to give up." Then she stood up and shouted something that sounded like "*Tozzfiika!*" down the hill.

She dropped back down just before a shot glanced off the rock parapet. I raised my eyebrows at her in a query. "I told them no," she said matter-of-factly.

"She didn't exactly say that," whispered Hadley to me. "She said they could go fuck themselves."

I grinned. "That's our Nadia." I was rather starting to like this woman.

A moment later, both men started up the hill. They walked slowly and confidently, holding their pistols out in front of them.

"They don't know that we're armed," I whispered to Hadley. "Otherwise, they'd never come at us this way."

"What are you going to do? Shoot them?"

"Not unless we have to," I said grimly. "How good are you at throwing rocks?"

Hadley nodded. "I played softball at the University of Vermont."

"Don't you pitch underhand in softball? That's not going to do us much good."

"I wasn't a pitcher," she said. "I played second base. Watch this."

Hadley picked up a rock about the size of a tennis ball, stood, and threw it overhand with surprising force at the lead man, hitting him full in the chest. He yelled in surprise and fell backwards a few steps. His companion shot twice in our general direction, both shots pinging uselessly off the rocks.

"That was impressive," I said.

"Second base is one hundred and thirty feet from home plate," she said. "He's closer than that. I can smoke one in there any time I want. If he gets a little closer, I might be able to hit him in the head."

They were less than thirty meters away from us now, advancing warily up the hill toward the rock walls. You can, if you're good, hit something with a pistol at that range, but it's much better by far if your target is twenty meters away, and better still at ten meters.

Let's keep them thinking that we're unarmed, I thought. I picked up a rock myself and hefted it experimentally. Then I stood up and threw it down the slope at the second man, walking right beside the first. It went wide, and I heard him chuckle as he snapped a shot back in my direction. "You dead now, mister," he shouted up the slope.

From my side, Hadley thew another rock, hitting the first man again on the shoulder. Damn, I thought, she's good.

As I'd hoped, our rock barrage had the desired effect of pissing our two attackers off. And as a result of that, making them impulsive and careless. They quickened their steps up the hill. They were about ten meters from our protective wall when Nadia moved out from behind the end of the rock wall, her pistol raised to fire.

And promptly slipped on the rock scree and went down, in full sight of them.

Everything then happened very quickly. I stood up, just as the lead guy brought his pistol up and fired at Nadia. She hit the ground rolling, and his shot went wide. The second shot won't miss, I thought. I brought my gun up and fired twice.

I did it almost without thinking. My 9mm slugs hit the man center mass and he dropped like a stone, without a sound. The second man stopped in his tracks, looked up at us, and then turned, starting to scramble back down the scree toward his vehicle. A single shot from Nadia's gun put him down.

Both bodies lay still below us. I'd gone numb from the shock. It had been a long time since I'd actually killed someone. There are quite possibly others on this earth who can do this kind of thing repeatedly and not feel all that much. Maybe snipers are like that. Maybe SWAT team people are like that.

I'm not like that. I sat down on the rocks, letting my gun drop from my hand. Then I bent over and vomited into the sand.

When I looked up, Nadia was standing over me. She put her hand on my shoulder and squeezed. "It was necessary, Max," she said in a quiet voice. "They gave us no choice."

"I know," I said dully, wiping my mouth. "I know that. You're right. I realized that as soon as I saw them shooting out our tires."

She nodded. "They had no intention of letting us leave here. So it was either us or them. It would have come to that sooner or later, no matter what we did."

I looked up at her and smiled weakly. "You're a good shot," I said finally.

Hadley was approaching, a worried look on her face. "And you're not bad with a rock, either," I said to her.

I stood up, scanning the horizon. Nothing in sight. Good, I thought, we have a little time. We're going to need it.

CHAPTER TWENTY

First, we checked the Land Cruiser the Libyans had come in. Inside it, we found little more than a collection of empty food wrappers, old cigarette packets, and a few extra magazines for their guns. Their Tokarev pistols used different ammunition than our weapons, so the only really useful things were a couple of liters of warm water in bottles and an extra jerrican of fuel.

In the back seat sat a bulky military radio with Cyrillic labels on the controls. I called over to Nadia, asking her to come check it out.

"It's Soviet, all right," she said, glancing at it. "A lot of our military equipment is. I recognize this, it's a UHF transceiver. They were probably using it to talk to their bosses, wherever they were."

I looked at the radio, picked up the mike, hefted it. "Can we call people on this? Maybe get some help down here?"

Nadia shook her head. "Better not to try. This is a fixed-frequency rig. It's specially set up for military operations."

"Meaning what?"

"You can only transmit to one frequency. In other words, to the military net. Anything you say on this radio will be picked up by the Libyan military. You can only send to them, on their frequency. Nobody else."

I shook my head. "That doesn't help much, then, does it?'

"I'm afraid not, but–"

Just then, the radio gave a loud squawk, startling both of us. I dropped the mike. A second later, a voice began speaking in Arabic over a low layer of background static. Nadia leaned across me to listen.

"It's somebody wanting a status report."

The voice continued, ending in a question of some sort. After a moment, the question was repeated, louder and more urgently this time.

Nadia picked up the mike and thumbed it twice, the universal military signal for 'I hear you.' The voice came on again and another string of incomprehensible Arabic followed. Hadley came up to stand beside us, her expression quizzical. I put my finger to my lips, and we all listened as the speaker wound down.

Nadia thumbed the mike again, twice, and the carrier wave disappeared. Whoever was at the other end had gone off the line.

"What just happened?" said Hadley. "I didn't understand all that much of what they were saying."

Nadia set the mike back onto its holder. "Well, it wasn't good news," she said. "The guy speaking must be their controller, their commanding officer. He was asking for an update on the operation. 'Have you found it?' he asked. 'Are they dead yet?'"

"Jesus," breathed Hadley beside me. "But why were you clicking the microphone like that?"

"That means you acknowledge the message, but you can't talk back. Usually that's because you're in the middle of something, or you're trying to keep quiet."

"Yes," I said. "Our guys have the same system."

"Well, he said something interesting, after I gave him the double-click. He said he's going to be sending more guys down to the *ksar*, to help out. But not until tomorrow – they don't have enough people in place right now."

"Well, that's a bit of good news," I said. "Do you have any idea where he was broadcasting from?"

"None. These things are ultra-high frequency, they have a pretty long range. Could be Tunis, could be Tripoli." She looked again at the radio. "But since this one doesn't have much of an antenna, I'm guessing that whoever was talking to us is a lot closer than that."

I nodded. They wouldn't be coming from Tripoli; that was too far away. If they were in Tunis, it would take them most of a day to get down here. But if they were closer – Sfax, say, or Gabès – it wouldn't take nearly that much time at all. Either way, we didn't have long.

I stood up. "Okay," I said. "That makes things a lot simpler. Let's find some shade and talk about what to do next."

* * *

We moved up against the wall of the *ksar* out of the sun, and sat cross-legged in the warm sand. The wind had picked up, and was helping to dry our sweat a bit, although it really just felt like being close to a hair dryer. I picked up the map of Tunisia that had come with our rental car and unfolded it.

"Here's the situation," I said, pointing to a spot on the map. "We're about here, just off this road–"

"It's a track," said Hadley.

"Road, track, whatever," I said. "We can't stay here forever–"

"And we've got almost nothing left to eat," said Hadley.

I gave her a look. "I'm getting to all of that, okay?"

She gave me a cool-eyed nod. "Sure, Max," she said. "Just pointing things out."

I went back to the map. "We've got to get away from here, and the sooner the better. Friends of these two guys down the hill are probably on their way to us right now."

Nadia nodded. "They'll have the main roads under surveillance, and by tomorrow, a team headed our way," she said. "They'll know we've got their car, and we don't exactly blend in with the local population." She paused. "At least you two don't."

"Exactly," I said. "If we go north we're heading straight into danger." I traced my finger down the map. "South leads to the border of Algeria and Libya, where they come together. I don't think we want to wind up in either of those places."

Hadley spoke. "All very calm and logical. But perhaps instead of going over all the things that won't work to save us, let's focus instead on whatever will." She looked at me, her glasses glinting in the sunlight. "Any bright ideas?"

"Just one," I said. I pointed to the map again. "A little bit south of here, there's a junction with another road, going west. If you follow that road west far enough, it winds up in the oil camp at El Borma, right on the Algerian border."

"And how does that help us?"

"El Borma has an airstrip and a radio. I used to fly out of there when I was doing prospecting work. Once we get there, I've got a guy in the American embassy I can call. He'll be able to get us out."

Nadia looked at the map. "How far is it?"

"Hard to say," I said. "I've never been on the road, actually – just seen it from the air. It curves back and forth a lot, to avoid some of the worst of the dunes. I'd say fifty kilometers from the turnoff, which is" – I turned around to look south – "about ten kilometers from here."

"And you think the road is drivable?"

I shrugged. "I have no idea. But if it's like this, it ought to be manageable." I held up my hand. "I know, that's not much of an answer. But supply trucks used it from time to time when I was flying out here. So yes, it should be okay."

They both looked at me dubiously.

"In principle," I added, just for good measure.

Nadia narrowed her eyes. "You know that in French, *en principe* signifies a negative, don't you?"

I grinned. "Yeah, I found that out quite some time ago."

She stood up. "Well, it sounds like our only option. The wind's picking up, it should cover our tire tracks. If we're going to go, we'd better go soon. We haven't got much daylight left."

"We can't leave just yet," I said. "We've got a couple of things to do first."

* * *

We buried our would-be assassins in shallow graves dug into the soft sand beside our useless car. "They might have been trying to kill us," Hadley had said, "but we shouldn't leave them out here for the buzzards." And she was right. We'd gone through their pockets, finding nothing of interest except a few hundred dinars, which I appropriated for the communal treasury. Their Tokarev pistols got buried alongside the bodies.

"Once we get to safety," I said, "we can tell the cops where to find these guys."

Nadia looked at me. "Perhaps we'd better all be out of the country before you do that, don't you think?"

I nodded. "I suppose you're right. I don't want to get caught up in anything involving the authorities right now. And I'm sure you don't either."

She gave me a thin smile. "You're so perceptive, Max," she said.

We smoothed the sand over the graves and then inspected the Land Cruiser. It had numerous dents and scratches as well as worn tires, but it was what we had, so it was going to have to do. It was a gasoline model, which meant that the fuel we'd bought earlier for our Peugeot would work in it. And it was a four-wheel drive, which would make navigating the sand a little easier.

Like us, the Libyans had brought extra water and gasoline, so combined with ours, we had plenty. No food, though, which bothered me. We'd eaten all our fruit and most of our dates, and I was starting to get hungry. I assumed the others were, too. There was no sense in bringing that point up, since there was no way we were going to get any food until we reached El Borma.

What I was really hoping for was more firepower. We'd checked the Tokarevs and found one empty and the other with only two bullets left in the magazine. A search of the Land Cruiser had turned up no spare ammunition, and their guns were in a worse state than ours were, so we were leaving them behind. Nadia and I both had reliable Makarov 9mms, but these were mostly for confidence-boosting. Don't kid yourself, Donovan, I told myself; if we get into a situation where we actually have to use them, we don't have anywhere near enough ammunition to do the damage required. We would just have to cross our fingers.

I wiped sweat off my face and spit. Five o'clock now. I got everyone into the truck and settled down, our gear stowed away. Hadley sat in the back, Nadia in front with me. We were hot and sweaty and covered with dust and grime, but I detected a slight lightening of the mood as I started the truck and put it in gear. We were on our way to safety.

CHAPTER TWENTY-ONE

We were following what might be called a road only by a very generous stretch of the imagination. Flying over it years ago, it had looked clear and distinct. On the ground today, it was an entirely different story. I was beginning to wonder whether I'd made a big mistake.

It was clear that there hadn't been a vehicle across this part of the desert in weeks. I remembered that supply convoys sometimes came to El Borma, but most of the time, stuff got flown in. I knew that, of course, because I'd been one of the folks doing the flying. But I'd expected more in the way of land traffic.

So quite possibly, we'd made an error here. Maybe a big one. The track – for that was what it was – was barely discernible, most of it covered by soft and drifting sand being blown around by the incessant wind. Underneath lay harder ground, but the sand drifts, often a meter deep, were more than enough to get you stuck. I remembered seeing this track from the air as resembling a kind of serpent, tracing lazy arcs through the desert as it followed what was presumably harder, more solid ground, in and around the large dunes that characterized the area. Off the track, of course, the sand was often much deeper.

That's why the job was to stay on the track if you possibly could, and while on the track, try and power through the drifts of sand that covered most of it up. The only good thing about any of this was the fact that the wind would cover our tracks quite effectively.

I'd figured out – once again – that I wasn't very good at desert driving. We got stuck almost immediately and spent twenty minutes digging and rocking the Land Cruiser back and forth to free it. Half an hour later, we got stuck again, and it took longer to get us free.

It was almost dark by this time. We sat on the sand beside the Land Cruiser and wiped sweat and grime from our faces. "This isn't going well," said Nadia after a moment.

"That's putting it mildly," said Hadley. She pulled at the fabric of her sopping T-shirt. "Look at this. I can actually feel the water leaving my body's cells. If we keep this up, we'll be nothing but husks."

"Don't exaggerate," said Nadia. "We've got plenty of water. Just keep drinking."

"'Plenty' is a relative term," said Hadley. "We're drinking it at a pretty fast clip. Sooner or later, we'll run out."

"It's not the water I'm worried about," I said, pointing to one of the back tires. "Take a look at that."

They all looked over at the tire I was pointing to. It was nearly bald, with white threads showing through the rubber here and there. There was also what looked like a split in the sidewall.

The other tires were almost as bad. We'd been in such a hurry to get away from the *ksar* that none of us had paid much attention to our vehicle. But after our first encounter with the deep sand, I started looking a little harder at the Land Cruiser.

It wasn't in such great shape. The tires were bad, the suspension was shot, and I'd been hearing a low noise from the rear which might indicate a bad bearing. The exhaust was smoky and there was a definite lack of power, even in low gear. The Libyans must have picked this thing up in a yard sale, I thought.

"Not good," said Nadia. "What do we do?"

I shrugged. "Not much we can do, I'm afraid. It's not like we had a choice of cars, after all."

She nodded. "How far along do you think we are?"

I considered my answer carefully. "In a straight line, the El Borma camp is probably fifty kilometers from where we started. It's more than that, of course, because of the way the road twists and turns. I'd say we've made no more than fifteen or twenty kilometers since we began."

Hadley stood up. "Then we've got a way to go, don't we?" she said. "Bad tires or not. Let me drive for a while. You know I'm better in this sand than you are."

I hated to admit it, but she was right. With Hadley driving, we made marginally better progress across the dunes, but by the time we got stuck again, it was fully dark, and now we had pretty much lost sight of the track altogether. I suggested we call it quits, and no one really objected.

We sat on the back tailgate of the Land Cruiser, sipping warm water and mopping the sweat off ourselves. Hadley looked up at the cloudless night sky, at the brilliant band of stars that formed the Milky Way. "When the sun goes down out here, things cool off fast. It's a good thing we bought those blankets. We'll probably want to spend the night inside the Land Cruiser. It'll be a little warmer that way, all of us in there together. And safer."

I looked at her. "Safe from what? There's nothing out here."

Hadley snorted. "I can see that you know practically nothing about the desert, Max." She turned to Nadia. "What about you?"

Nadia shook her head. "Don't look at me. Lebanon doesn't have any deserts. And most of my time has been spent in Tripoli, inside headquarters at Bab Al-Azizia. Hardly the desert."

"Well," continued Hadley, "I got to know this place pretty well when I was searching around down here. There are scorpions, and there are snakes. Especially scorpions, they're everywhere. One of the most poisonous kinds is called the deathstalker. There's a reason for that."

"Great," I breathed. "I had no idea."

"Cobras and horned vipers, too," Hadley continued. "The vipers hide in the sand, they're almost impossible to see. I'm telling you, we ought to spend the night in the vehicle."

"Well, that's settled, then," I said, standing up and dusting the sand off my palms. "We're here for the night. And inside the car. We'll recalibrate in the morning."

I looked at the water jerricans. "Everybody take a drink before bedtime, another one for breakfast in the morning. If you have to pee in the night, keep your shoes on, take one of the flashlights, and watch the ground." I pointed over at the horizon. "There's an almost full moon coming up, though. That will help."

I looked back at the way we'd come, noting that our tire tracks had almost completely disappeared. The Libyans, when and if they got down here, would have a hell of a time finding us.

"This is jolly," grumbled Hadley as we started rearranging things in the back of the Land Cruiser. "Stranded out in the middle of the desert. Exactly what I was worried about, and what I very much hoped wouldn't happen." She turned to me. "Max, I hope you know that if we don't figure a way out of this, we're going to be sucking pond water in a day or two."

I smiled and clapped her on the shoulder. "Cheer up, Hadley, look on the bright side. We've been sucking pond water ever since we got started on this. Now, there's just going to be a whole lot more pond water for everyone."

From the side, Nadia watched us, her face expressionless. "Sucking pond water," she murmured. "I'll have to remember that one. Pass me one of those blankets, will you?"

* * *

We spent a pretty miserable night in the Land Cruiser. Hadley claimed the back seat, where she could stretch out fully. Nadia and I shared the front bench seat, wrapped in

130

our blankets. As Hadley had predicted, the temperature dropped quickly as soon as the sun went down, and by midnight, all of us were chilly despite our blankets. Hadley, oddly enough, seemed less affected by the cold than the rest of us, and actually managed to get some sleep. Naturally, she snored.

It wouldn't have mattered in my case. I was wide awake for most of the night, my mind turning over plans and possibilities, weighing the odds, estimating the chances. Thinking is free, and if you have the luxury of time, it's good to take advantage of the occasion to put your mind to work.

It helps, of course, to have a bit of raw material to actually work with, and in this case, we didn't have much. No food, no medicine, no transportation, and a dwindling supply of water. We more or less knew where we were, but nobody else did, and unless we could change that situation, things were going to get dire pretty soon.

So, I thought and thought. Eventually, Nadia and I drew close to one another and wrapped our arms around each other for warmth, snuggling down in our blankets. That helped a bit. But by the time the sun came up again, I still hadn't come up with a plan.

CHAPTER TWENTY-TWO

We rose at dawn, chilled, sore and tired. Everyone looked as though they'd just come through a couple of sessions of bull riding. I picked my boots up off the sand and turned them over, only to see a small lime-green scorpion fall out of one and go skittering off across the sand, its stinger cocked and ready.

"That would be the deathstalker," said Hadley, stepping on it with an air of satisfaction. "Told ya."

We drank some water, finished the last of our dates, and got the Land Cruiser going again. Hadley took the first shift, and half an hour later, handed it back over to me. I cursed under my breath as I wrestled the Land Cruiser through the sand. I was getting better at this, I thought, but it was still exhausting work, no matter how you sliced it.

The sun's intense reflection made it all but impossible to spot variations in either texture or topography. It had to be well over a hundred degrees in the cab. Sweat ran down my forehead and into my eyes, and my headscarf was soaked. The shocks and springs of the Land Cruiser did almost nothing to cushion the unending bumps and jolts as we crawled along. Through it all, I had to keep shifting down and up, looking for a gear ratio that would keep us going.

We were no longer anywhere near the track by now, having gradually drifted away in search of firmer ground. The track lay somewhere to the north of us, but I no longer could say how far. This wasn't going well at all, but I wasn't going to voice my concerns to the others. There was nothing to be done in any case.

But sooner or later, I knew, our systems would fail. A four-wheel drive is a complex piece of machinery, one which almost by definition gets regularly abused and is very rarely well maintained. That was certainly the case for the piece of crap that I was attempting to push through the sand at the moment.

We were overtaxing the vehicle, and I knew that eventually, something would break. It could happen in so many ways. We could develop a radiator leak, or suffer a break in one of the hoses. We could get sand in the carburetor, or in the fuel pump. We could crack the oil pan on a rock. Our exhaust smoke told me that we were burning oil, and I hadn't seen any spare cans in the back.

And so forth and so on. As we struggled along, we were really nothing more than a hot, sweaty, very uncomfortable breakdown just waiting to happen.

It happened less than an hour later.

We had just topped a small rise when I felt the wheel go mushy in my hands. As the vehicle slowed, I hit the gas, and felt the tires spinning in the soft sand. Here we go again, I thought. We'd had to dig out half a dozen times already, and in addition to being physically exhausting, the time and effort involved were starting to get seriously on my nerves. I gave the accelerator one more jab, and felt the vehicle dig itself even deeper into the sand.

"It's that time again, folks," I said. I turned off the motor, opened the door, and stepped out into the sand. Then I saw the left rear tire, completely flat. The weakened tire wall had finally burst, leaving a six-inch gash in the sidewall. I walked around to the back of the vehicle and stared wrathfully at the mounting bracket for the spare tire, which was of course empty.

Hadley and Nadia had climbed out of the Land Cruiser by this time. We all stared at the ruined tire. "Sonofabitch," Nadia muttered softly.

"And so our desert holiday comes to an end," murmured Hadley.

"*Akh!*" Nadia threw her hands in the air in angry frustration. "Look around." She swept her arm across the horizon. "Does anyone see a gas station? A telephone? A water faucet? What the hell do we do now?"

It was an excellent question, and I'd already started thinking hard. We were still at least thirty kilometers from El Borma, by my reckoning, but it might as well have been a hundred. There was no possible way we were going to get that tire repaired, and so the vehicle was now useless except as a small piece of shade. That was the first priority, I decided: get us under cover.

"There's a coil of rope in the back," I said. "And we've got the blankets. We'll use those to rig up a shelter from the sun. Come on, let's get moving."

Twenty minutes later, we were all sitting somewhat uncomfortably in the sand beside the vehicle, the blankets above us providing at least some protection from the sun, which was now doing its worst to bake us. We sat wedged in together, out of the direct sunlight.

It was nearly noon, and I decided to bring the meeting to order. "First," I said, "we need to do an inventory. What have we got?"

"We have three shovels," said Hadley.

"We have two pistols," said Nadia. "Mine, and the one Max took off that *mukhabarat* agent in the Medina."

"How much ammunition?" I asked. I already knew the answer to this, but I wanted to make sure.

She frowned. "I have a nearly full clip in mine, and another two clips in my bag."

I took my pistol out of my shoulder bag and popped out the clip. "Six shells left," I announced.

"We have the radio," said Hadley. "For all the good it will do us."

Nadia sighed. "I already explained. It's a military radio, fixed frequency. If we use it, all it will do is alert the Libyans that we're here."

"Okay, what else do we have?"

"I have my knife," Nadia said, holding up her long and wicked-looking military-issue dagger.

"I have my Zippo lighter," I said.

"We have the chelengk," said Hadley, holding up the leather bag. "And a dozen or so other jewels."

Nadia cleared her throat, and then said the quiet part out loud. "But we have no food."

"We do have water, however," I said, pointing to the jerricans in the back of the Land Cruiser.

Nadia stood up, walked over and looked at the jerricans. "Yes, we have water," she said. "Yesterday, we had forty liters. Today, quite a bit less than that. That's not a lot, Max."

I knew what she meant. Adults need at least three to four liters of water a day; out in the desert, probably even more. And, I thought, if we were going to try to walk anywhere while the sun was up, more still. With four of us drinking, the water wouldn't last long.

So our next moves, I realized, would determine whether we lived or died.

Water was what was going to keep us alive. At least for as long as we had any. The choice was very simple, really. Either stay where we were and hope that somebody passing through noticed us, or tie our shoelaces, hike up our pants, and set out on foot with whatever water we could carry, head more or less west, and hope to hell we didn't walk right by El Borma before we dropped dead from dehydration or heatstroke.

There had to be other options, but I was damned if I knew what they were.

"We're still a long way from El Borma," I said at last. "We know that it's west of here, but we've been off the track for some time now, and although we can walk west, nobody's got a compass. We might miss the settlement altogether. If we do, there's nothing but more desert, all the way into Algeria. There are no other intersecting roads, no way to really tell where we are. That's a big risk."

I wiped sweat out of my eyes. "I think the worst thing we could do is to try and walk out of here. I've crash-landed in some remote places and when that happens, the best thing is not to leave the site of the crash, but to stay in one place until someone spots you. Wandering around trying to get back to civilization is usually a quick way to die."

"But nobody even knows where we are, Max," Hadley pointed out. "How are they going to come for us if they don't even know we're missing?"

"Well, this may be a desert," I said, "but it's not completely devoid of human activity. The track is used by other vehicles. How often, I have no idea, but the fact that it's here tells you that once in a while, someone drives through."

"But we're not even *on* the track anymore," Nadia pointed out. "So how is that going to help?"

"True," I said. "But El Borma has an airstrip, and folks fly in there from time to time. We'll see and hear planes."

Hadley shook her head. "What are you planning to do, wave at them to come get us?"

I gave her a grim smile. "No," I said. "We'll set the Land Cruiser on fire. That would get their attention."

"Either way," I continued, "if we just stay alive long enough, somebody will spot us. So that's our priority – staying in place, and staying alive."

Nadia shook her head. "But we don't have anything to eat. We're going to starve to death eventually."

"It'll take us weeks to actually starve," I pointed out. "We'll be dead from lack of water long before that."

Hadley looked up at me, her face pinched with worry. "So we're basically screwed. How long, exactly?"

I thought for a moment. "We've got about thirty-five liters, and there are three of us. If we each drank a liter every day, we could do ten or eleven days." I paused. "But we really need to drink more than that, even if we're just sitting still. So, say two liters each, per day. Do the math."

Nadia nodded slowly. "Five days. Not a lot of time, when you think about it."

"Not a lot of time," I agreed. I kept my voice steady and confident, but inside, I was beginning to feel the first tremors of fear and doubt. I could deal with an inboard fire in an aircraft. I knew how to hide in the jungle from men who were hunting me. I wasn't afraid to walk down a dark alley at night.

But I admitted to myself that I knew next to nothing about the North African desert. Flying over it didn't really count. Nor did driving along through it on a nice, paved road, knowing that there would be something to eat, something cold to drink, and a reasonably comfortable bed at the other end. No, this was a case of what they called the cold equations – stuff you really couldn't bargain with.

All of this was starting to give me a headache. So maybe it was time to take a break, pull my thinking cap off, and shut the brain down for a while. I stood up, stretched, and opened the door to the Land Cruiser. "Folks, I'm going to suggest we all take a breather right about now. It's what people in hot countries do around noon, and it's a sensible practice." They were both staring at me.

"I'm dead serious. We need rest, and we need to conserve water and energy. The way to do that is to hole up during the day as much as you can." I reached in and pulled the seat back as far as it would go. "Now, you two can do whatever you like, but I'm going to try and get a little sleep."

I'd learned many useful things during the time I'd spent in Asia, and one of them was that reality was kind of like a kaleidoscope. The pattern you see right now is not necessarily the same one you'll see a little later on. Waiting enables a couple of things to happen. One is that if you wait, and keep looking at the pattern, you'll probably start to see things in it that you'd missed before. And another is that no pattern stays the same forever. If you wait long enough, the kaleidoscope will shift. Something will happen to shake up the pattern and give you a new set of options.

This had worked once in a while for me in the past, and I was hoping that it might work again. I lay back on the car seat, wrapped my *shemagh* over my face, and tried to think cool and peaceful thoughts as I willed sleep to come.

CHAPTER TWENTY-THREE

I woke up a few hours later with a plan forming in my head. Well, a kind of plan.

The only plan we had, I thought soberly. I checked my watch; four in the afternoon. My headache, thankfully, had gone. The heat should start to retreat now as the sun began to sink.

I climbed out of the Land Cruiser and waved to the two women, who were sitting together on the tailgate, talking quietly. Nadia held out a cup of warm water to me and I accepted it gratefully, sipping it slowly, enjoying the sensation of wetness sliding down my dry throat.

I ran my hand over my face, feeling my three-day stubble, and wondering if I looked as scruffy as I felt. It would have been easy to get up and walk over and look in the rearview mirror, but I decided I was probably better off not knowing. The only person who looked at all composed was Nadia, and even she was showing a bit of wear around the edges.

I'm not sure we can take more than another day or two of this, I thought as I handed her back the cup. If my plan worked, maybe we wouldn't have to. I cleared my throat to get everyone's attention. "I've been thinking."

"No, Max," said Hadley, "you've been sleeping. Like a log."

"And snoring," added Nadia with a small smile.

I smiled back. "That's called power breathing," I said. "But while I was sleeping, an idea came to me that I want to talk to you about. We're in a lifeboat in the middle of a very dangerous sea."

"We're in the freaking *desert*, Max." This from Hadley.

"I'm speaking metaphorically," I said testily. "Okay, we're stuck in the middle of a sand ocean, is that better? And if we're going to survive, we have to work together." I looked at them. "Now, each one of us has a particular set of skills or talents. And if we combine these in the right way, I think we can get out of here."

I paused. "What I'm about to propose is going to sound a little crazy, but hear me out, and think about it. It won't work unless we all agree, and if you give it some thought, I think you'll see that it's our only good option."

"The long, slow curve," murmured Hadley. "And soon, the fast break. I can't wait to hear this."

I got up and opened the back of the Land Cruiser. Inside, lying on its side, was the radio that we'd found when we took the vehicle from the Libyans. "This," I said, "is a Soviet transceiver. We saw some of these in Vietnam, years ago."

"It's an R-311," said Nadia. "They call it the Omega model."

"So you know how it works, right?"

She nodded. "But I told you, it's hooked into the Libyan military net; it's of no use to us at all. But yes, I know how it works. Why?"

"I think we can get it fired up," I said. "And if we can, I think you should call the Libyans on it." I paused. "And ask them to come and get us."

They both turned to me, their mouths open. "Are you crazy?" hissed Nadia. "We're running *away* from the Libyans. I thought you were helping me. Call them? Never. You're out of your mind."

I held up my hand. "Hear me out," I said. "Each of us has something special. Hadley has the chelengk, which we know the Libyans want very badly." I turned to Nadia. "You speak Arabic, and you know Libyan military protocols. You can talk to them. You get them on the radio, and you explain that you joined up with us right from the start as a ruse, in order to get the chelengk back, and now you've got us cornered in the desert, and it's time for them to come collect their prize. You're not a deserter, you're a hero. Think you can make them buy that?"

She shook her head. "No, I don't. I don't think they would believe that for a second." She thought for a moment. "But they probably would come for the chelengk."

I beamed at her. "I think so, too. And I'll bet you could pull it off. I really do."

"Maybe. Possibly. There's a military base at Ghadames, not far from here across the border. They have a helicopter base there. Let's suppose we persuade them to come. What then?"

"Yeah, what then?" said Hadley. "You say we've each got something special. What have you got? What's your contribution to this crazy idea?"

I gave her my best smile. "I can fly," I said. "I can fly just about anything. And," I added, "I'm also a very good thief. If they come, I'm betting they'll come in a helicopter. Which I will promptly steal."

Both of them were staring at me now. Nadia spoke first. "This is insane."

Hadley nodded. "Deranged. Totally."

I smiled. "Do either of you recall what Sherlock Holmes said? '*When you have eliminated the impossible, whatever remains, however improbable, must be the truth.*'"

"Sherlock Holmes," said Hadley, "isn't real. You know that, don't you?"

"What I know," I said evenly, "is that we don't seem to have any other options. Like it or not, this is what's left. And," I added brightly, "I really think it will work."

Hadley looked at our two pistols, and at the extra ammunition clips beside them. "This isn't a lot of firepower," she said after a moment. "You think we can hijack a military helicopter with just what's here?"

I tapped my forehead. "We've got what's up here, too, don't forget. Attitude's very important in situations like this."

She frowned. "How's attitude going to help us?"

"Because we're desperate, that's why. I don't know about you, but I'm prepared to do just about anything to get us out of here."

She grinned then. "I see what you mean. Okay, what the hell – I'm in."

Nadia had been staring at the radio. "You know," she said after a moment, "it might work, at that." She stood up. "Okay. What do we do?"

"Hadley and I will work on the radio, see if we can get it going. While we're doing that, you work on your script – your story."

I put my hand on Nadia's shoulder and gave her what I hoped was an encouraging and confident squeeze. "Your story is simple: you didn't desert, you pretended to team up with us in order to get your hands on the chelengk and bring it to Tripoli. You're not a deserter, you're an undercover operative, and now it's time for them to send a chopper to come and rescue you. You've got us under control – hell, tell them you've killed us all if it helps the story – and now you want to come home. With the chelengk." I paused. "Think you can do that?"

She nodded. "I just hope you know what you're doing."

I snorted. "I hardly ever know what I'm doing, but I'm pretty good at getting myself out of tight spots."

"You'd better be," said Nadia. "Okay, when do we do this?"

CHAPTER TWENTY-FOUR

It took us a while to figure out how to get the radio going. "Ugly thing, isn't it?" Hadley said, staring at the two-toned green metal case festooned with switches and dials.

"Ugly, yes, but it ought to work, if we can get it connected," said Nadia. "Here, help me move it." She took the handle on top, I took the sides, and together we pulled it back onto the tailgate.

It was heavier than it looked, weighing somewhere around twenty-five kilos. Behind it was a tangle of cables and plugs, together with a microphone and what looked like a battery pack.

Hadley shook her head. "I still think this is nuts."

I smiled and nodded. "I do, too. But until one of us comes up with a better idea, this is what we're doing. Help me untangle these cables, will you?"

* * *

An hour later, we were ready. The sun was low in the sky by this time, and things were finally starting to cool off. We'd discovered that the battery pack for the radio was very weak, so we stripped wire from the Land Cruiser's engine and used it to rig a connection to the vehicle's battery. "Clever Russians thought of everything," I muttered as we twisted the connections tight. We'd also laid out the antenna and raised it as high as we could.

Nadia walked over and inspected our work with a critical eye. "This thing would work better with a nice strong charge and a long antenna," she said. "We don't have either, so we'll just have to try to broadcast with what we have."

I nodded. "Something just occurred to me," I said. "I know that this is a fixed-frequency rig, but others could pick up the signal on that same frequency, right?" She nodded. "So there's a chance the Tunisians will hear it, too, isn't there?"

"Yes," she said. "I'd thought of that. But the Libyan bases at Ghadames and Al-Watiya are a lot closer to us. There's no guarantee that the Tunisians will hear us, and even if they do, no guarantee they'll come." She grimaced. "And no reason to suppose they'll get here first. So I would suggest, Max, that you stop thinking about all that. Is it ready to go?"

"Yes, give it a try."

She picked up the microphone. "This will either work, or we'll blow the circuits out." She reached over and snapped on a switch.

The dials sprang to life, and a red light blinked on. She turned up the gain dial, and the sound of the carrier wave came out of the speaker. "Oh, good," breathed Nadia. "It's working."

"Okay," I said. "The house lights are on, the curtain's going up. You remember your story?"

"Of course I do," she said. "Let's get going." She adjusted a few controls, turned up the gain, and began to speak. "Mayday, Mayday, Mayday," she began in English, and then switched to Arabic. She paused, and then repeated the sequence.

The hiss coming through the speaker didn't change. Nadia repeated her call sequence three more times, without result.

She sat back down on the sand and shook her head. "Something's wrong, Max," she said in a low voice. "Either the radio's broken, or the signal isn't really going anywhere."

Suddenly the speaker erupted in a blizzard of noise, followed by a stream of what sounded like angry Arabic. All of us turned toward the radio. The voice repeated itself.

Nadia grabbed the microphone again and began to speak slowly and deliberately. There followed a long series of exchanges, punctuated by even longer silences, as whoever was on the other end of the transmission presumably consulted with colleagues or superiors.

Hadley sat beside Nadia, listening intently, nodding from time to time. At one point there was a pause in the exchanges, and Nadia turned to us. "I asked them to send in people to get us out. An extraction team. They said they have to talk to the higher-ups but they haven't made any promises. This frequency is that used by the central military command at Tripoli," she said. "They picked up our transmission at the military base at Ghadames, and patched it through."

After a few more exchanges, Nadia signed off, put down the microphone and snapped off the transmitter. "What do you think?" I asked. "Did they buy your story?"

She blotted sweat from her face with her headscarf. "Hard to say. They're definitely interested in getting their hands on the chelengk, but whether they'll cross Tunisian territory to lay their hands on it is another matter."

"Well," I said, "let's just hope they make the right decision."

"Be careful what you wish for," she said.

* * *

Sunset came quickly after that, and as before, the temperature dropped dramatically. The breeze disappeared as darkness descended and the first stars began to appear. The desert was absolutely still, holding its breath as it silently awaited the rising of the moon. In other circumstances, it might have been mystical, perhaps even romantic. Instead, however, it held a distinct air of menace.

We sat huddled together inside the Land Cruiser. After a few moments, Hadley was the first to say what was probably on everyone's mind.

"What happens if nobody comes?"

There was a long silence. Then Nadia spoke. "Then, my dear Hadley, we're screwed. We've already drunk half our water; we've only got one jerrican left. And that's not going to last much beyond tomorrow."

I grimaced, trying not to think about what would happen when the water ran out. This was all my fault, I told myself. We could have tried to make it back up the road, toward Tunis, despite the near certainty that the Libyans would be waiting for us.

But, I reasoned, an escape to El Borma had seemed both logical and feasible at the time. Of course, I hadn't counted on the realities of the desert track, the softness and depth of the sand, and, above all, on the poor state of our tires.

Piss-poor planning, Donovan, I told myself. All your fault. You thought you knew what you were doing, but it turns out you didn't know Jack. And now as a result, you've put everyone's life at risk.

I suddenly felt dizzy and nauseous. I'm going to throw up again, I thought with some surprise. I mumbled something to Nadia and stood up, holding on to the side of the vehicle for support. I staggered off into the darkness.

I made it to the top of the nearest sand dune before I started retching. Bent over, I was throwing up practically nothing, but clearly, larger forces were at work. I sank to my knees, deathstalkers and horned vipers be damned, and bent forward, my forehead touching the sand. Shit, shit, shit, I thought.

I'd always carefully avoided death in the past. But although luck and skill had so far kept the Reaper from my door, now my bad judgment had put two other lives in danger as well as my own. And thanks to my fecklessness, it looked as if we were all going to die in one of the worst ways possible.

And all for what? A piece of jewelry which looked like something a ten-year-old kid would make in his school art class. My stomach heaved again, with no result.

After a long moment, I pulled myself together, wiped the tears from my eyes, and stood up. Bad show in front of the others, I thought. I took a deep breath and stared up at the sky. The moon had risen well above the horizon, bathing the sand sea in an odd silvery light. Despite the moonlight, most of the stars were still visible. Not too surprising, I thought, given the total lack of light pollution.

I tuned slowly, taking in the scene. From the top of the dune, I had a panoramic view. The moonlit sand spread out before me in all directions, seemingly to infinity. Everything was peaceful and utterly still.

But wait; not entirely still. My eye caught movement on the horizon. I peered into the darkness, trying to make it out. Something moving. An animal?

A tiny bolt of fear shot through me. Did they have lions in Tunisia? Unlikely. Maybe a hyena? No, it was too big for that. I could discern nothing but a distant dark shadow. It was definitely alive, and big. And moving slowly toward us.

In fact, whatever it was, there were now several more of them. As my eyes grew adjusted to the darkness, I could make out more than two dozen shapes, moving slowly across the sand toward us. Maybe they *were* hyenas, I thought. A pack of hyenas? Then why were they moving so slowly, and in such a deliberate manner, one after the other? Almost as if—

Camels, I thought. Damn, they were camels. A whole caravan of them, plodding along westward, about half a kilometer away from us. And drawing closer.

I ran down the dune to where Nadia and Hadley were watching me with wary interest.

"Max, are you okay?" asked Nadia. "We heard—"

"Everybody on your feet," I said. "We've got visitors."

CHAPTER TWENTY-FIVE

There seemed to be about forty of them, all men. Several sat quietly in front of us on the sand while we waited for their leader. Behind them, some of the other men were busy setting up what looked like an open-fronted tent. In the background, the camels had all decided that the day was over, and were kneeling on the sand, muttering quietly to themselves. Each was heavily loaded with parcels wrapped in burlap.

We stood beside our dead Land Cruiser, watching them. Two men came forward and spread a large mat on the sand a few meters away from us. Another man approached with a lit Petromax lantern and set it carefully at the edge. He then motioned for us to approach and sit down.

When we were seated cross-legged on the mat, I got my first good look at one of our visitors. The man who had beckoned us forward stood in front of us, staring with frank curiosity. What I could see of his face under the turban was lined and weathered, crisscrossed with an elaborate pattern of tattoos. I started to speak to him, but Nadia's hand on mine was a signal to keep my mouth shut for the time being.

Just beyond the circle of light, other men had spread out around us in a rough semi-circle, speaking in low tones to one another. After a few moments, the crowd parted to let a new arrival in. He spoke briefly to several of the men, and then came to sit directly in front of us.

This is the guy, I thought. The chief, the main man. The leader of whoever or whatever these folks are.

He spent a long moment taking us in. His piercing dark-brown eyes shone with curiosity and intelligence, and perhaps a touch of humor. His face was nut-brown, creased and weathered from the sun and wind. He had a wispy Van Dyke beard underneath a strong aquiline nose.

He was dressed in a similar way to the others, but his turban was white, and he wore a large, heavy medallion of some sort around his neck. The wicked-looking curved sword at his waist was held in place by a wide leather belt. He spent a few moments carefully arranging his robes, and he smiled, showing us a set of crooked teeth, several of which were gold. Then he began to speak.

His voice was clear and strong, but it didn't sound like Arabic to me. "Who are these guys?" I whispered to Nadia.

"I think they're Tuaregs," she whispered back. "They're speaking Tamashek."

"Tuaregs," breathed Hadley. "Unbelievable. Look at those knives."

The man addressed what was obviously a question to me. "Do you understand what he just said?" I asked Nadia.

"Not a word. But let me handle this." She raised her head and brought up the fingers of her right hand, pursed together, in the near-universal sign that means, 'wait, slow down.' "*B'il arabi, min fadli'k*," she said. "Speak Arabic, please."

He looked momentarily surprised, and then began to speak to her in Arabic. He seemed to be asking questions.

"What's going on?" I asked Nadia after a moment.

"Shut up and let me work here," she said in a low voice. "Don't either of you say a word."

They talked together for some minutes, during which time I inspected our surroundings. All of the forty or so men who now stood looking at us had either a sword or dagger at their belts, and several of them had long rifles. It was hard to see them in the dark, and even harder to read their expressions, since most of them had head coverings which obscured everything but their eyes and part of the nose. I was particularly interested in the heavy loads the camels were carrying. Who were these guys, where had they come from, and where were they going? I started to think that maybe we weren't going to be much better off than before they showed up.

Finally, I sensed that the conversation going on in front of me was drawing to a close. Nadia turned to us. "Okay, here's the story. As I thought, these guys are Tuaregs. This is a trade caravan, headed into Libya from Algeria. Their chief is called an *amghar*. That's this guy right here; his name is Sayyid Zerhouni, and the other men are members of his clan."

I nodded. "What have you told him about us?"

"As little as I could. They think we're on an archeological field trip. I figured with Hadley to back me up, we were on reasonably solid ground with that one. We were on our way to El Borma when the vehicle broke down."

I nodded. It was a good story. Particularly since so much of it was actually true. "You didn't mention the Libyans and all that stuff, did you?"

She gave me a scornful look. "Of course not. What do you take me for?"

"Just checking."

Sayyid Zerhouni smiled at us then, his gold teeth glinting in the light of the Petromax. He turned and barked something to his men. They all immediately rose to their feet and began unloading the camels.

"He's agreed to help us," Nadia said. "They're going to make camp here, and talk with us again in the morning. In the meantime, they have food and water."

"Great," I said. "So far so good."

Even as I spoke, one of the Tuaregs hustled up with a goatskin filled with water, which we passed around gratefully. Then came a round tin platter piled with flatbread and a small pyramid of dates. I'd had enough dates to last a while, but it had also been a longer while since I'd had anything to eat at all, so I smiled, nodded my thanks to Zerhouni, and dug in.

I spoke around a large chewy piece of bread. "Well, this is a change," I said. "An hour ago, we were broken down and lost in the desert, getting ready to die of thirst. And look at us now."

"Ever the optimist, aren't you?" said Nadia. "Let me point out a couple of things to you. First, these people are not going in the right direction. They're coming *from* the west, and headed into Libya, which is not a place any of us want to go right now."

I chewed, absorbing that piece of news. "You said a couple of things. That means there's at least one more. What is it?"

"I think they're smugglers, Max," she said. "They move at night to avoid detection. I'm not really sure how this helps us."

Hadley spoke up. "Smugglers? Of what?"

Nadia shrugged. "Who knows? Libya's got, shall we say, difficult trade relations with many parts of the world. There's a black market for all sorts of stuff. Guns, drugs, medicine. Cigarettes. Even people."

I thought about that for a moment. There was quite a bit more I wanted to know about smuggling in this part of the world, but maybe now wasn't really the time. We had other more pressing concerns. "Okay," I said finally. "What do you think our next move is?"

She shook her head. "We don't have any moves, Max. Look around. We're in the middle of nowhere. We have no food, no water, and no means of transportation. The Tuaregs have all of these things."

"So we're just stuck here, aren't we?" said Hadley.

Nadia nodded. "For the moment, yes, I think so."

I had to agree. We really didn't seem to have a lot of room to maneuver.

Sayyid Zerhouni was looking intently at me as I talked with Nadia. He asked her a question. She turned to me. "He wants to know if that's English we're speaking. He says he doesn't speak English, but he does speak some French."

I brightened. Finally, something I was somewhat good at. "*Je parle français, moi aussi*," I said to him. "I can speak French, too."

Zerhouni clapped his hands together delightedly. "*Formidable!* We shall all be close friends! And we shall all speak French from now on!" He looked at each one of us in turn. "A strong man, two beautiful women, Allah be praised." He indicated Nadia with an upturned palm. "Your wife?"

I shook my head. "No," I said. "My, ah, colleague."

"Colleague," he repeated, as if he'd never heard the word before. "And the other one?" He was pointing at Hadley now. "Your sister?"

"Another colleague," I said, wondering where all of this was going.

"Excellent, excellent," murmured Zerhouni. Behind him in the darkness, I could see his men erecting tents, untying loads from the camels, and setting up small firepits. "We will camp here tonight. You are our guests. It is the desert way to show hospitality to strangers. Especially," he added, with a glance at our vehicle, "to those who are in distress." He barked an order to one of the men, who hustled over.

"Rachid will show you to your tent, and he will bring you more food and water if you require it. You are certainly very tired after your difficult day. Eat, drink, and then rest. We will speak again tomorrow."

"Best idea I've heard all day," said Hadley, getting to her feet. "I don't think I'll have any difficulty sleeping tonight."

* * *

We lay spread out across a large mat in a kind of three-sided tent structure that Rachid had rigged up for us. The front was open, and through it, we could see the moonlit desert – and our vehicle – just down the slope from us. Rachid and several helpers brought in coarse woven blankets, and shortly thereafter, more water and something containing couscous and boiled meat in a battered metal pot. The water was in what had once been a four-liter plastic motor oil can, and despite the fact that it still carried the taint of hydrocarbon, it tasted delicious. We took turns eating the couscous using the single large metal spoon provided.

I scraped the last of it out of the pot, offered it to the others, and when both of them shook their heads, I gulped it down. Then I turned to Nadia. "Tell me," I said, "about the smuggling."

She smiled. "Is this professional interest?"

"In a way. People smuggle some strange things. I like to keep up with the trends." I was thinking, in particular, of some folks I'd encountered a few years ago who'd smuggled birds. And wound up dead because of it. I waved my hand out the door of the tent to the desert scene beyond. "I wouldn't have thought there was that much to smuggle out in a place like this."

"You'd be surprised," said Nadia. "Any time there are borders, there are variations in supply, demand, and price."

"Well, that's certainly been my experience," I said. "But what sorts of things might they be carrying out in a place like this?"

She shrugged. "Gaddafi's crazy, but people in Libya are actually pretty well-off in some ways. Despite what the Western press says. Electricity is free, for example. Gasoline costs pennies per gallon. But not everything's cheap. Or even available. So, they could be smuggling all sorts of things. Medicine. Rolex watches. The latest Paris fashions."

"Or guns," I said. "Or heroin. Or people."

She shifted beside me. "In theory, yes. But I doubt it's guns, hard drugs or people out here. There's too much risk."

I nodded. "Granted. But they're obviously carrying something into Libya. What do you think it is? Barbie dolls? Illegal copies of *People* magazine?"

She gave me a poke. "Be sensible. The couscous has obviously gone to your head."

Hadley spoke. "If you two are done talking nonsense, I have a different question."

I raised myself up on one elbow. "Fire away."

"Well, what now?" asked Hadley. "I mean, what do we do next?"

"That's easy," I said. "We rest. We see what things look like tomorrow, and then we make a new plan. How's that sound?"

She gave me a dark look. "Well, you're right about one thing," she said. "We need a new plan." She paused. "One that works out a whole lot better than the last stupid plan you had." She turned on her side away from us, and closed her eyes.

A moment later, I did the same.

* * *

I woke up to someone poking me. Gently, to be sure, but poking nonetheless. Nadia's voice was soft in my ear. "Max?"

"Nuh?" I grunted, coming slowly awake.

Her hand was on my shoulder. "I wanted to say something, Max. Day before yesterday, you saved my life. Back at the *ksar*. I'm alive because of you. I wanted to say thank you. I… I don't know what else to say. No one's ever saved my life before."

I squeezed her hand. "You don't need to say anything. We were all just looking out for each other. We did what we had to do."

"Yes, I understand that. But we killed two people, Max."

"Who would have killed us if we had let them. You know that, right?"

She nodded. "It's just hard to think about, that's all." She leaned forward and kissed me softly on the cheek. "Anyway. Thank you."

"Try to get some sleep. And with any luck, nobody else will die."

"I hope you're right." She snuggled up against me, and we both fell asleep holding hands.

CHAPTER TWENTY-SIX

"Max, wake up! Wake up!" Someone was shaking me. I shook my head to clear it, blinked twice, and sat up. Hadley and Nadia were both looking at me.

"What's up?"

"Our stuff, Max. They've got our stuff!"

I looked down to where my shoulder bag had been the night before. Right beside me. It was gone. I looked over across the mat at where Nadia and Hadley had been curled up. Their things were gone, too.

"What the hell?" I breathed.

"They've robbed us, Matt," said Nadia. "They took everything."

They had indeed taken everything, from what I could see. My shoulder bag had contained my passport, my money, and most importantly, my pistol. Nadia's bag had held her pistol and her commando knife.

And Hadley's bag had contained the chelengk.

I got up and went to the entrance of the tent. As I stepped outside, someone moved in front of me. It was

Rachid, one of Zerhouni's men, a short, curved sword at his belt and an ancient rifle in his hands, held at port-arms. "*La*," he said. No.

Nadia poked her head out of the tent and fired off a stream of Arabic at him, only to receive a short, terse sentence in reply.

"You're not allowed out, Max," she said. "None of us are. We are to stay here until Sayyid Zerhouni sends for us."

I looked the man up and down. He wasn't that big, and I didn't think he'd actually use the rifle. But there were dozens of other men in the camp, all of whom seemed to have swords or guns or knives of one sort or another. Nadia and I could probably bring this one down, but what then?

I nodded. "Prisoners," I said quietly in English.

"I think so, yes," Nadia said. "Perhaps this isn't the time to challenge them."

I went back inside and sat down. After a long moment, Nadia said to Hadley, "Well, this is a fine mess, isn't it? What do you think happens now? You know more about this part of the county and the people here than either Max or I."

Hadley shook her head. "The best case," she said, "is that after they take what they want from us, they let us go."

"Into the desert?" I said. "We wouldn't last two days on our own."

"Well, there's that," said Hadley. "But as I said, letting us go might be the best thing that could happen."

That got my attention. "Dying in the desert is the *best* option?" I said.

Hadley shrugged. "They could just kill us, Max," she said. "Take our things and kill us. Or they could keep us."

"Keep us and do what?" I wasn't sure I really wanted to know the answer to this one.

"Some of these desert tribes have a tradition of taking captives," she said. "Not all of them do it, but it's a common practice."

I nodded, thinking back to what my Senegalese friend had told me years ago about the Mauritanian raiders coming down from the north to seize captives. And then I remembered that in some places, laws against slavery had only been in existence a few years. "And what is normally expected of a Tuareg captive?" I asked.

"A lot of hard work, I expect," Hadley replied. "And not very much in return."

"So, if we don't die, slavery is our next best option, is that what I'm hearing?" Nadia's voice was indignant. "To be dragged around the desert by these... these idiots?"

"Some of the captives move around with the caravans," Hadley said. "Others get sent to one of the desert oases. Their job is to grow food for the group, for when they pass through."

"Kind of like a truck stop on the interstate," I said.

"Don't joke about this, Max," snapped Nadia. "We're talking about *slavery*, for God's sake."

"Sorry," I said. "Just trying to get a sense of how it all fits together." I turned to Nadia. "What do *you* think's going to happen?"

She shook her head. "I've no idea. I know a little about these people, but not very much. I'm neither Libyan nor Tunisian, remember. It's impossible to generalize about the Tuareg and the other Berber groups in the desert. Some of them are pro-Gaddafi. Some of them are fighting Gaddafi. Either way, I don't think it would be a good idea at all to tell them I've been in the Libyan military. Some of them are smugglers, like these people." She paused. "I have no idea what they plan to do with us. All I know is that we won't like it, whatever it is."

Hadley nodded at this, her face grim.

I thought for a moment. "We don't know enough yet," I said. "They're probably all over in Zerhouni's tent now, talking about what to do next. Once they've made up their minds, they'll tell us. Until then, there's really nothing we can do. Let's wait a bit and see what the situation is once they've finished their conclave or whatever it is." I peered out the front of the tent at the desert beyond. It was only midmorning, but already the heat was building, making the dunes in the distance shimmer in the thermals.

"We could try to run," I said. "But we're no longer armed, and they are. I don't think we could get very far on foot, and I don't think any of us know how to saddle and ride a camel. And there are too many to kill, I think." I thought for a moment. "Although we might be able to think of a way to do that, eventually."

I stretched back out on the mat and closed my eyes. "In the meantime, I'd suggest that we wait, and get a little more rest. I think we're going to need it."

* * *

We were summoned at noon by another of Zerhouni's men. He stuck his head into the tent and uttered a single word, "*Yallah!*"

Even I knew what that meant. "Time to go, folks," I said.

We assembled outside and were led through what had now become a small tent city to where Sayyid Zerhouni sat under an awning. Behind him stood a dozen men, all watching us intently as we came forward and sat down on the carpets.

Our stuff was spread out on the carpet beside Zerhouni. Guns, money, passports, the chelengk – all of it. Even my Zippo lighter. Over to the side lay the dismembered hulk of the radio, its parts piled up beside the empty metal case. Beside the radio, the rest of our equipment – shovels, jerricans, the Land Cruiser's jack and a few small tools – lay piled in a heap.

"Sit. Please sit." Sayyid Zerhouni was beaming, his arms open wide in welcome, a smile putting his gold teeth on good display.

He barked an order, and one of the men rushed forward with a battered coffeepot and a stack of small cups. We each took a cup and waited for it to be filled. I took a sip. It was hot and bitter. I supposed it was coffee, but I wondered what it was really made from.

Oh, well. Better than nothing. I turned to Nadia. "I think it's better that you do the talking here," I said. "And I think you should do it in Arabic. His French isn't bad, but using Arabic will give us a couple of seconds after each exchange to figure out what to say next."

She nodded, and launched into what I took to be an elaborate set of greetings, salutations, and general inquiries after health and other important matters. After a minute or two of this, Zerhouni's expression changed into a more businesslike one.

Nadia listened closely. "He says he understands we were going to El Borma. Unfortunately for us, he is headed in the other direction."

I nodded. "Ask him what the camels are carrying."

"Max, this isn't the time. I—"

"Naw, go on, ask him," I said. "These guys are businessmen, right? Maybe we can make a deal or something."

"With what? They've already got all our stuff, remember?"

"Ask anyway, okay? It won't do any harm."

She asked, and Zerhouni's face again split into a broad smile. He turned to me. "*Des cigarettes,*" he said in French. "*Beaucoup de cigarettes. Pour le marché noir.* Cigarettes. Lots of them. For the black market." He gave a low laugh. "*Nous sommes des contrebandiers — contrebandiers professionnels.*" He laughed again. "We are professional smugglers."

Beside me, Hadley stirred. "The news doesn't get better, does it?" she said quietly. "If they're smugglers, they're not going to want to deal with the authorities on our behalf, are they?" She turned to me. "Still think you can make a deal?"

I shrugged. "It was worth a try." A moment later, two men approached, carrying something bulky in a dirty sheet. They laid it down beside Zerhouni and proceeded to unwrap it. A battered wooden case emerged.

Zerhouni opened it with a flourish and peered inside. He beamed. *"Ma boîte à trésors,"* he said in French as he opened it. "My treasure box."

Inside, I could see wads of currency and a heap of what looked like gold and silver jewelry; rings, gold chains, pendants. He began to put our things into the box.

"Stop! You can't do that!" I raised my voice. "All that stuff belongs to us! You just can't take it like that."

Although I'd spoken in English, my meaning was crystal-clear to Zerhouni. He smiled again, and as he talked, Nadia translated.

"He says we're very lucky that they found us. We have no food, very little water, and our vehicle is useless. We are very far away from help."

He finished putting our things into the box, and shut the lid. Then he said, in French this time, "We are not thieves, we are smugglers. We are keeping your possessions safe, while you benefit from our generous hospitality. And," he added with a glint in his eye, "as a guarantee of your good behavior."

"This is bullshit," muttered Hadley. "They're going to kill us, aren't they?"

I shook my head. "I don't think so. If they'd wanted to kill us, they could have done so easily. They've got something else in mind."

Nadia nodded. "I'm afraid you may be right."

Zerhouni reached back into his treasure box and pulled out a plastic laminated card.

"Oh, shit," whispered Nadia.

"There's one other problem," he said in French. He held up Nadia's military ID card. "It appears that one of you works for our enemy. We have long been opposed to the antics of that fool Shafshoufa in Tripoli. We keep to ourselves, conduct our business, and have as little to do with the government as possible." He waved the ID in front of us. "Now, however," he said, his eyes blazing, "we find an infiltrator, a traitor, a spy in our midst."

He was just getting started on a rant now, and I was sure it wasn't going to end well. The men around him were quiet, listening raptly, even though I was sure that not one in ten of them could understand French. He wasn't speaking for their benefit, of course. He was talking directly to us.

"The desert way is to be hospitable to strangers, to welcome the outsider with open arms. To share what little we have with them, and to care for them." He raised his voice another notch or two. "But this – this is betrayal! This is provocation! We cannot let this challenge go unanswered."

He spoke again, this time in Tamashek. The men around him started smiling and nodding. He was building up to something, and the atmosphere around us was changing fast.

Zerhouni resumed talking in French again. "As is our custom, we met this morning for several hours to decide what to do. Some among us wanted to kill you. But this is not the desert way, not *our* way. You may be foreigners and spies, but you are not animals, to be sacrificed." He raised a finger. "No, the desert way is to show compassion and mercy. And so, after much discussion, we have found a solution."

He turned to me. "As for you, Monsieur Donovan, we will let you go. We did discuss admitting you into our group, but most of us thought you were not up to the high standards we set for ourselves." This came out in French as "*pas à la hauteur*," which sounded worse, somehow.

"You are therefore free to leave us," he continued. "We are not only hospitable and compassionate, we are also generous. Tomorrow morning at *fajr*, the hour of the first prayer, you will be given a camel, together with food and water. I would advise you to travel mainly at night, however, to avoid the heat. Use the star in the north, the one we call *najm ash-shamal*, to guide you. With God's mercy, you have a chance of reaching El Borma alive."

"*You* get a camel," muttered Hadley darkly. "What do *we* get?"

"Wait for it," I whispered back. "I don't think you're going to like it."

"Oh, I'm sure of that."

Zerhouni turned to the women. "As for these two women, we must make other arrangements. It is well known that women do not do well on their own. Unsupervised women are a danger to themselves and to others in the community."

"We're both right here, you know," muttered Hadley in English.

Zerhouni barely hesitated. "We have been given a great responsibility with the appearance of these two strangers; women without husbands, women without even a suitable *mahram* to accompany them as they travel." He shot a disapproving glance in my direction. If I wasn't good enough to be a Tuareg, he seemed to be saying, I certainly wasn't good enough to be their required male companion.

"So, we faced a great dilemma." Here he raised his bony finger again. "We could abandon these women to fate, or we could accept our responsibilities, and find another solution. After much discussion, we found that solution."

"Which is?" I asked.

He turned to me, beaming. "It should have been obvious to us all along. The women require a *wali*."

"A *wali*?"

"That's a male guardian," whispered Nadia. "Kind of like a godfather, only more so."

"As the chief of my clan, I have appointed myself as *wali*. I now have the authority to arrange marriages for both women." He sat up straight and raised his head high. "We will find them suitable husbands from within my clan here. Once the marriages have been carried out, our caravan will resume its way. And, of course, the women will accompany their new husbands."

He beamed. "It is an excellent solution, is it not? Once again, the generosity and mercy of the people of the desert will be there for all to see. And admire."

Everyone stayed perfectly quiet after Sayyid Zerhouni had finished speaking. I noticed that all eyes were on the two women.

Hadley broke the spell. "What the fuck?" she muttered. "Married, seriously?" She started to get up. "I've had enough of this—"

Nadia put her hand on Hadley's shoulder. "Stay right where you are," she said quietly, locking eyes with her. "I agree, it's crazy. But right now, reacting isn't going to help. They've got our money, our passports, and our weapons. We need time to figure this out."

She was right. But time, I thought, was something we had very little of. Hadley sat back down, her face a mask of anger.

Zerhouni was talking again. "We'll have the celebration this very evening," he said. "Roasted goat, plenty for everyone. I will lend the women jewels from my treasure box. They will both look beautiful, and everyone will dance all night." He swung around to face me. "And tomorrow morning, Monsieur Donovan, you will be on your way." His eyes shone with excitement. Behind him, the men began to talk in low voices among themselves.

We sat there, stunned, for a long moment. I thought I should say something. "Let's not panic," I said. "We can still—"

Hadley put her hand on my wrist and gave me a hard stare. "I'm not panicked, Max," she said calmly through gritted teeth. "I'm *pissed.*" She flashed Zerhouni a quick smile then, and added, "And when I'm through with this bunch of miserable losers, they'll wish they'd never set eyes on us."

CHAPTER TWENTY-SEVEN

Just past seven now, and the day's heat was starting to dissolve into early evening. The camp had been buzzing with activity for most of the day, and now things were nearly ready. Goats had been slaughtered and food prepared. The large campfire, built earlier in the afternoon using some of the caravan's precious wood, was slowly burning down to form a bed of hot coals. Under the coals lay the bodies of three butchered goats, now roasting.

Earlier, Nadia and Hadley had been led into a tent and prepared for the ceremony. They emerged an hour later, their hands covered in designs picked out in henna. They wore flowing white *abayas* embellished with intricate embroidery, a headscarf and niqab, covering all but their eyes. They sat side by side on camel saddles in front of the area where the food was being prepared. With ceremony, Zerhouni then proceeded to decorate each woman with a variety of jeweled ornaments from his treasure box. I sat off to the side, ignored by everyone.

By the time Zerhouni was finished, both of them sported a collection of necklaces, bangles and rings which must have been worth a small fortune. While the women were being attired, the men of the caravan came by, one by one, to admire them and offer congratulations.

Two of these guys, I thought, were slated to be their future husbands. I wondered if they had any idea what was really in store for them.

"Beautiful, aren't they? Zerhouni had finished his final touches and come over to sit next to me. He gestured with his hand. "These embroidered *abayas* are silk, nothing but the finest. We acquired them in Algeria, for our wives at home." He winked at me. "We won't be mentioning that to the wives, however. The jewelry either."

The overall effect was quite stunning. Both Nadia and Hadley wore huge gold earrings. Gold and silver bracelets climbed halfway up their arms. Nadia wore a heavy necklace of gold chains and gold coins. Hadley's was of silver. Both women also wore elaborate headdresses incorporating gold and silver coins, gold braid, and cascades of flat rings looking a bit like silver and gold faucet washers.

Zerhouni noticed my interest. "The rings, we call *rayhana*. All women love these."

Maybe not these two quite so much, I thought. But in truth, the women were beautiful nonetheless. I glanced over at them, sitting stiff as statues on their camel saddles. "It's not a bad look, I have to say," I said to them.

"Fuck off," hissed Hadley, turning her head away.

Having hit a conversational dead end with her, I tried Nadia. "Any idea what happens now?"

"I don't know much about these people," she said. "But they say Tuareg women are somewhat liberated. For desert nomads, at least." She paused, looking thoughtful. "They don't do bride kidnapping anymore, or so I've heard. And I don't think the Tuareg practice female circumcision."

Hadley's head snapped around. "What, now?"

"It's okay," I said in my most soothing voice. "Nadia just said they don't do that kind of thing here."

"I'd like to see them try," muttered Hadley. "Oh, God, I'd so like to kick someone's ass right now."

For most of the afternoon, while the decoration of the brides had been going on, there had been dancing and drumming. Half a dozen of the men had produced flat drums of goatskin from somewhere, and someone else appeared with a long flute. Zerhouni leaned over to me. "According to our custom, only our women are allowed to play the real drums. These noisemakers you see here are coming from Algeria, cheap tourist things. Our men amuse themselves at night sometimes with them. But we are doing our best, as you can see."

The men had moved off into a large, open space and arranged themselves in a loose circle, beating their drums. Other men came to encircle them in turn, clapping their hands in rhythm while uttering short, piercing cries. In and out of it all, the flute wove an odd, haunting melody.

After an hour or so of this, a dozen men wearing full desert robes and turbans appeared, each holding a long saber. Using a skipping, hopping and shuffling dance step, they began to prance around the drummers, waving their weapons. Everyone else moved back and forth, clapping and ululating, becoming more and more excited.

Then the camels appeared. All of the caravan's camels formed a line and paraded in slow and stately fashion around the outside of the circle of dancers and drummers, their footsteps in synch with the music. Nadia, Hadley and I watched, open-mouthed, as this continued through the late afternoon.

"I apologize," said Zerhouni after a while, "for the poor quality of this celebration. As I said, the women normally play these instruments. And they are generally much better dancers than these hopeless men." He smiled. "But here in the desert, we have to make adjustments.

"However," he added, "we do have your tents ready." He pointed behind us to where two small tents had been set up, side by side. "In our clan, the tents belong to the women, and so each of you will have your own tent. This is where you and your husband will live."

Over her veil, Hadley was staring daggers at him. "And who exactly are we going to be married to?"

His smile broadened. "That, my dear, is the best part. It's going to be a surprise. After the feast, we will escort you to your tent. There, you will wait for your new husband. He will enter through the back of the tent."

Hadley shook her head. "If you think I'm sleeping with somebody I've never met—"

Sayyid Zerhouni raised his hand in a gesture of supplication. "No, no, of course not. Closeness takes time to develop. In our tradition, the man and wife do not, shall we say, fully join together until three days have passed." He nodded. "You will have plenty of time to get to know your new husband. To develop interest and affection."

Hadley glared at him, and seemed about to say something, but Nadia put her hand on Hadley's, and stopped whatever was about to be said.

While the goat was roasting, we all drank mint tea, served on a metal platter in very small glasses. Zerhouni explained the process. "Tea is a very social occasion for us. It is one of the ways we honor our guests." He gestured to the two women. "The first round of tea is bitter. We say that it is as bitter as death." He glanced meaningfully at me as he said this.

"The second round of tea," he said a few minutes later, "is as strong as life." Later, he held up the tray containing the final round. "And this one," he said, "is as sweet as love."

"What a bunch of bullshit," muttered Hadley under her veil. "I can't believe this is happening. When are we going to start kicking some ass? In a few hours, if these jackasses have their way, I'm gonna be someone's wife. I—"

From the vicinity of the campfire came a shout. Zerhouni rubbed his hands together and stood. "*Yallah.* Let's go. The goats are ready," he said. "Now the wedding feast can begin. Come."

The daylight was fading fast into dusk as we walked down the sloped dune to the remains of the campfire, by now just a bed of coals. The men had spread mats around it, and were busy bringing bread, dates, and other morsels of food and setting them down. While they did this, Zerhouni's men were using the shovels from our Land Cruiser to push the coals and sand aside, uncovering the baked goats underneath.

Zerhouni knelt down and poked the carcass experimentally with the point of his knife, nodding with satisfaction. "It's done," he pronounced. He turned to me. "Come closer," he said.

As I approached, he pinched his nostrils and blew a plug of snot into his hand. He flicked it away, and then, using the same hand, reached forward and popped out one of the goat's eyeballs.

"*Tiens, chef,*" he said, handing it to me. "*C'est le meilleur.*" "Take this, chief. It's the best part."

The eyeball was hot and slimy, and I juggled it awkwardly in my hand. I looked at Nadia for help. "Do I have to do this?" I said in English.

Hadley was watching me, her eyes twinkling with amusement. Nadia nodded slowly. "I'm afraid you do, Max."

I held the steaming eyeball in my palm, regarding it warily. One of the men closest to the fire pit said something, and Nadia gave a low chuckle.

"What did he say?" I asked her.

"He said, 'Look out, I think he's going to vomit.'"

"Never," I whispered. I drew myself up and popped the eyeball into my mouth. A ragged cheer went up from some of the men.

Just then, I became aware of another noise, coming from behind us, and growing louder by the second.

We all turned to see a helicopter approaching, flying fast and low over the sand.

CHAPTER TWENTY-EIGHT

The thumping of the rotors grew louder as the machine approached, its landing lights probing the sand beneath. I moved over beside Nadia. "Is that—"

"Yes," she said. "It's ours. It's got Libyan military markings."

It did indeed. Even in the gathering darkness, I could see the big green rondel on the tail structure. As the chopper drew closer, I recognized it as a Soviet-made Mi-8, the one we used to call a 'Hip' back in the day. The Soviets had manufactured tens of thousands of these things and sent them all over the world, including to a few places I'd happened to be at the time. It was a sturdy, dependable, tough workhorse, used both as a troop transport and an attack helicopter.

As the chopper approached, I was relieved to see that it wasn't kitted out for combat. This was an extraction. Exactly what we'd asked for.

Everyone in the caravan had heard the chopper by this time, and some of them were running for their tents, presumably to grab weapons. Nobody was paying the slightest bit of attention to us. We all moved back behind the camel saddles.

Hadley grabbed my arm. "We've got to find the chelengk, Max. I'm not leaving here without it. And," she added, her face grim, "not before I've kicked some ass. Hard."

"I'm with you on both of those things," I said. "But we need to wait just a bit, see how things play out here." I had no idea at all about what was going to happen in the next few moments, except that it represented our only real chance to get out alive. We'd sent the distress call a day ago, when we were on our own. The Libyans who were just now arriving probably hadn't expected to encounter an entire caravan, and I wondered what they were going to do. An extraction is just what it says – roar in, pick up the package, and take off. Of course, it sometimes happens on hostile territory, with incoming fire on the approach. In that case, you need to have people inside the chopper capable of delivering suppressive rounds – lots of them, and fast.

So far, though, the folks in the chopper hadn't said boo. It thundered in right overhead, the rotors raising big clouds of grit, making one big, low circle before settling to earth thirty meters away. Behind me, the camels were growing alarmed and restless.

Three armed soldiers hopped down from the open side door and fanned out across the sand, their assault rifles up and ready. The chopper's rotors continued to turn slowly, and I knew the pilot had turned the throttle on the collective to idle. They weren't waiting around. They were here to find, grab, and take off, as quickly as possible.

The soldiers slowly approached our group across the sand, coming into clear view now as they drew closer. "God save us," whispered Nadia. "These are people from my unit." I looked more closely and saw that she was right. All of them were women. One of them was none other than Major Fawzia Al-Sharif, the woman with the eyepatch who'd thrown me to the floor in the Hilton dining room. It seemed like centuries ago.

Nadia stood up, pulled off her white veil, and waved it at the approaching soldiers. "We're here! We're here!"

Zerhouni's men were pouring out of their tents now, and as I had feared, many of them had weapons. One man in particular was in the lead. He wore a bright blue turban and carried an ancient Enfield rifle, and as he ran toward the Libyans, he raised it in one smooth motion and fired.

"Shit," I murmured, pulling Nadia down flat on the sand beside me.

The Libyan response was immediate and devastating. They brought their assault rifles up and unleashed a short burst into the camp. Screams and cries indicated that more than one Tuareg had been hit. I glanced up to see four men lying on the ground. The rest had dropped their weapons and were running as fast as they could away from the campfire, trying to get to shelter behind the tethered camels.

I looked over at the helicopter, its navigation lights blinking in the gathering darkness, the rotors still turning on idle. I was trying to estimate force levels. Three soldiers were advancing toward us, but no more had yet appeared. That left whoever was still inside the chopper. Something the size of an Mi-8 would normally have a crew of three — a pilot, a co-pilot, and a navigator. If they'd brought the full crew, that meant that there might be as many as six of them altogether, all armed.

That many troops made what I had in mind a little difficult, but not impossible. I looked around. Almost all of the Tuaregs had vanished, leaving four dead tribesmen sprawled out on the sand around us. The rest of them were hunkered down now behind the camels, almost a hundred meters away, taking occasional potshots at the advancing Libyans. At that distance, they were unlikely to hit much.

In response, the Libyans continued to let off short bursts of suppressive fire in the general direction of the camel herd, which appeared to be finally waking up to the situation, and they were not pleased. Some of the animals were already on their feet, pulling their tether stakes out, grumbling and bellowing as they started to panic.

I took Nadia's arm. "In a minute, I want you to stand up, make sure they see you, and walk toward them. Identify yourself, explain the situation, and tell them we all want a ride. Don't let them take you by yourself."

"They won't," she said. "They want the chelengk more than they want me."

"Perfect. Tell them they're going to get it, as long as we can all get a ride in that helicopter. You need to keep them busy for only a couple of minutes."

"Why? What are you going to do?"

"Hadley and I are going to go on an errand," I said. "Aren't we?"

She nodded, excitement building in her face.

"And when we get back," I continued, "we're going to need to overpower the soldiers if we want to get away. So, we'll need the element of surprise."

Both women were paying close attention now. Around us, a few of the Tuareg continued to fire sporadically at the Libyans from a distance, but they seemed more interested in keeping their camels from running away.

"There are three of them and three of us," I continued. "The crew will have to stay in the cockpit to keep the chopper running. That means we only have to deal with these three right now. Each of you pick one, and on my signal, we bring them down. Get their weapons first if you can." I looked at Nadia. "I want Fawzia, the one with the eyepatch."

She grinned. "Fine. I'll take the tall one. Hadley, you take the one with the red beret. Hit the solar plexus as hard as you can with your fist. By the time you do that, I'll have finished with mine, and I can help you."

"That's the spirit," I said. "We'll wait until all of us are close to them. The trigger phrase is 'It's Howdy Doody time.' Think you both can remember that?"

Both women stared at me. "What's a Howdy Doody?" they said in unison.

I sighed. "Oh, hell, never mind, just try and remember it." I took Hadley by the hand and pulled her to her feet. "While Nadia goes and talks to the soldiers, you come help me."

I glanced back at the camp. Sayyid Zerhouni was nowhere to be seen. Here we go, I thought. To Hadley, I said, "Let's go."

Crouching low, we ran inside Zerhouni's tent. It was thankfully empty. This will make what happens next much easier, I thought. I spotted his so-called treasure box over in a corner, and beside it, our empty shoulder bags and Nadia's duffle. The treasure box was an ornate carved wooden chest, but without any sort of lock. "Honor among thieves," I murmured as I flipped it open.

Inside, our passports and money lay on top of a layer of gold and silver ornaments, odd wads of currency, and, underneath it all, the chelengk. Our two Makarov pistols were also there. I stuffed the pistols into my shoulder bag. I handed Hadley her passport, put mine and Nadia's into my pocket, and pawed through the currency. Zerhouni had a nice fat collection of Algerian, Tunisian and Libyan dinars, together with a not inconsiderable quantity of French francs. The dinars weren't an easily convertible currency, I knew, but I decided to take them anyway. We weren't out of the territory yet, and given the way that things had gone so far, who knew what tomorrow would bring?

I grabbed Nadia's duffle bag and handed it to Hadley. "Hold that open." I began to shovel money, jewels and ornaments into it, together with the chelengk. I emptied the treasure box, zipped the duffle shut and stood up. From outside the tent, I could hear more gunfire, and screams from the camels. A French phrase I'd heard before came back to me, *Ça va faire du vilain bientôt.* Gonna get ugly now.

Hadley picked up her shoulder bag. I grabbed mine and Nadia's duffle, now heavy with loot. I headed for the door of the tent.

"Wait," said Hadley. "There's one thing more."

She moved to the Petromax lamp in the corner, picked it up and shook it. She grinned. "Nearly full." She unscrewed the filling cap and upended it, shaking fuel over the sides of the tent.

I spotted one of our jerricans of gasoline in another corner, and ran to open it, joining Hadley in our act of impromptu arson.

When we had splashed all the fuel out around the tent, I pulled out my Zippo and got it going. I turned to her. "Ready?"

Her eyes glowed with mischief. "Born ready, Max," she breathed.

I touched the lighter to the edge of a piece of canvas. In two seconds, the tent began to burn very nicely, flames shooting up the walls, adding a new and exciting element to the chaos unfolding in the camp.

Clutching our new acquisitions, we ran outside.

CHAPTER TWENTY-NINE

As we fled the burning tent, the rising full moon helped illuminate what was going on outside. It was almost fully dark now. Most of the Tuaregs had disappeared, presumably hiding out somewhere in the camel enclosure. Several bodies lay sprawled on the sand near the firepit. A few hardy souls had stayed behind, but they were holding very still, their arms in the air. Most of the camels seemed to have disappeared.

The Libyan recovery squad stood facing them, at a distance of about twenty meters, their weapons raised. Fawzia, the major with the eyepatch, was talking intently to Nadia. Hadley and I paused at the edge of the firepit. I noticed with some relief that the troops didn't seem to be wearing body armor. That would make things a little easier.

We approached cautiously and stopped about five meters away from the group of soldiers. Nadia turned and spoke to us in English. "It's okay, I think," she said. "They asked me to explain what happened here."

Another exchange in Arabic between Nadia and the team leader followed, during which we kept a respectful silence. This has to work, I thought. And it has to work right now, before those Tuaregs recover their camels, and their courage.

"They've agreed to take us," said Nadia a moment later. "They need us to come with them right now. Before anything else happens."

I had no idea whether any of these soldiers spoke English. Or even French. So I needed to play along. "You bet," I said, nodding. "Here we come."

"Tell me the plan again," hissed Hadley beside me as we walked slowly toward the group.

I gave her what I hoped was a confident smile. "We're going to steal that helicopter," I said in a low voice. "But in order to do that, we need to disarm these folks, just like we discussed, remember?"

"Hard fist to the solar plexus," she growled.

"Wait for the signal," I reminded her.

She looked past the group at the helicopter, its rotors turning on idle. "Can you really fly that thing?"

My smile widened. "I can certainly try."

She shook her head in disbelief. "This is all kind of made up, isn't it?"

I beamed at her. "Now you're getting it. Look sharp; here we are."

The Libyans didn't look that happy to see us, but I assumed that Nadia had somehow persuaded them not to shoot. We all started walking together toward the chopper.

Fawzia hopped aboard through the side hatch, motioning me to climb in. Once inside, I looked around, my heart beginning to pound. Only one pilot, still in her seat, and with her seatbelt still buckled. Luck, I thought, was finally on our side. It was about time we had a break.

Fawzia racked her assault rifle against the rear bulkhead and pointed to one of the jump seats behind the cockpit. I smiled and nodded, but instead of sitting down, I turned and stuck my head out the hatch. Down on the sand, Hadley and Nadia stood next to the two remaining guards. Perfect. Time to get started.

"Hey kids, what time is it?" I yelled down over the noise of the rotors. Everybody looked up at me. *"Why, it's Howdy Doody time!"*

Things happened then very quickly. I turned, grabbed Fawzia by the belt, and spun her around so that she was facing the open hatch. With my free hand, I popped open her holster and extracted her pistol. Then I hit her over the head with it, hard, and pushed her out the hatch door.

Below on the sand, I saw Hadley sucker-punching one of the soldiers, while Nadia was in the process of flipping the other one in the air. "Don't forget their weapons!" I yelled, and turned back to face the pilot.

She was just coming up out of her seat, eyes wide in fear, as I racked the slide on my newly acquired pistol and steadied it between her eyes. Summoning one of my few useful words of Arabic, I whispered, *"Shwaya, shwaya."* "Take it easy."

She nodded. I motioned for her to hand over her pistol, and when she did, I booted her out the hatch as well.

She fell nearly on top of Hadley and Nadia, just below. Nadia tossed me two assault rifles, Hadley plopped two more pistols down on the floor, and I kicked them all back into the aircraft.

Nadia was struggling with her robes as she boarded the chopper. "I need to get this stuff off," she said, starting to remove her heavy gold and silver wedding necklace.

I grabbed her wrist. "Wait until we're in the air," I said. "We don't have time now. You're leaving just as you are." I leaned in and gave her a quick kiss. "Besides," I added, "I really think you look great all dressed up like that."

"Did you forget somebody?" Hadley's voice floated up from below.

I grabbed her and pulled her up through the hatch. "Good work back there," I said.

Her eyes were glowing. "Yeah, it was, wasn't it? She went down like a telephone pole."

A volley of shots crashed into the cockpit from outside, and we all flinched. I turned to see Fawzia, the eyepatch major, climbing back through the open hatch, her combat knife in her hand and fury in her single eye. She launched herself at me.

"*Merde*," muttered Nadia as she pivoted and with a single strong sidekick, sent Fawzia back out the door and onto the sand. She peered cautiously out the hatch. "Those shots didn't come from her," she said. "The Tuaregs are regrouping, and one of them must have an automatic rifle."

Nadia scooped up an AK-47 from the floor, brought it up and fired a few bursts out the door. She turned to Hadley. "Make yourself useful," she said. "Grab one of those guns and help me out here."

I tossed Hadley one of the AK-47s from the bulkhead. "Know how to fire this?"

She shook her head. "But it's never too late to learn."

"Nothing to it," I said, glancing out the hatch to see four or five Tuaregs with rifles advancing slowly across the sand toward us. Or toward the soldiers, I couldn't tell which.

"Hold it like this," I said, taking her hands and positioning them on the grip and the handguard. I took the AK by the barrel, pointed it out the door for her, and flipped the selector up. "Lean forward," I said. "Now just pull the trigger."

There was a long burst of explosive noise, and Hadley fell backwards. I grabbed the gun from her hands. I'd forgotten that there were two firing positions on these things. She'd just loosed off an entire thirty-round magazine in the general direction of the rising moon. Beside me, Nadia was working the other AK effectively, firing one burst at a time in the general direction of the Tuaregs, laying down suppressive fire.

I slapped another magazine into Hadley's gun and set the selector properly. "Better now," I said as I handed the gun back to her. "One trigger pull, one shot. Try not to kill anyone unless they get way too close."

She nodded, stuck the muzzle out the hatch and started firing.

Nadia turned to me. "You know, if you really can fly this thing, now would be a good time to show us," she said calmly, continuing to fire rounds in the direction of the Tuareg camp.

"On it," I said, as I hopped into the pilot's seat.

CHAPTER THIRTY

If you don't fly, then the cockpit of anything bigger than a Piper Cub can look pretty daunting. All those lights and switches. A chopper pilot might go through thirty or more pre-flight checks, but we weren't bothering with pesky details like that here. If all you want to do is get into the air and put some distance between you and the opposite party, then you just need to keep your eye on two or three of the instruments.

The dials and gauges in front of me were labeled in Cyrillic, but someone in Gaddafi's military had helpfully pasted English stickers on most of them. Probably for the benefit of their Cuban and North Korean friends, I thought, as I checked the fuel and oil pressure. We appeared to be good on both counts. I scanned the board for signs of red lights or other warning indicators. All good.

We were lucky they'd kept the rotors turning. Although, I reflected, that was probably standard procedure for an extraction in unknown territory. Having the Mi-8 warmed up and ready to go was a big plus; starting a military aircraft often involved complex security measures, and I had no idea what those might possibly be for this machine.

I grabbed the collective lever with my left hand and gave it a nudge upwards as I twisted the throttle. The chopper began to hum and vibrate, bringing back memories of other places and other situations. Behind me, Nadia and Hadley continued to fire short bursts, keeping the Tuaregs and the Libyans at bay. Keep focused, Donovan, I told myself. Let them do their jobs, and you do yours. Be here now. Right here. Right now.

I raised the collective some more, altering the blade pitch. When I felt the wheels go light, I pushed the cyclic stick forward with my right hand, tilting the rotor disk slightly. We lifted into the air, wobbled for a second, and then began to move forward, gaining speed. I heard Hadley's cheer from somewhere behind me.

I pushed at the anti-torque pedals with my feet, remembering at the very last second that the blades on Soviet helicopters turn in a clockwise direction, unlike US military equipment. It wouldn't do to send this bird spinning back out of control toward the Tuareg camp.

But no. Everything worked, and we rose smoothly into the gathering night, the burning camp behind us receding fast. I felt a rush of relief, coupled with a sense of pride. I'd actually remembered how to fly one of these damned things. Hot damn, as we used to say.

Pilots will tell you that most types of fixed-wing aircraft actually seem to *want* to fly. They're built for the air, and they seem to know it. You're just there to nudge them along. Helicopters, by contrast, are an affront to nature. They're not really supposed to work at all, and flying one of them requires intense concentration. What helicopters really want to do is to turn themselves upside down, spinning wildly around as they head for the ground. And they will do this given the slightest opportunity, so it pays to be alert, calm, and composed when you fly them.

I was alert, all right, but hardly calm and composed. So okay, one out of three. Not so bad, really.

I was a little worried, however, about what sort of damage those last shots might have done. As we rose and put distance between ourselves and the burning nomad camp, I scanned the cockpit. One shot had gone through the window on the right side but hadn't shattered it. I could live with that. Two other shots, however, had gone into the instrument panel in front of me. One appeared to have done no real damage. The other had gone straight into our radio. I reached forward and toggled the switch. Nothing. Completely dead.

I took the chopper up to five hundred meters while Hadley and Nadia set about removing their wedding jewelry, stuffing it all in Nadia's duffle bag. The moon was fully up now, giving me good visibility from the cockpit. The stars above us were brilliant, but there was nothing at all to see on the ground below except the burning tents of the Tuareg camp, fast receding into the distance. I picked out Polaris – the star that Sayyid Zerhouni had called *najm ash-shamal* – and brought the chopper's nose around in a half circle until we were heading roughly north by northeast.

There were headphones clipped to each of the seats. I picked one set up and flipped switches until I heard a hiss through the earpieces. We've got internal comms at least, I thought. That will make talking to each other a lot easier over the racket of the rotors. People who fly commercially have no idea how loud it can get inside an aircraft's cockpit.

I beckoned Nadia up to sit beside me in the copilot's seat, gave her a pair of headphones, and showed her how to turn them on and adjust them. "These stars are just magnificent," she said after a moment. "It's almost romantic."

"Yes, it is," I said, glancing sidewise at her. This would be the moment, I told myself, to hold her hand. But I needed both hands to fly the damned helicopter, so I had to satisfy myself by simply saying, "I meant what I said about how you looked in all that gear, you know."

She gave a soft laugh. "I'm glad you approve, Max."

Hadley came up behind us and pulled down the navigator's seat, putting on a pair of her own headphones as she did so. She sat facing forward, so now there were three of us in a rough line, gazing out at the stars as we flew over the desert. If you ignored the rotor noise coming through faintly on the earphones, you could almost imagine that you were drifting along in a hot-air balloon. Not a care in the world, the desert below nothing but inky blackness, the stars above a magnificent glittering canopy of pinpoint galaxies. And over it all, the huge orange moon.

Hadley draped an arm around each of us and pulled us in for a group hug. "We did good, didn't we?" she said.

"Yes, we did," I said. "We kicked some ass, just like you wanted. We're all still alive, we're on our way home, and we've got the chelengk."

"We accomplished much more than that, you know," said Hadley with a grin. "We found the Tuaregs four new candidate brides, all of them in superb physical condition."

All of us burst into laughter.

After a moment, Nadia put her hand on my knee. "It's not over, I'm afraid."

"What do you mean?"

"I need to tell you what Fawzia said to me, just before we attacked them and stole their helicopter."

I could feel the tension in her voice, even through the earphones.

I turned to stare at her. "I'm not going to like this, am I?"

She shook her head. "No. Not at all."

CHAPTER THIRTY-ONE

Nadia's voice came through the headphones clear and measured, blowing the tranquil moonlit scene away. "They mean to kill your ambassador, Max."

"What?" The chopper wobbled slightly as my hand gripped the cyclic in surprise. "How do you know this?"

"Fawzia – your friend with the eyepatch – told me just before they took us to the helicopter, while you and Hadley were burning down the tent and stealing Zerhouni's treasure. She said there's going to be a reception at the American ambassador's residence in Tunis, tomorrow afternoon." She paused. "They're going to try to kill him. We need to contact your embassy as soon as possible."

Tomorrow, I thought. The Fourth of July. The day for a traditional celebration, no matter where on the globe you might be. I'd attended a few of these over the years. Fun occasions, for the most part. Hot dogs, pizza, and cold beer, some speeches, and then maybe a softball game or fireworks in the evening. A family event, bring your friends.

"Why kill the ambassador?" asked Hadley.

"It's a revenge killing," Nadia said. "Payback for the American pilots shooting down two of our planes a while ago."

"Did Fawzia tell you how they were going to do this?"

Nadia shook her head. "Not exactly. All she said was that they were hoping to kill him in front of everyone. To be a lesson, she said."

"That's horrible," Hadley said. "Is there any way we can stop it?"

"Not until we can get to a phone or some kind of secure radio transmission," I said. "We don't have comms, remember?"

Nadia touched my arm. "She didn't tell me how they were planning to do it, but she told me who." She paused. "Rachida Al-Mansouri is the assassin. She was my unit commander two years ago. I got to know her pretty well."

"And this Al-Mansouri is going to kill the ambassador?"

"Yes. Rachida left the Amazons to join the Intelligence Service. There, they trained her to be an assassin. They get given targets in different countries, and then work with people at our embassies, who help them get set up and escape afterwards."

"Jesus," I said softly, "so it's a whole government program, this stuff?"

"It is," said Nadia. "They mostly go after Libyan dissidents living overseas – students, businessmen, that sort of thing. But we used to hear wild stories, about plans to kill President Reagan, the British prime minister – all sorts of people."

I thought about this for a moment. "And are they, ah, any good at this stuff?"

"They've killed dozens of people, Max," she said. "Mostly Libyans, it's true, but they are dead serious about this. It's what we call *al-antiqam* – revenge. A very old concept with us. And a big deal."

I nodded. "It is with us, too. 'Don't get mad, get even,' is how I learned it." I paused. "And you know this Al-Mansouri, the killer?"

"Oh yes," said Nadia. "We worked side by side for some months."

"You'd recognize her, then, if you saw her?"

"Absolutely."

I pulled up the collective a bit, trying to get a little more speed out of the chopper. "We need to get to a phone. In the meantime, I'll keep us low to the ground, so we'll have a better chance of avoiding radar contact."

"Why wouldn't contact be a good thing?" asked Hadley.

"We don't know whose radar it would be," I said, as I adjusted the rotor pitch slightly. "We're down in a kind of wedge, with Algeria on one side and Libya on the other. If we show up on the radar of either of those two countries, who knows what they might do. And if the Tunisians spot us, they might think we're an invading force. So the best thing to do," I concluded, "is to be invisible for a while. Until we get back to civilization, so to speak."

"Won't we be able to see city lights, stuff like that, eventually?" asked Hadley.

"We will once we get further along," I said. "Right now, I'm on a course that will take us up to where we intercept the coast a bit south of Tunis. Once we see the beach, then we can turn north and follow it right up to the nearest city. We'll get help there."

Nadia's voice was quiet in my ears. "Unless," she said, "something goes wrong."

"Well," I said with a grim smile, "there's always that, of course."

* * *

Flying a helicopter takes concentration at the best of times, and it's even worse in the dark. Especially when there's nothing underneath you but featureless sand. No lights, no settlements. Up in the air, it's easy to lose track of exactly where you are, particularly when there's nothing much to see.

I was doing this more or less on instruments, using the compass, the altimeter, and the altitude indicator. I was being very careful, trying to stay high enough to clear rises, but low enough so that I wouldn't show up on somebody's radar. I was assuming that the altimeter in front of me had been calibrated to sea level, but I had no way of really knowing that, so from time to time I flipped on the landing lights to see how far below us the ground really was. So far, it all seemed good.

I leaned forward and tapped the fuel gauge. Half full. The Libyans must have been flying search patterns for a while, looking for us before they spotted the camp. I had no idea what the range of one of these Soviet helicopters was, but I was reasonably confident that we'd at least get out of the desert. And with any luck, to a small town or city that had a telephone.

The one good thing was the moon. It shone big and bright, providing a nice, highly visible reference point as we skimmed along. The only thing bothering me – apart from Nadia's unwelcome news about the ambassador – was the rapidly deteriorating weather.

Helicopters don't generally have radar screens, and this one was no exception. All I had to go on was how the air felt and looked, and on both scores, things were starting to worry me. The wind out of the west had picked up quite a bit in the last ten minutes. Sudden gusts were starting to push us around a little, and I was having to fight the pedals to keep the chopper headed where I wanted it to go. Nothing I couldn't handle for now, but the weather was changing fast, and not at all for the better.

"Just a few gusts," I said into my mike. "Nothing to really worry about."

I wasn't being entirely truthful here. The really worrying thing was visibility. Off to our left side, I'd noticed that the stars were going out. The sky still remined clear to my right, but darkness was advancing fast, moving from west to east, blotting out everything in its path. Even the moon, now high above the horizon, was beginning to get occluded.

Just then, we were hit by another sharp gust of wind, harder than before, and then another. I made a sharp correction, only to feel a third gust, even harder than the first two.

Everybody was paying attention now. "What's going on?" Hadley was looking anxiously out into what had suddenly become a pitch-black sky.

I shot a glance at Nadia, and she gave me a small nod. Both of us knew what this was. "*Haboob,*" she said quietly. "A big one, too. Coming straight for us."

"What?" Hadley's voice was tight with anxiety.

"It's a sandstorm, Hadley," I said, fighting the controls.

CHAPTER THIRTY-TWO

Nadia had called it, I thought as I peered out into the black void. The sandstorm was indeed big, and coming straight for us. Another blast of wind hit the chopper, threatening to push us over. I pulled on the cyclic to get us back on track, only to feel a second blow from the wind, even stronger this time.

We were being overtaken, the storm closing fast, and there wasn't much we could do about it. I glanced down at the airspeed indicator. No way we were going to be able to outrun this thing.

Two things suddenly happened. The moon disappeared altogether, plunging us into near-total darkness, and the first grains of sand struck the chopper. They made an odd hissing noise against the hull, which I could hear even with my earphones on. The noise got rapidly louder until it was hard to talk, even through the mike.

Sand and dust are bad for any aircraft, but especially so for helicopters, which are unstable machines to begin with. Turbine choppers usually have efficient filters which take care of the dust and grit thrown up on unimproved landing sites, but a sandstorm was a different kind of beast. It brought kilos of coarse, heavy sand, driven by winds that could easily reach seventy kilometers per hour, going straight into the air intakes above me. A lot of it was being filtered out, but a lot of it wasn't, and it didn't take much of this kind of punishment to block things up and generate an engine flameout.

Added to all of this was the fact that we were now, for all practical purposes, flying blind. We couldn't see the ground, and we'd lost the moon. All we had left was the compass, the altimeter and the artificial horizon. I'd been flying well under the radar, so to speak, but that only really worked if you could see well enough to avoid whatever might be coming up on you, such as an escarpment or bluff.

We needed to be higher. I pulled up on the collective, changing the rotor pitch to get us climbing, and as I did so, I goosed the throttle as much as I dared, trying to coax a little more power out of the engines. Maybe we could get enough height to clear the storm.

No such luck.

As I clawed for altitude, I heard a change in the engine noise. Not a good one. Nadia heard it, too. "What's happening?" she said.

"It's the sand," I said. "It's getting into the intakes, and from there, into the turbines." The engine noise was growing louder.

"Is the engine going to blow up?" asked Hadley.

"Not likely," I shouted over the noise of the engine and the sand. "It'll flame out first, by cutting off the air-fuel mixture."

Just as I spoke, I felt the chopper yaw hard to the right. I glanced down at the instruments, to see that the right turbine had stopped working. We'd lost one of our engines. Above me, a line of red lights came on. I had no idea what they signified, but it wasn't anything good.

"Everybody relax," I said, hoping that I sounded more confident than I felt. "These things are designed to run on just one of the two engines." As I spoke, I looked frantically around the cockpit instrument panel for something that resembled a starter or ignition button. It might still be possible, I thought, to get the first turbine going again.

Suddenly, the second turbine quit. I swore under my breath as I fought down creeping panic. "Okay," I said a second later. "Get your safety harnesses on, everybody. Pull them tight. We're going to go into autorotation, and get this thing down on the ground."

Autorotation is easy to do. You get the rotors turning thanks to the air generated by your descent, and the turning rotors then help slow your fall and let you control it. Up to a point, that is. If your rotors stop turning, you'll drop like a stone.

Normally when you do this, there are all sorts of safety precautions to take. Shutting this and that down, making sure everything's all set up for an emergency landing. Not only didn't we have time for any of that crap, but I had no idea, in a Soviet-built craft, where half of those controls might be.

I lowered the collective to change our rotor pitch, and as we began to come down, I pushed the cyclic forward a bit to get the air underneath us lifting the rotors. I watched the rotor RPM indicator carefully, wanting to get it back up nearly to normal.

The problem was the ground. I couldn't see it at all, because of the blowing sand. The altimeter had me at five hundred meters and falling steadily, but that was only marginally useful. Aircraft altimeters are usually set to what's known as MSL, or mean sea level, which in this case, had probably been calibrated off the coast of Tripoli somewhere.

I'd been making allowances for that as we flew. I'd been flying at about seven hundred meters above sea level, figuring that that altitude would give me a decent chance at avoiding detection. But as we'd traveled to the north, the altitude of the ground below us slowly decreased to less than two hundred meters, and I'd been bringing our aircraft down a bit as we traveled. It was all guesswork. I had no real idea where we were, and no idea how far above the ground we were. If I couldn't figure this out, I knew from past experience, I was risking what pilots termed a CFIT – controlled flight into terrain.

A crash, in other words.

I snapped on our landing lights to see if they helped, but it was like peering into brown fog.

The altimeter read three hundred meters now, and the needle was dropping fast. I turned us into the wind, got the speed down a bit, pulled the cyclic back aft, and lowered the collective fully.

Two hundred meters. We *had* to be close to the ground now, I thought, fighting the pedals to keep the damned thing pointed in the right direction. And yes, there it was, in the glare of our landing lights, solid ground, less than fifty meters below us. I pulled the cyclic back to begin a flare prior to setdown.

I heard Hadley's cry of "There's the ground!" In that moment, an enormous gust of wind turned the chopper on its side.

"Brace!" I yelled as I fought the controls, trying to get us upright. But I knew it was too late; we were going to fall.

And fall we did.

CHAPTER THIRTY-THREE

We hit hard. I heard a screech as one of the rotors snapped off, and then there was silence, broken only by the pinging of hot metal.

The helicopter lay sideways on the sand, crumpled and broken, the hatch door facing upwards. I unbuckled quickly and turned around. Hadley and Nadia were still in their harnesses, looking shaken but unhurt. "Can both of you move?" I asked.

Weak nods from both of them. Nadia was struggling with her harness, and I helped her unbuckle it. On the panels in front of me, circuits were sparking and popping, never a good sign. I couldn't smell fuel yet, but that didn't mean that the chopper wasn't getting ready to catch fire.

"Grab all your stuff," I said. I pointed to the hatch door, now above us. "Once we get that open, get out, and as far away from this thing as you can. Don't wait for me, just run."

I pulled the hatch release lever, and tugged at the handle. To my vast relief, it moved. The airframe was obviously bent, but the hatch door still opened halfway before getting stuck. I turned to the others. "Let's go," I said. "Hadley, you first."

I boosted her up and out the door. Then Nadia. Finally, I scooped up the two shoulder bags and Nadia's duffle – the one containing our loot – and pushed them up and through the hatch. I took one last look around, wondering if I should grab one of the assault rifles from the bulkhead rack. Don't borrow trouble, I told myself. We've each got a pistol, and that ought to be enough.

Then I smelled the fuel; one of the tanks must have ruptured in the crash. Time to leave. I hauled myself fast up through the hatch, dropped to the ground, grabbed the bags, and started running toward where the other two were waiting, two hundred meters away across the sand. Just before I got there, the helicopter went up with a dull boom, sending a billowing ball of fire into the night sky.

* * *

"Down flat on the ground," I barked. We all lay on the sand facing the chopper, presenting as small a profile as possible. Nobody said a word. Then some of the ammunition clips inside the chopper started cooking off, with a noise like popcorn. We stayed in place until the popping stopped, and got slowly to our feet.

The wind had dropped a bit, and although sand still stung our faces, the storm seemed to be moving on beyond us. I checked my watch. A little before 11 p.m. "We've got about six hours until sunrise," I announced.

"Any idea where we are?" asked Hadley.

I thought for a few seconds. "We were in the air for less than two hours. During that time, we were going at something less than two hundred kilometers an hour. So, we're somewhere in the middle of Tunisia, for whatever that may be worth."

Nadia looked around. "I don't see lights, I don't see a glow anywhere."

"We might still be in the desert," I said. "If we are, we're not much better off than before."

Hadley gave a little snort of indignation. "Look on the bright side, Max. Have you forgotten already? Nadia and I were about to get married to a couple of desert desperados that we hadn't even been introduced to yet. But we're both still single, and the Tuaregs have four brand-new wives in our place. We've got all our stuff back, and more besides. Oh, yeah," she added, "and we've all just survived a plane crash."

Nadia nodded. "Yes, Max, cheer up. This is quite an improvement over our earlier situation."

I smiled then. "All true," I said. "But we still don't know where we are."

The nighttime chill was starting to seep into my bones. I looked around. No trees. No bushes. Therefore, no warming fire. I glanced back at the crashed helicopter. The flames were dying down now. I looked up at the sky. The night air was finally clear, the storm having passed over to the east. I found the Big Dipper and followed one of the edges to the North Star, Zerhouni's *najm ash-shamal*.

"I think we should stay right here for a while," I said after a moment. "We need to catch our breath and pull ourselves together. In the morning, we can talk about next moves."

"I agree," said Nadia. "There doesn't seem to be much around here, but maybe in the daylight, we'll see something."

"In the meantime, we're freezing to death once again," said Hadley, her arms wrapped around herself. "And on top of it all, I have to pee." She looked around.

I looked out into the darkness across the empty flat. "Just walk out there a little ways," I said. "Nobody here will be able to see you. I'll even turn the other way."

She gave me a dirty look and moved off.

"Mind the scorpions," I called out after her.

"Wait," said Nadia. "I'll go with you."

Hadley nodded gratefully, and the two women set off across the sand.

I sat on the sand by myself in the dark and thought about why women always seemed to like to visit the ladies' room in pairs. Bone says it's an example of female bonding. And that the bathroom is a 'safe space' – whatever that means – for the exchange of information.

Maybe like guys in bars or locker rooms, I thought.

Then I heard a shout, and Hadley was running back towards me. I stood up. "What's wrong?" I said.

"Oh, Max, you won't believe it," she shrieked. "We found a *road*!"

CHAPTER THIRTY-FOUR

I walked back with Hadley to where Nadia stood waiting for us, a wide smile on her face. The sandstorm had passed now, the moon was still high in the sky, and although there wasn't a light to be seen, the road they'd found was clearly visible in the moonlight. We hadn't seen it after the crash because of the low embankments on either side, but here it was, an honest-to-God modern, two-lane tarmac road, running straight through the middle of nowhere.

We all stood there admiring it for a moment. No lights, no noises except for the soft whisper of the wind, just the tail-end of the sandstorm saying goodbye. Apart from that, the desert was as quiet as the grave.

Finally, Hadley spoke. "Where do you think it goes?"

"More to the point," said Nadia, "where exactly are we?"

I looked up at the stars, found good old *najm ash-shamal* again, and used it to orient myself. The road was running southeast/northwest. I stepped off the road and onto the desert hardpan, scuffing it with the point of my boot. Then I bent down, picked up a handful, and poked it experimentally with my tongue.

Salty.

I looked at the road again. "What on earth are you doing?" asked Nadia.

"Trying to figure out where we are," I replied. "And now I think I know."

That got everyone's attention. "We're in the middle of the Chott El-Djerid," I said. "The salt lake. Completely dry most of the time. But there's a road through it that connects the town of Tozeur at one end with Kébili at the other. There's really nothing in between. I used to overfly this area on my way up from El Borma."

"We're in the middle of the *chott*," said Hadley. "Big deal."

"Well, as you both pointed out, we're better off than we were a while ago," I said. "This isn't the south; there are going to be people going back and forth. Sooner or later, somebody will come along. We wait for someone going east, and then we're on our way to Tunis." I paused. "I just hope we reach a telephone in time to warn the embassy about what's about to happen."

I looked at my watch. "Let's wait for dawn."

We sat on the tarmac at the edge of the road waiting for the day to start. I was really hoping that someone, or something, would appear before then, because I didn't feel much like sitting around unprotected for yet another day under the desert sun.

"What's the plan now?" asked Hadley.

I shrugged. "Simplicity itself this time," I said. "Flag down a ride, find a telephone, and warn Boomer." I paused. "And then get the hell out of the country, as fast as we can."

"Sounds good to me," said Hadley. "But have you considered that we're all probably targets by this time? The Libyans seem to have spies everywhere. What makes you think we won't be spotted as soon as we get back to Tunis?"

"If they see me, they will probably try to kill me," added Nadia.

I shook my head irritably. It was cold, and it was dark, and aside from a goat's eyeball, I'd had very little to eat. I was dirty and I was sore, and the events of the past two days had filled my brain to the point that I had very little space left for figuring out what to do next. "Look, I can't think of everything, all right? Let's just take this one step at a time."

Everyone went silent after that, each of us retreating into private thoughts.

The roadway was still warm from the day. I lay down on it, stretched out fully, and shut my eyes. I figured the noise of an approaching vehicle would probably wake me up before it hit me. Part of me didn't care much whether it did or not.

In seconds, I was asleep.

* * *

The rising sun had climbed two diameters above the horizon now, and I could feel the night's coolness starting to evaporate. Very soon now, the heat would start. Just then, I saw movement on the road. A wavering, shimmering shadow, down at the very base of where the two sides of the road came together in the distance. It could be just a mirage, I told myself, as I got to my feet.

We all stared as it approached. It wasn't a mirage. "What are we going to do?" asked Nadia.

"We're going to get a ride, of course," I said.

"And kick their asses if they give us a hard time," added Hadley.

"And what if they don't stop?"

I pulled out my pistol from my shoulder bag and racked the slide. "We're not going to give them that choice, are we?" I said. "This is just for backup. Remember what Al Capone said? *'You can get a lot more done with a gun and a kind word than you can with a kind word alone.'*"

Hadley snorted with laughter.

"But I'll put my gun away now," I said. "And just remember where it is."

We could see the vehicle clearly now. It was a camper van of some sort, chugging down the road towards us. We all moved out into the center of the road, spacing ourselves a few meters apart.

The van slowed, and then stopped, ten meters away from us. "Stay here," I said to the others. "Stand in front of the van so they can't take off. I'm going to talk to them."

Hands empty, arms out to the side, I walked slowly toward the van. They're tourists, I thought. A family of tourists. I stopped five meters away. Through the windshield glass I could see that the guy driving was wearing a too-tight Union Jack T-shirt. Brits, I thought with relief. They still had the windows up. I waved in what I hoped was a friendly manner. "Ahoy the van," I shouted in English.

The driver's side window came down an inch or so. "What do you want?" The tension in his voice was unmistakable.

I looked through the window into the van. T-shirt Man, a woman who might be the wife beside him on the front seat, and two kids in the back seat. I had only a few seconds to get this right. "Look over my shoulder," I said. "Tell me what you see."

The window came fully down. Everyone inside the van stared out at the burned wreckage of our helicopter, a hundred meters away.

"Crumbs," said the driver after a moment. "That's yours?"

I nodded. "It used to be. I'm Max, by the way. We were on our way to Tunis when we got caught in a sandstorm. Our radio's busted, so we can't call for help." I gave it a beat. "We were kind of hoping you'd be able to lend a hand."

He shook his head. "I know bugger-all about fixing helicopters, mate."

"*Basil!*" The woman's voice was a sharp crack. "Watch your language in front of the children."

"Can I approach?" I asked.

The driver nodded warily.

"We don't need help fixing the helicopter – it's wrecked. We need to find a telephone. As soon as possible." I gave him my best smile. "My name is Max Donovan. I was the one flying the chopper when it went down." I turned and motioned the others to come forward. "This young lady is Hadley Holloway. She's a PhD student at Cambridge, studying history. And this," I said, indicating Nadia, "Is Captain Nadia Khoury. She's our security person." As I spoke, I was acutely conscious of the fact that the two women were dressed in what looked like dirty white bedsheets.

His eyes had narrowed as we spoke, flicking back and forth from us to the helicopter. "That," he said finally, "is a military helicopter. In fact, it's a Libyan military helicopter. What the bloody hell were you doing flying around in that?"

"*Basil!*"

Impressive, I thought. How'd he pick up on that so quickly?

His next words cleared that up. "I know what Libyan military equipment looks like, mate. I live in Tunis, work one of the rigs in Libya, down south of El-Sharara. Three weeks on, one week off. Which," he added pointedly, "I am presently enjoying with my family."

I lowered my voice. "Basil – it is Basil, right?" He nodded. "Well, Basil, we have no desire whatever to get in the way of your family holiday. It would take a while to explain everything to you, but suffice to say that we're on a top-secret government mission, the Libyans are chasing us, and time, as they say, is of the essence."

Basil's wife spoke up. "You're all absolutely filthy. And these two women – why are they dressed like that? What exactly have you three been up to? No, you're not getting in our van."

I turned imploring eyes on Basil. "I'm serious, man," I said in a quiet voice. "We need a ride, and you're the only one out here with transport. Help us out." While I was speaking, my hand moved inside my shoulder bag and grasped the handle of my pistol.

Basil looked us all over for a long moment, and then came to a decision. "Get in," he said at last. "We're headed to Sfax. I reckon we can take you that far." He turned to his wife. "And, Penelope, I'll thank you to just belt up now. Dirty as they may be, these people obviously need our help."

* * *

We piled into the van, and found seats in the back facing the two young children, a boy of about twelve, and his sister, a year or two younger. They stared at us with frank curiosity. The boy looked out the window at the wrecked and burned helicopter. "Is that your helicopter, then?" he asked.

"Ah, no, not exactly," I said. "We borrowed it from some other people."

He smirked. "You stole it, didn't you?"

I looked at him. "Borrowed," I said evenly.

"Liar," said the kid.

Out of the corner of my eye, I caught Nadia's grin. It was going to be a long ride, I could see that.

The girl piped up. "Why'd it crash?"

"We ran into a sandstorm," I said.

She crossed her arms and sniffed. "You can't be a very good pilot, then," she said. "Your friends aren't going to be very happy with you."

"The ones you 'borrowed' it from," added her brother, with just a bit of a sneer.

I nodded. "I think you're right. So we're not going to mention it to them right away."

The mother turned around in her seat to peer at me. "You're not criminals or anything like that, are you?"

"No, ma'am," I said in what I hoped was my most sincere and convincing tone. "We're exactly what we appear to be – surviving passengers from a helicopter crash. We need to find a telephone, and once we do, we will be quickly out of your hair."

"There'll be a phone in Gabès," said Basil. "That do you?"

I looked at my watch. Every minute counted, now. "Sure," I said. "But do you think you could get a little more speed out of this thing?"

And then I pulled my *shemagh* down over my eyes and tried to imagine that I was somewhere else.

CHAPTER THIRTY-FIVE

We reached Gabès an hour later, and after a few missed turns, found the local post office. One of the telephone cabins was free. Nadia and I wedged ourselves inside, and I placed a call to Boomer Quackenbush at the embassy in Tunis. As I waited for the call to go through, I could smell the woodsmoke from the Tuareg's campfire fire on Nadia's skin, feel her warmth.

There was the usual farting around with the switchboard and various transfers, but eventually, Boomer's muted bellow reached my ears. "Nice of you to call, Max," he roared. "Thought you'd perished in the desert or something."

"You've got no idea," I said. "But that's not why I called. Listen to me carefully." I began to tell him about the assassination plot, but after the first two sentences, he cut me off.

"Stop talking," he said. "This isn't a secure line. Where are you right now? What's your situation?"

"We're in Gabès, traveling with a British family of tourists in a camper van."

He was silent for a moment. "Can you get up to Skhira? It's up outside Gabès, on the road to Sfax."

"Yes," I said. "They're going to Sfax, in fact."

"Good. Go to the Garde Nationale in Skhira. It's right on the main road. I'll call ahead and make the arrangements. Let the Brits go, and stay with the Garde until I get there. Don't leave the compound. And Max–"

"Yes?"

"Shut up about all this. Not another word to anyone. Got it?"

"Yep." I hung up.

* * *

A little over two hours later, we pulled into the parking
lot of the Garde Nationale in Skhira, north of Gabès. The
Garde was housed in a modern whitewashed one-story
building behind a low wall right off the main road. The red
and white Tunisian flag flew proudly from the roof of the
entryway.

"You can drop us here, thanks," I said to Basil.

I hopped down, shook his hand, and nodded to his
wife as Nadia and Hadley got out. We all waved as the van
turned out of the parking lot and onto the main road.

"Thought I might kill those two kids at one point,"
muttered Hadley.

I grinned. "Don't be so grumpy. Come on, let's go
meet the Garde."

We went up the steps and into an airy reception room.
The two uniformed men inside went on alert as soon as
they saw the three of us. Not too surprising, I thought,
considering what we probably looked like at this point.
Once they heard my name, however, their demeanor
changed completely. Boomer must have a real way with
words, I thought.

In five minutes, we were comfortably installed in soft
armchairs in a room off to the side, and one of the Garde
was bringing in a cold bottle of Garci mineral water and
three glasses. We drank it all down in seconds. More Garci
soon appeared, together with several assorted bottles of
gazouza. Half an hour later, bowls of *lablabi* chickpea stew
were brought in, together with half a dozen pieces of
deliciously crusty French bread.

We were then left completely alone. We ate with quiet
intensity, as if we were starving. Which in fact we were.
Hadley looked up at me eventually and spoke around a
large piece of bread. "Who is this guy Boomer, anyway?
Some kind of miracle worker?"

I smiled. "Just a friend who works at the embassy," I said. "He obviously knows the cops around here, though."

"And he's coming to get us?" asked Nadia.

I nodded. "Just as soon as he can. In the meantime, this is about as safe a place as we can be."

* * *

An hour later, a large black van entered the compound and stopped in front of the door. Boomer stepped down from the driver's seat and raised his eyebrows at me in greeting. "Still in one piece, I see," he said with a grin.

I nodded. "You made good time. You came alone?"

"Faster that way," he said. "This trip is kinda off the books, so to speak." He looked past me at Nadia and Hadley, coming out the door. "This your posse?"

I nodded. He gave the women a quick going-over glance, and then he pulled the side door of the van open. "Hop inside then. We need to get going."

I went in with Boomer to say quickly goodbye to the Gardes. "Thanks for the hospitality," I said to the commandant as I shook his hand. "I doubt we'll see you again."

Boomer winked at him. "You didn't see them this time, either, *mon ami*," he said.

The commandant looked puzzled. I patted his shoulder. "Don't worry about a thing. In a few moments, we'll be just a memory. And shortly after that, nothing at all. Forget you ever saw us. But thanks for everything. The *lablabi* was delicious."

I pulled myself up into the van behind the others and shut the door. We exited the parking lot and started up the highway toward Sfax, and beyond it, to Tunis.

Boomer drove like a demon, but with skill and care. I looked around the van. "I assumed they'd send some folks with you."

He grimaced. "Nobody at the embassy knows I'm gone, Max. I'll get into that a bit later. Why don't you introduce me to your traveling companions first?"

"This is Hadley Holloway, the doctoral student I told you about. She's studying at Cambridge."

"Impressive," said Boomer. "Your taste in friends is obviously improving." He looked at Nadia through the rearview mirror. "And you are?"

"Nadia El-Khoury," she said, looking him straight in the eye.

"Have I seen you before, Miss Khoury?"

"No," said Nadia, "I don't believe you have."

Boomer nodded slightly. "No, probably not. But I've seen your picture. In one of our intelligence briefings. You're a captain in Gaddafi's bodyguard, aren't you?"

"Not anymore."

I put my hand on Boomer's shoulder. "And therein lies a tale, so if you'll keep your eyes on the road, I'll tell you all about it."

***

For the next half hour, I told Boomer the story. All of it, starting with Bone's message to me in Indonesia, my trip to Cambridge, and the rest that followed. I stopped when I got to the crashed helicopter. When I had finished, Boomer nodded, and said, "Trabelsi."

"Who?"

"Ali Akbar Al-Trabelsi. The guy you met at dinner in Cambridge. Didn't you say he was from the Libyan embassy?"

I nodded.

"Well, he's almost certainly one of their cowbirds, and in all likelihood, the dude who set all this off. After his little attempt to run you over failed, he probably phoned somebody down here. By the next morning, they'd have had guys at the Tunis airport looking for you."

Nadia nodded. "You're probably right. They have people everywhere."

"Yeah, we know that all too well," said Boomer with a grimace. "Okay, Max, let's talk about what you started to say on the phone this morning. Something about assassination. There's more to that story, I assume?"

"Lots more," I said, "but it's probably better if Nadia tells it."

"Well, Ms. Khoury," said Boomer, "we've got a few more hours before we reach Tunis. Let's hear it – what do you know?"

"I'll tell you everything I can," she said. "It wasn't as if I got a full briefing or anything. I had only a couple of minutes with my squad leader down at the Tuareg camp before – well, before things started happening. She said that they'd decided to kill the ambassador during the Fourth of July reception. They'd given the job to one of their best people."

"And your squad leader told you this why?" Boomer sounded skeptical.

"She told me out of spite," Nadia said. "When we made the call for help, the story I gave them was that I had only pretended to defect – that I was doing it in order to recover the chelengk. We thought it might fool them, but of course it didn't. She told me about the assassination to show me that they intended to win."

She paused. "They knew I was a defector; they were going to take us all back to Tripoli as prisoners, for questioning. I would be court-martialed and probably shot. Probably Max and Hadley as well. They were convinced that Max was CIA. And, of course, they were going to bring the chelengk back. That's basically what got them to come for us in the first place. We were just extras. Otherwise, they'd have let us die in the desert."

"Ah yes, the famous chelengk. You've still got it?"

Nadia nodded. "Hadley does. Show him."

Hadley opened her rucksack, felt around inside, and came up with a cloth parcel. She carefully unwrapped it, and there was the chelengk, looking just as it always had.

One hand on the steering wheel, Boomer picked it up and turned it around, examining it from various angles. "Ugly damn thing," he said after a moment. "Hard to believe it's caused so much trouble. What happens to it now?"

"It goes back to England," said Hadley. "After that, I have no idea. To a museum eventually, I suppose."

"Yeah, well, the sooner it's gone from here, the better," said Boomer, handing it back to her. He turned to me. "I've got some bad news, Max."

"What is it now?"

"Well, right after you called me, I went down to see Security. I told them exactly what you'd said about an assassination attempt. Security went into a huddle with the ambassador, and fifteen minutes later, the word came back. The reception's going ahead."

I looked at him, my mouth open in surprise. "Boomer, that can't be right. You've got a serious threat, and the source is totally credible. Are they crazy?"

"Well, there's some context here. The ambassador's new, I think I told you. A political appointee, out of the current administration. Big fan of private enterprise and all that. You know how it works, right?"

I sighed. "Unfortunately I do. Is there more?"

"Yeah, there is. The ambassador's a bit of a macho man, fancies himself out on the range with a horse and a six-gun, leading the charge. Great admirer of President Reagan, likes to show his old movies in the canteen on weekends."

"And backing down isn't his style," I said.

Boomer nodded. "You got it. His precise words to Security were 'no pissant Arab's gonna take away the celebration of our sacred heritage, no way, José.'"

Nadia had been listening to us. She leaned forward over the seat. "Doesn't he understand how dangerous Gaddafi's people can be?"

Boomer shook his head. "The man's an idiot, I don't mind saying so. Course it didn't help that your name came into it, Max."

I shot him a glance. "What are you talking about?"

"Well, when I told Security what you'd told me, he naturally asked me where the hell I'd gotten that information from. When he heard your name, he kinda blew up. Arnold's a bit of an uptight asshole sometimes, but I was really surprised to see him lose it like that."

"Arnold?"

"Arnold Shacklady, the security guy."

I groaned. "Oh, no. Damn."

"What's the matter? You know him? He sure seems to know you."

"Shacklady?" I said. "Yeah, I know him. Tall skinny guy, carrot hair, pinched face, long bony nose? Likes to wear seersucker suits?"

Boomer looked at me suspiciously. "Yeah, that's him all right. What did you do to him?"

"I tried to burn down his embassy," I said after a moment.

"You *what*?"

I shrugged. "It was nothing personal, believe me. Anyway, this was a while ago, in a country far away from here. You'd think the man would have put it all behind him by now."

Boomer grimaced. "Well, he hasn't, that's for sure. That's why this little trip of mine is off the books. Shacklady said that if he ever saw you on embassy property, he'd have you arrested. I think he means it, too."

Hadley leaned forward. "You burned down an embassy? Really?" She sounded impressed.

"I didn't really burn it down," I said. "I only tried to. Their sprinkler system turned out to be first-rate. And I only did it to create a diversion."

I spent the next few minutes giving them a few of the details surrounding the incident, trying, of course, to make myself look as good and brave as possible.

"This is what Uncle Isaac talked about," said Hadley thoughtfully after a moment. "Your gift – that's the word he used – for wrecking things."

Nadia piped up. "Like helicopters."

I decided that this had gone far enough. I turned back to Boomer. "Is the ambassador dug in on the question of holding the reception?"

"He most certainly is," said Boomer. "He's of the opinion that cancelling would be a sign of weakness. And in any case, he doesn't take the threat seriously."

"What about radio chatter, talk on the street, that sort of thing?"

Boomer shook his head. "Quiet as a tomb. Nothing at all out of the ordinary."

"There wouldn't be," said Nadia. "Gaddafi's people are very good at keeping quiet when they have to. There won't be any warning, I'm sure of that."

"Well, there it all is, Max," said Boomer. "Shacklady doesn't want you around, and nobody wants to believe your story anyway."

"Then we'll just have to take matters into our own hands," I said.

Boomer's eyebrows rose, and Hadley's eyes did a quick roll. But Nadia actually smiled.

"Good," she said, giving me a quick wink. "We've got a couple of hours before we get to Tunis. Plenty of time to make one of those plans of yours, don't you think?"

CHAPTER THIRTY-SIX

Nadia made a final small adjustment to my headdress and then stepped back. "Not bad," she said to me. She turned to Hedi, who was standing behind her. "Put the beard on him."

Hedi nodded, bending to pick up a small wooden stepstool. Hedi was a short man, and he needed some altitude for detailed work. He stepped up and began to attach a goatee and mustache to my face with spirit gum. Nadia, Boomer and Hadley looked on with amusement.

Finally, he was done. He stepped down and back to take a good look. "*Behi*," he said. "*Maintenant, sidi, tu as une bonne tête d'arabe, wallahi.*"

"Yes," said Nadia. "He's got the look of an Arab, all right. All except for the eyes."

Hedi drew himself back in mock horror. "But, madame, I myself have blue eyes, as you can see."

"And as anyone would know from your name as well," Nadia said.

Hedi Zarg Al-Aiyoun beamed. He was small and dark, but true to his name, had striking blue eyes. More evidence, if any were needed, of the long-term genetic effects of successive wars, invasions, migrations and shipwrecks in this part of the world. In this time and place, however, Monsieur Zarg Al-Aiyoun was neither a sailor nor a conqueror. He was a clothier and tailor. He had come recommended by Boomer Quackenbush not only for his sartorial skills, but also for his ability to keep his mouth firmly shut.

We'd snuck into Tunis in the early afternoon, by which time the rough outlines of a plan had taken shape. Boomer brought the van up to the back of Hedi's establishment, and we came in the rear door, out of sight. At a word from Boomer, Hedi closed the shop and pulled down the metal shutters, shielding us from passersby on the Avenue de Paris. We had the place entirely to ourselves.

Getting me kitted out hadn't been much of a problem, in the end. Most of Hedi's stock ran to fine woolen blends and high-end suits with a decidedly Italian flair. For me, however, we'd decided that something more traditional was the only thing that would really work, so Hedi was asked to produce a full-on "sheik suit" – Boomer's term – as a disguise.

Hedi turned out to have a whole rack full of options. "Not something any self-respecting Tunisian would wear, of course," he murmured as he flipped through the hangars. "But we get a lot of people from Saudi Arabia and the Gulf during the summer. They're all filthy rich, of course. They rent villas out on the beach and race their sports cars up and down the corniche. They're the only people who buy these things."

And there I was, decked out in full regalia. I wore a long, ankle-length white collarless *thobe*, over which Hedi had draped a *bisht* robe of dark, rich brown, topped with a flowing white *ghutra*. The thobe was more like a dress, and limited the length of my stride, but I supposed that, if necessary, I could always hike up my skirts and run for it.

"Wait," said Nadia. "Put these on." She plucked the sunglasses out of Boomer's pocket and handed them to me. I put them on, took several steps and faced the full-length mirror. In spite of myself, I was impressed. Half an hour earlier, I'd been a scruffy foreigner in dirty, wrinkled clothes. What stared back at me from the mirror now was a distinguished Arab gentleman, refined, elegant, aloof. A player. The getup covered all but a part of my face, and the false beard and sunglasses did the rest.

Boomer nodded approvingly. "If we were going whole hog, you'd need a Rolex and maybe a diamond pinky ring, but I think this'll get you in the door."

"As long as it fools Arnold Shacklady, I'm happy with it," I said.

Nadia frowned. "This man Shacklady isn't your biggest problem, Max. There may be Libyan agents there. Some of them may have seen your photograph," she said.

I nodded. "But that goes double for you," I said. "There might also be people there who know who you are."

She nodded. "Don't worry, gentlemen, Monsieur Hedi and I have that problem well in hand." She steered Boomer and me over to the side of the shop, where Hedi had tables and a small coffee bar set up for waiting customers. "You two have a nice cup of coffee and relax. This won't take long." She and Hadley disappeared into the back room with Hedi.

Boomer and I sipped our coffees slowly, and in silence. Finally, he spoke. "Your Captain Khoury."

I looked up at him. "Nadia? What about her?"

"You trust her?" He spoke softly, his eyes holding steady on mine.

I thought back to our raid on the house in La Marsa. To our time in the desert together. Her pushing the last Libyan paratrooper out the door as I was trying to get the helicopter into the air.

I nodded. "Indeed I do," I said. "With my life."

"Good to know." He took a sip of coffee. "You might have to, you know."

"I'm aware of that."

Boomer had been thinking along the same lines as I had, I realized. Both of us had been involved in enough of these kinds of things to know that once the curtain went up, almost anything could happen. And often did. And when it did, it was absolutely necessary that we had total confidence and trust in one another. Because otherwise, it would be all too easy for things to fall apart, once the first unexpected event occurred.

And as we both knew, in this kind of situation, unexpected events were to be expected.

The door to the fitting room opened, and Hedi Zarg Al-Aiyoun appeared, grinning like a raccoon eating a sweet potato. *"Messieurs, voilà,"* he breathed. He moved aside and Nadia stepped into the room.

I caught my breath.

"Whoo," breathed Boomer.

Nadia was a vision of loveliness, pure and simple. Hedi had dressed her in a flowing embroidered *abaya* with matching headscarf, all in a tasteful cream color designed to complement my own outfit. Despite the fact that she was effectively covered from head to foot, she radiated beauty and poise. She'd done something to her eyes to make them even bigger and more luminous, and they danced with mischief as she took in our reactions.

"Like it? Hadley's still trying things on. We're going to use some of Zerhouni's jewelry, too, if nobody objects."

Finally, Boomer found his voice. "You – ah – look incredible, Captain. Ah, Nadia. But you and Max are supposed to be undercover. Looking like that, you'll have every person in the room staring at you. All the guys, anyway."

She smiled. "That's rather the idea, Monsieur Quackenbush. Hiding in plain sight. They're looking at an Arab princess, not at me. And Max – well, Max will be almost invisible."

I could see her point. "But aren't you afraid someone will recognize you, even still?" I asked.

She turned to Hedi, who handed her a scrap of cloth. "Not with this on," she said, fixing the *niqab* in place. Now all but her eyes was entirely covered.

"I see what you mean," I said after a moment. "You're still – well, stunning."

She batted her long lashes at me. "Why, thank you, Max."

Boomer coughed. "If you two kids are through flirting with each other, I think we need to talk strategy." He looked at his wristwatch. "It's just past four o'clock, and we should be heading out to the ambassador's soon. He'll make a speech at about six, and then there are the fireworks."

"Wouldn't want to miss the fireworks, now, would we?" I said.

CHAPTER THIRTY-SEVEN

We parked Boomer's van in the lot below the house and walked up the tree-lined drive to the ambassador's residence. Like just about every other building in Sidi Bou Said, it was white with blue trim on the doors and windows. There was, of course, an American flag flying out in front, together with a large hand-lettered sign saying 'America's Birthday! Welcome all!'

"This is a security nightmare," I muttered, looking at the throngs of people coming up the walk. "How do they expect to keep control of a crowd like this?"

"They don't," Boomer replied. He pointed up ahead of us at the entrance to the residence, where two embassy staff were giving each guest a quick once-over with a metal detector wand. "That wand's about the extent of it. The ambassador likes to think of himself as a man of the people. Back in Kansas he used to do hog roasts for the folks a couple of times a year. He thinks this is kind of the same thing."

Nadia wrinkled her nose. "Hog roasts?"

I nodded. "A little like what the Tuaregs were doing with the goats," I said. "Only I don't think they bury the hogs."

"Good barbecue's better'n most anything," said Boomer with a smile. We were approaching the door. "Now shut up and let me do the talking."

We stood still while the wands checked us out. Over to the side, I spotted Arnold Shacklady in one of the doorways, overseeing the process of admitting guests. He hadn't changed much. Skinny, tall, and pale, with a shock of carrot hair over a pinched, suspicious face. In my limited experience of the man, he'd favored seersucker suits and wingtips, and he didn't disappoint today. As I watched, he pulled a walkie-talkie from his pocket and spoke quietly into it.

We moved into the entrance foyer. Shacklady gave me a quick glance, nothing more, and then he spotted Nadia and Hadley, and started forward. Oh, shit, I thought.

"Welcome, ladies," said Shacklady in a voice laced with corn syrup. "Welcome to our July Fourth celebration. And where are you two lovely creatures from?"

They were both lovely, all right – Hedi Zarg Al-Ayoun had certainly seen to that. Both wore flowing abayas edged with intricate gold and black embroidery. They'd also raided Sayyid Zerhouni's treasure chest – now our treasure chest – for various pieces of gold jewelry, which they had arranged to great effect. They'd spent quite a while in Hedi's shop making up their eyes, which of course was all that Shacklady could see over the *niqabs* covering their faces.

"*Vous venez d'où, mesdames?*" Shacklady repeated in French.

There was a momentary flash of panic in Nadia's eyes, and then Boomer stepped in to save the day. "Sorry, Arnold," he said. "Neither of 'em speak French. Or English, for that matter." He turned to me. "This here is Sheik Abdel-Aziz Mustafa, from the Sultanate of

Antabaranta. He's only here for a few days. I thought it might be the neighborly thing to invite them out."

"Welcome, Mr. Mustafa," said Shacklady, shaking my hand. Now we'll see, I thought, how good this disguise is. His eyes showed absolutely no sign of recognition.

"A great pleasure, sir," I replied, pitching my voice low and trying to sound like Omar Sharif.

I turned to the ambassador and swept my hand out in what I hoped was a royal gesture toward the two women. "My wife the Sheika, and my niece, ah, Noura. We are most honored to be here."

The ambassador grabbed my hand and pumped it. "Howdy, Sheik. Real glad you came. You're in for a real treat today."

He was tall and broad, with a W.C. Fields face and a low-hanging potbelly. Instead of a suit, he'd decided to wear his national dress, which consisted of a Western shirt and a pair of low-cut jeans over ostrich-skin cowboy boots, topped off with a ten-gallon felt cowboy hat. His jeans were held up with a leather belt sporting a huge brass buckle featuring an American flag with the word 'FREEDOM' across it. To complete his ensemble, he wore a bolo tie with an enormous piece of turquoise set in silver.

He kept hold of my hand and tightened his grip. "We're gonna show you folks some good old USA hospitality," he boomed. "We got barbecue." He pronounced this *'bobby-queue.'* "We got hot dogs. We got good ol' American beer."

He winked at me. "We even got lemonade for those that don't partake. And cake! We got a special big ol' Freedom Cake, everybody gets a piece!" He pulled me closer. "You play softball, sheik? Game starts after we eat, just before the fireworks."

He looked me up and down. "Might be a bit difficult for you in that getup, though." He gave an explosive laugh and turned to the next person in the receiving line, but not before slapping me on the back and saying, "Mighty glad you're here, boy."

Hadley and Nadia and I regrouped on the porch, behind one of the columns.

"Well, that was interesting," said Nadia.

"Where do guys like that even come from?" wondered Hadley.

Boomer caught up to us just in time to hear Hadley's question. "There are millions of guys like him back home, in case you hadn't noticed," he said. "This guy was a used-car dealer in Wichita, sent a ton of money to the re-election campaign. They say his car commercials were better than standup comedy." His face grew serious. "Okay, folks, what now?"

I'd kind of been dreading the question. "Nadia is the only one who knows what Rashida Al-Mansouri looks like," I said. "She and I will make the rounds and try and pick her out. Boomer, you and Hadley separate off, but stay close. Once we find her, we'll have to figure out what to do."

Boomer snorted. "That's easy. We grab her up. End of story."

I shook my head. "She might not be working alone."

Nadia interrupted. "No, she'll be alone. I'm sure of it. If this goes the way her other assignments have, she'll be working by herself. That's what she prefers. She's very proud of the fact that she doesn't need help."

I nodded. "That makes things a little easier, then. And I assume she doesn't have suicidal tendencies?"

Nadia shook her head. "That's not how she operates. She's been very good – so far – at getting away afterwards."

"Until now," I said. "But first, we need to find her." I turned to look at the crowd of people below us in the garden. "Let's get started."

* * *

Nadia, Hadley and I started working the crowd, which was growing bigger by the minute, as more guests streamed into the reception. The ambassador's house was large, but all but one or two of the public rooms had been closed off. Instead, guests were funneled through the reception line onto the back patio, and from there, down onto the wide lawn beneath. The centerpiece of the lawn was a full-size swimming pool, and beyond it, a spectacular view of Sidi Bou Said Bay and the deep-blue Mediterranean beyond.

Whoever had picked this spot, I thought, knew what they were doing. The entry to the residence was down a closed street, easy to block at the entrance off Rue de la Méditerranée. The grounds were surrounded by a high wall with wire, lights and the occasional security guard. All very discreet and designed to blend in, but there nonetheless.

The house itself sat on the edge of a steep hill, not quite a cliff, dropping down just past the swimming pool to the coast road some hundred meters below. Hard to get in, hard to get out. And this is what had been bothering me all day. Nadia said that Rachida Al-Mansouri liked to work alone, and that she had no desire to become a martyr in the cause of the Socialist People's Libyan Arab Jamahiriya. She'd also told me that Rachida seemed to be quite proficient in the use of several different types of weapons, from pistols to knives and back again.

Given all of that, I thought, we had to start making some assumptions. One, she wanted to kill the ambassador here, in a public place, in front of a bunch of people. To make a statement. Two, she wanted to survive the attempt, and get away. Three – and here I was stretching things – she intended to do it using something relatively small that could be hidden. The security at the gate wasn't great, but it was certainly good enough to pick up a pistol or a long gun. And everyone, as far as I could see, was being checked.

That eliminated a few things, but not many. It pushed my thoughts in the direction of a knife. All houses have knives somewhere, usually in the kitchen, and many of those knives are quite big enough to inflict a fatal wound, especially from someone trained in the art of killing.

But as Nadia and I scanned the crowd, I kept coming back to the question of the getaway. You could stab someone in public, but how would you then escape? That line of thought went unfortunately to the idea of accomplices, people inside the compound who could, at the moment of the assassination, set off a diversion to permit an escape.

The worst thing, of course, was that only one of us knew what Rachida Al-Mansouri even looked like. So, I let Nadia take point as we circled slowly through the crowd. She was focused on facial recognition, while I watched body language. I was hoping to spot postures, expressions, movements – anything that might signal an intent to do murder.

The crowd were a mixed lot. The international set was there in force, diplomats and attachés from the various embassies, representatives of the aid organizations, and some of the international companies. Representatives of the various Tunisian offices and companies were there as well. The conversations swirling around us were a thick mixture of French, English and Arabic, as people stood, drinks in hand, sweating lightly in the warm air, and told each other stories. I caught the tail end of a joke as we moved past one group. "…*wear whatever you like,*" one man was saying to his companions. "*It's just the two of us.*" His companions exploded in loud guffaws. All while the serving crew, dressed in nondescript white smocks and aprons, moved silently among them.

Most of the crowd was American; embassy employees, aid workers, teachers, students and tourists, all out to have fun, eat barbecue, and toast the nation's birthday. Unlike the internationals, who had actually dressed up for the occasion, the Americans had gone more for a Spring Break look featuring Bermuda shorts, T-shirts and sandals. And true to form, most of them were talking to each other about details of life on the edge of the world. One sharp-eyed woman was complaining to her friends about the decline of polite manners in Washington under the current administration. "Republicans are so incredibly impolite," she was saying peevishly. "It's not 'just say no to drugs.' It should be 'just say *no thank you*.' I honestly don't know what things are coming to." I smiled politely and moved on.

Nadia turned to me, her eyes anxious. "This is impossible, Max. There are too many people."

I nodded. "We've got to keep trying." My eyes scanned the crowd. "Where the hell is the ambassador?"

Boomer stepped up beside me. "Reception line's finished. He's gone inside to change."

"Into what?" Hadley spoke softly from underneath her niqab. "A frog?"

Boomer chuckled. "He's got an Uncle Sam suit he likes to wear sometimes. I'm thinking that's his plan right now." He glanced up. "Well, shoot, look at that, will you?"

We all turned to look. A line of waitstaff had appeared from around the corner and were busy setting up a table beside the swimming pool. As we watched, two men carried a wooden podium over and positioned it beside the table.

"Guess that's where he's gonna speak," said Boomer. "He always gives a speech at these things. Man likes to talk, though he don't say much, really, when you think about it afterwards."

As we watched, two women in aprons and headscarves appeared from a side door, pushing a low wheeled cart. On the cart sat an enormous cake done up in red, white and blue frosting, and topped with an American flag. "That must be the Freedom Cake," I whispered.

Nadia grabbed my arm. "There!" she hissed. She raised her chin sharply to the right. One of the cake-bearers was standing at the side of the veranda, but the other one was moving back away from the pool, heading for the side of the house.

"That's her, Max!" said Nadia. "That's Rachida Al-Mansouri."

CHAPTER THIRTY-EIGHT

We watched as the woman disappeared around the corner of the house. "Are you sure?" I asked.

"Absolutely," Nadia replied. "It's her. Come on."

I turned to Boomer. "Stay here and keep an eye on things. We'll deal with this."

He nodded. "Good luck, bud." He turned back to scanning the crowd.

Nadia and Hadley and I hurried around the corner. There was no sign of Rachida Al-Mansouri, but halfway along the wall, I saw a blue metal door. "In there," I said. "She's gone inside."

I was expecting the door to lead into the residence itself. If you were trying to find the ambassador, that's where he would most likely be. But instead, the door opened onto a flight of stairs leading downward, into some sort of basement. Nadia looked at me, a question in her eyes. I nodded. "Let's go."

We crept down the stairs, and along a corridor at the bottom. I was sweating profusely in my getup. At the end of the corridor, I saw a set of stainless-steel steam tables and a long gas range. Alongside us, pushed against the wall, were several rolling tables holding metal trays of hot dog and hamburger buns. "It's the kitchen," I whispered. "She was dressed as one of the catering staff."

The kitchen lay empty now, everyone up on the lawn, arranging things for the barbecue. Then I heard a noise off to the right. One of the pantry doors stood ajar. I flung it open to see Rachida Al-Mansouri, now changed out of her catering costume, and fiddling with a small black case. She looked up, saw us, and dropped the case, her eyes widening in surprise. Beside me, Nadia drew in her breath sharply.

Neither woman hesitated for a second. They flew at one another with silent but deadly force. Nadia was a hand-to-hand expert, but so apparently was Rachida. The two of them fought like tigers in the enclosed space of the pantry, knocking over shelves and boxes, splitting open bags of flour and sugar. Neither of them said a word apart from grunts and short intakes of breath.

It was all happening too fast for me to do anything, but I thought I ought to try. I made a grab for Rachida's arm, and got immediately brought down by a sweep-kick that knocked me back against one of the shelves. The shelf promptly toppled over on me, covering me in flour. I struggled to my feet, ripping off my *bisht* robe so that I could actually move, only to be slammed back again, harder this time, into the opposite wall.

I must have blacked out for a few seconds, because when I staggered to my feet again, Rachida had Nadia in a chokehold, and was dragging her toward the door. She obviously knew how to apply a chokehold, and she was doing it deliberately. If I couldn't break the hold in the next few seconds, Nadia would probably die.

I needn't have worried. As Rachida backed out of the pantry room, Hadley appeared behind her holding one of the heavy metal serving trays. She swung it hard against the back of Rachida's head with a loud clang. She dropped to the floor, poleaxed.

Nadia was on her knees, hands to her throat, gasping for breath. "I'm okay, Max," she said hoarsely. She glanced up at Hadley. "Thank you."

Hadley's eyes were shining. "My little contribution," she said modestly. She looked at me. "You're covered in white stuff, you know."

"It's just flour." I looked down at Rachida's body. "She'll regain consciousness pretty soon," I said. "We need to figure out what to do with her."

Hadley pointed to three stainless-steel doors at the other end of the kitchen. "I'll bet those are the cold lockers," she said. "We can shut her up in there." She smiled. "Only until we figure out what to do, of course. Otherwise, she'd freeze to death. And we wouldn't want that, would we?"

"Remind me never to get in a fight with you," I said. My headdress had gotten knocked off in the fight, and my outer robe lay on the pantry floor under a layer of spilled powder.

"Give me a second here." My *thobe* was binding me at the armpits. It had been tight around my legs during the fight, restricting my movements, and I decided it was time we parted company. I quickly unbuttoned it and shucked it off, throwing it in a corner. Now, I thought as I turned from side to side, I can finally move properly.

Hadley stared down at my boxer shorts. "Mickey Mouse, seriously?"

"I'm quite proud of these, in fact," I said with offended dignity. "You can admire them later. Help me drag her in here, will you?"

Hadley and I got Rashida stretched out on the floor of the freezer just about the time she woke up. She looked up and gave us a strange, slow smile. Then she whispered, "*Laqad fat al'awan,*" and passed out again.

I looked at Hadley, a question in my eyes. "Did you understand that?"

She nodded. "She said, 'it's too late.'"

I shut the freezer door and secured it with a metal skewer from one of the trays. Nadia came out of the pantry holding the small black box that Rachida had been messing with when we caught her. "Max, you need to look at this."

My heart sank as I stared at the small metal case. It was a timer of some sort, and it was counting down. "Shit," I breathed.

"It's a bomb, isn't it?" said Nadia.

"Yeah, I think so," I replied, my heart starting to hammer. "But *this* isn't the bomb, it's just the timer. The trigger."

"Can we shut it off?"

"I don't see any way to do that," I said, turning the case over in my hands. "And in any event, it won't stop the bomb from detonating. This thing is nothing but a switch – once you turn it on you can't really stop it."

"Then what are we going to do?" said Hadley.

"We're going to have to find the device, and we've got" – I glanced down at the timer – "just about four minutes to do it. Hadley, you stay here, keep an eye on that freezer door. Nadia and I are going to go topside and see if we can find this thing."

She nodded, and I sprinted for the stairs.

* * *

I took the stairs three at a time, my thoughts racing. A bomb made sense – death at a distance, highly dramatic, and the killer gets away. Perfect, actually. I shot out through the door, Nadia close behind, to hear the crowd around the swimming pool burst into pleased applause just as a musical number ended. There were loud whistles and one or two rebel yells.

I came racing around the corner and skidded to a stop, searching the scene in front of me frantically for clues. Downstairs when we'd grabbed the trigger mechanism from Rachida, there had been just over four minutes left on the countdown timer. Less than that now, I figured, which was not very much time at all to find a hidden bomb and figure out what to do about it.

In front of me, a crowd of several hundred people stood spread out around the large swimming pool below the raised porch of the residence. Drinks in hand, they'd been listening to an impromptu band up on the veranda. As I stood and frantically scanned the scene, the band wheezed into their next number, an off-key rendition of *Sweet Home Alabama*. A few of the crowd had spotted me and turned, staring curiously at this new arrival.

Stay calm, Donovan, I told myself. Stay focused; look around. The crowd was off to my left. The swimming pool in front of me. To the right, steps going up to the porch, the band on one side. And at the top of the porch, a long table, where the catering staff had placed the Freedom Cake on top of a white linen tablecloth.

There it was, a good three layers high, red, white and blue, with lit sparklers on top. Below it, marzipan letters around the base spelled 'Happy Birthday America.' As I watched, the ambassador himself came through the double doors, dressed in an Uncle Sam suit with an improbably tall stovepipe hat. The crowd roared, and he raised his hand in greeting. In his other hand, he held a large chef's knife.

He stepped forward, getting ready to cut the cake. It hit me then like a thunderbolt. *It's the cake*, my mind screamed. *The bomb's in the damned cake*. Nadia's train of thought reached the station at exactly the same time. She pointed at the cake, her mouth open in a horrified O, as the ambassador prepared to bring the knife down.

I took off like a sprinter for the veranda, a good ten meters away. The next few seconds were a slow-moving kaleidoscope of images: people in the crowd still smiling, turning now to look in astonishment at the guy in whiteface and Mickey Mouse boxers running up the steps; Arnold Shacklady stepping out from behind the ambassador, outrage building on his face; embassy security people starting to react and move in on me from the side.

I had a couple of meters on all of them, and I used it well. I bounded to the top of the steps and body-checked the ambassador, pushing him out of the way. He fell off to the side with a whoosh of outgoing air, taking Shacklady with him.

I gathered up the cake in the white linen tablecloth. Then I picked the whole thing up and whirled it around my head twice, like a hammer-thrower at a track meet.

With a grunt I let the whole thing go. It arced high out over the veranda and down into the swimming pool.

With a splash and a burble, the cake slowly sank to the bottom of the pool, the rest of the tablecloth spreading out over the water above it like a shroud.

There was deep silence from the crowd. Half of them were staring at the swimming pool. Half of them were staring at me. Two of the ambassador's security guys grabbed my arms just as Boomer appeared at the top of the stairs. "Max," he gasped. "What the fuck–"

I heard a sound, like an enormous timpani drum being struck, a deep vibrant boom which shook the ground and rattled the building. In the same instant, a massive fireball shot up from the bottom of the pool and into the air, sending water everywhere and soaking all of us. The pressure wave rocked everyone back, sending the glasses and bottles on the table crashing to the floor.

The crowd screamed and scattered as shards of pool tile clattered down around us, scraps of charred tablecloth floating gently down behind. The ambassador, hauled up by two security men, stared numbly at the wrecked pool, and then at me. He opened his mouth to say something, and then shut it. Shacklady was still on the floor, curled up in the fetal position.

Boomer looked out at the scene. "Dawg," he said finally. "Well, this is one Fourth they won't forget in a hurry."

He turned to me. "How'd you know it was in the cake?"

I shook my head. "I didn't know for sure. It just seemed like the best place for it. Nadia had spotted Rachida dressed up as one of the catering staff, helping put the cake on the table. We followed her down to the kitchen where we caught her setting a timer. We knew we only had a couple of minutes. It was timed to go off while the ambassador was making his speech."

Boomer lowered his voice. "I hope these dumb sonsabitches know how lucky they are."

I grabbed Nadia's hand and pulled her close. "I don't much care whether they do or not, Boomer," I said. "We're all still alive, and that's the main thing."

Then I had a thought. "When he gets up, go tell Arnold Shacklady to look in the freezer down in the kitchen. Tell him to bring three or four of the Marines with him, though. And send Hadley up here to us."

I brushed flour off my face and took one last look at the wreckage of the pool. "And then maybe you could work on some way to get all of us the hell out of here."

CHAPTER THIRTY-NINE

We backed the trailer down into the water on a deserted stretch of the Plage de Sidi Mansour, just north of Kelibia. There was nobody around to wave goodbye and wish us safe travels, probably because it was well after three o'clock in the morning, and we were hoping to slip away unnoticed. I helped Boomer untie the straps and we eased the Zodiac inflatable off its trailer and into the water.

We pulled it back up onto the sand just a bit to let Hadley and Nadia hop in. Boomer moved to the back and started fiddling with the engine controls as I pushed us out slowly, climbing aboard just as the water started coming up toward my knees. I wasn't worried about getting wet. I was just anxious to get as far away from Tunisia as I could before the sun came up.

Because they would be looking for us by now, everywhere. And in a country like this, anyone could be a spy, anyone could say something. After yesterday's circus, our faces would be all too recognizable to all the wrong people.

So it was time for us to bid our farewells. We'd left a hell of a mess behind, I had to admit that. The ambassador's wrecked swimming pool was the least of it. There were going to be questions asked in the coming days about the rental Peugeot and what lay buried alongside it at the *ksar*, about the crashed helicopter in the *chott*, and about the disappearance of an elite Libyan military unit. Boomer assured me that he and the cowbirds would be able to take care of it all, quietly and without fuss. "You did your job, fella," he'd said to me. "Now we'll do ours."

With a cough and a burp, the Evinrude motor started, and Boomer gave me a thumbs-up. I nodded, turned to the man on shore, and did the same. He gave me a wave back in return, climbed into the van, and started it up.

I watched him pull the boat trailer up out of the water and drive the van and trailer up across the sand to where the coast road ran down to Kelibia. He was one of Boomer's diving cronies, sworn to silence. He'd keep driving, through Manzil Tamim and the other small towns until he reached Grombalia, where he'd pick up the *autoroute* that would take him right into Tunis. He'd be back there well before morning, with none the wiser.

Boomer had moved up to the steering console now, strapping himself into the seat and adjusting the throttle and fuel mixture. The sea was calm, hardly any chop at all, and I hoped that it stayed that way. The weather forecast had been good, light winds out of the west, sunrise at about five. And in the meantime, our old friend, the nearly full moon, was due to rise to see us on our way.

Out on the open water, the temperature started dropping as the wind picked up slightly. Boomer's Zodiac was a hard-bottom fourteen-footer, big enough to carry six people. But anyone who's used an inflatable knows that they're only really comfortable with half that many, so things were a little cramped on board. Nadia and I were wedged close together on the back seat, but neither of us seemed to mind one bit. Hadley was in the bow seat, clutching her backpack in her lap, singing softly to herself.

Boomer had brought parkas for all of us, some wrapped sandwiches from the reception, and a big thermos of coffee. We shared out the sandwiches and I poured coffee for everyone. I turned and looked back at the shore, several kilometers behind us and receding quickly. Already the lights had reduced themselves to pinpoints, and in a few minutes, they'd fade away altogether. The moon was rising, the sky clear and the stars bright.

I raised my voice and spoke above the growl of the engine. "How long?"

Boomer turned his head. "Say what?"

I spoke louder. "How long until we get to Pantelleria?"

He chuckled. "You sound like my six-year-old. Couple hours, maybe a little more if we hit some chop. We're doing about twenty knots right now, course 93 degrees east steady. No problem." He paused. "Unless of course we sink, or break down."

Nadia sat up. "Sink?"

Boomer laughed. "Just fooling with you, darlin. Nothing's gonna go wrong. I've done this a few times."

That piqued my interest. "Really? You do this a lot?"

Boomer grinned. "Well, not all that often, but it's been known to happen. Every now and then the cowbirds decide somebody has to leave the country in a hurry. So no, this isn't my first square dance. Probably won't be the last, either."

Nadia turned to me. "Who are the 'cowbirds'? You said that word before."

I spoke up. "He means the intelligence crowd – you know, CIA, DIA, like that?" She made a face. "Don't worry," I added. "I'm sure Boomer cleans out the boat thoroughly after each one of those trips." This brought a smile to her lips and a guffaw from Boomer.

Boomer cleared his throat. "I made a call to the *Commissario* in Pantelleria, just before we left Tunis," he said. "They're expecting us. There'll be no problems. I also alerted the customs boys. You're coming in under diplomatic rules, no baggage inspection." He winked at me. "But if I were you, I'd get rid of your weapons before we hit land."

"Thanks for reminding me," I said. I reached into my bag, pulled out the pistol I'd taken from the Libyan in the Medina, and tossed it over the side. I held out my hand for Nadia's.

"Is this really a good idea?" Nadia said.

"Yep," I said, taking the pistol from her. "The last thing we want is some guy with a uniform finding a gun in our bags. Especially one that's Libyan military issue. There's not going to be any more shooting." I tossed it over the side.

"I hope you're right," she said.

We droned on, bouncing gently over the waves. Nadia's hand found mine, and we sat that way for a while, our parkas snugged up against the stiff breeze now coming off the water. I took my other arm and put it around her shoulders. She leaned into me then, kissing my cheek and resting her head on my shoulder. We stayed like that for a long time, as I watched the stars and thought about the water underneath us, and what might be down there.

Snap out of it, Donovan, I told myself with a shake. Sharks wouldn't eat an inflatable. I was almost sure of it. Nadia stirred beside me. Neither Boomer nor Hadley were looking our way, so I leaned over and gave her a proper kiss, partly because I had been wanting to for a while, and partly to take my mind off the sharks. I felt her breath catch and deepen, but this was not the time or place to press my case, so I eased back. Her head went back on my shoulder, and we sailed on towards the coming dawn.

After an agreeably long time like that, I spotted the lights of the harbor on the horizon, a couple of kilometers out. "That's the Punta San Leonardo light," Boomer said. "Italy, coming right up."

He turned to me. "Just remember this, Donovan. Once you step off this boat, you're on your own. All of you are. You gonna be okay?"

I nodded. "We'll be fine."

"You got any sort of a plan? Other than staying alive, that is?"

I grinned. "I doubt they'll chase us," I said. "In any case, I'm pretty good at covering my tracks. We'll take a day or two to figure things out, and then Hadley goes back to the UK. Her uncle Bone will be glad to see her."

Boomer nodded. "And your paratrooper friend?"

"I'm not a paratrooper anymore, you know," murmured Nadia.

I looked over at her. "She and I have some things to talk over," I said. "It might take a while."

Boomer grinned, snorted softly, and turned back to the wheel.

Twenty minutes later, we approached the concrete landing at the end of the breakwater. A man in uniform waited for us at the edge of the dock. He saluted, and then leaned down to give Nadia a hand getting out of the boat. "*Benvenuta, signora.*"

She gave him one of her dazzling smiles. "*Grazie, signore.*"

"*Prego.*"

To the east, the sun was coming up spectacularly. It was going to be a beautiful day. We waved goodbye to

Boomer as he turned the boat around, gunned the motor, and started out of the harbor, on his way back to Tunis.

"*Donovan!*" he yelled back at me.

I looked up.

"*Good luck! And for God's sake, don't ever come back here!*"

I laughed and waved.

I turned around, looking across the boats in the harbor to the low buildings in the town, and the hills rising up behind them in the distance. I took a deep breath. Then I hitched up my shoulder bag, took Nadia by one hand and Hadley by the other, and said, "Let's go find some breakfast."

EPILOGUE

I woke to the smell of strong coffee and the gentle rocking of the boat. Through the open porthole I heard murmurs and splashings, and realized that Nadia was up and feeding the swans and ducks from the rear deck.

I swung my feet over the side of the bed, found the floor, and padded down the narrow corridor toward the galley, marveling once again at the compact and entirely sensible design of the narrowboat. There was hot coffee and a plate of nearly warm toast and jam set out on the small table beside the stove. I slipped a pair of shorts on, poured myself a cup of coffee, and went up the stairs to the deck, stuffing a piece of toast in my mouth as I climbed.

Nadia abandoned the ducks and turned to kiss me as I sat down. "*Sabah al-khayr,*" she murmured. "You sleep well?"

"*Sabah al-noor,*" I replied. "Good morning to you, too. And yes, I slept very well. *Keefik enti?*"

"I'm fine, *hayati*," she replied. "Never better." She cocked her head at me. "Your accent is improving."

"That's because I have an excellent teacher," I said, taking a long swallow of coffee.

She watched me closely. "And how's the coffee?"

Strong, I thought, nodding with satisfaction. Milk, no sugar, just the way I liked it. I smiled at her. The new short haircut looked great, I thought, and so did the understated blonde streaks they'd put in. As we'd hoped, it had changed her appearance considerably.

Couldn't do much about those gorgeous eyes, however. Or the brilliant smile. I reached over and traced her cheek with my finger. "*Enti helwa kteer*," I said softly. "You're beautiful."

She blushed. "Drink your coffee," she murmured. "We have a big day in front of us."

We did indeed. Today was the day we left for parts unknown. In a little while, I'd start the narrowboat's small engine, cast off, and turn our craft upriver, away from Cambridge and up towards Ely and whatever lay beyond.

I'd been teaching Nadia how to cook, and she'd progressed as far as non-burnt toast and excellent coffee. In exchange, she'd been teaching me Arabic. "Not that Tunisian stuff," she'd said disdainfully. "Proper Levantine Arabic, the way it should be spoken."

"Why would I want to learn Arabic?" I had said. "I've been told in no uncertain terms not to think about going back to Tunisia again."

"Precisely," she said. "Anywhere else in the Arab world, the Tunisian Arabic that you think you know how to speak will only mark you as a hayseed. Your vocabulary is very small and consists mainly of insults. Your accent is atrocious." She gave me her serious look. "It's time you learned to speak properly."

I couldn't object, really. The language was turning out to be nuanced and beautiful, and the fact that I was learning it from someone equally nuanced and beautiful, and under the most intimate of conditions, made it a deal I couldn't refuse.

We'd arrived in the UK from Turkey nearly three weeks ago. After two days in Pantelleria, eating decent food and catching up on sleep, it was time to make a move. Nadia didn't have quite the right passport for most countries, so we all went to Istanbul.

Hadley took the chelengk with her. Nadia and I took Sayyid Zerhouni's treasure. In Istanbul, I spent several days negotiating with a variety of backstreet types, and eventually sold off all of Zerhouni's loot for a surprisingly large sum of money. I had no idea that North African marriage ornaments could be worth so much. We split the proceeds three ways, and spent a few days converting it all into dollars, pounds and francs. Then Hadley parted company with us, flying back to London and going on to Cambridge. Taking the chelengk with her, of course.

We stayed on, enjoying Istanbul, the food, and the museums. I paused for quite a while one day before a portrait of Sultan Selim III in the Topkapi Palace, wondering what he might have to say about the adventures his precious chelengk had enjoyed over the years. While I was in the museum, Nadia visited a beauty parlor, coming out a few hours later with a new haircut and new hair color. With my help, she then purchased a remarkably good French passport, one that would pass muster anywhere in Europe.

We eventually flew to Paris, and several days later, on to London. Bone met us, as before, at King's Cross station. On the train to Cambridge, he fell completely under Nadia's spell, which was in no way surprising.

"Hadley is never better," he said in answer to my question. "She's holed up in a bed and breakfast in the Lake District somewhere, finishing her dissertation. Before she left, she gave that ridiculous piece of jewelry to Nigel Birdwhistle, who's apparently squirreled it away in one of the vaults at the Fitzwilliam Museum."

"I imagine it caused quite a stir in the British papers," I said.

Bone shook his head. "Not at all. Nigel insisted on absolute silence from the two of us. There are details to be worked out, he says. Until then, mum's the word." He put a finger to his lips and rolled his eyes, which made Nadia giggle.

"Fine," I said. "We weren't planning to tell anybody anyway." I shot a glance at Nadia. "Her passport is good, but it's probably best if no one looks too closely at either it or her. We're planning on, ah, keeping a low profile."

Bone gave a discreet cough. "Yes, I should think you would."

Someone three or four seats in front of us started playing punk rock music at top volume through a portable boombox. Bone frowned. "I curse the people who invented those things," he muttered as he rose. "If you'll excuse me for just a moment."

He made his way slowly up the aisle of the carriage. As he passed the young man with the boombox, the music abruptly stopped.

Bone walked to the end of the carriage and pretended to read a notice posted on the bulkhead. Then he came slowly back and sat down beside us again, the ghost of a smile playing across his face.

"Thank God that awful music has stopped," said Nadia.

I grinned. "You can thank your new friend Bone here," I said. I turned to him. "That was impressive. A sort of an escalation for you, isn't it?"

Bone nodded. "Well, someone had to do something, didn't they? Those boombox machines are proliferating like weeds. The whole point appears to be to annoy as many people as possible in your surrounding area." He gave us a sly smile. "But some of these people at Cambridge are quite ingenious, you know." He leaned forward and dropped his voice. "The electrical engineering people here were most helpful, after I explained the problem." He opened his coat slightly to show us a small black metal box with an odd assortment of buttons, switches and small red lights.

"Mum's the word," he said, closing his coat again. "I gather this sort of gadget is technically illegal." He sniffed, sending a dark glance up the train carriage. "As that infernal device should be, in my opinion."

Nadia's eyes were wide. "Did you actually destroy his music player?"

"Oh, no," said Bone. "Not at all. I merely disabled it temporarily." He patted his jacket pocket. "This has an operating radius of about twenty meters. He'll get his music back as soon as he leaves the train." The kid was fussing with his boombox, trying to get it to work. "Or moves to another car. That would also work, I suppose."

She smiled at him. "I can see why you and Max are friends."

* * *

Cambridge had been the perfect antidote to the chaos of the last few weeks. Peaceful, orderly, clean and quiet. We spent a few nights in one of the downtown hotels, and then looked for a different arrangement. One morning, as we walked beside the River Cam on Jesus Green, I noticed three or four narrowboats queued up waiting to go through the locks. I turned to Nadia. "I've got an idea," I said.

Two days later, we were moving into a newly rented narrowboat of our own. The *Drôle de Tête* was a 55-foot marvel of compact marine architecture and low-tech cunning. It made for squeezed but comfortable surroundings, which in fact was exactly how we wanted it. Once inside the narrowboat, with the hatches closed and the portholes covered, we were in a little world of our own.

We moored it a little ways upriver, by Stourbridge Common. We were far enough away from downtown to suit us, but close to the Tesco grocery store off the

Newmarket Road, and in the other direction, the Green Dragon pub and the shops on Chesterton High Street. There were three or four other narrowboats moored in the same area, plus a sizeable collection of ducks and swans who seemed to feel that this stretch of the river belonged to them.

We spent the next few days of our life on the river figuring out the next steps for Nadia. I'd gotten her out of North Africa in one piece, more or less as I had promised. Now what? Neither of us had much of an idea.

"I can't go back to Lebanon, Max," she said sadly. "Not now. The country is tearing itself apart. I will go back someday, though. But when I do, I want to bring something with me."

"Bring something with you?"

"A contribution of some kind. At the American University in Beirut, I studied English and history. Then I made a mistake; I became a soldier. Now, I think I know what I want to do."

"Which is what?"

"Teaching, Max. I want to become a teacher. Things won't be chaotic forever. And when the chaos dies down, the country will need teachers. People who can help the young to avoid the mistakes of the past."

"Otherwise," I murmured, "they will be condemned to repeat them."

She looked at me. "Exactly." She took a breath. "So, I need to go back to school. Your friend Bone thinks I have an excellent chance of getting into one of the universities here. Maybe even Cambridge. A master's degree in education."

"You're serious about this?"

"Absolutely. I talked with Bone about it earlier this week. He thinks he can get me into one of the teacher training programs here. He says with my background and the fact that I can pay full fees, I can probably start in a few months. He's going to write a letter of recommendation. I might even get a scholarship."

I thought for a moment. "Well, it beats driving around in the desert, I guess."

She laughed. "I would certainly say so." She moved close and put her arms around my neck. "It also means that we have about three months to play, before I start school. Do you have any ideas?"

And that was where the notion of a boat trip took hold. Although both of us were quite happy to stay where we were, it was, after all, a perfectly functional narrowboat, built expressly for traveling the extensive system of Britain's inland canals. How hard, we thought, could it be to learn to operate a boat like this?

Not very hard at all, as it turned out. We took a few trial runs up the Cam, with only one or two minor mishaps and no casualties amongst the ducks or swans. We bought maps and boat gear, and talked to our narrowboat neighbors over beers at the pub. We hiked back and forth to the Tesco, hauling in supplies.

And today was finally the day. I set down my coffee cup, finished the last slice of my toast, and stood up. "Are you ready?"

She looked up at me, her eyes bright. "Aye, aye, captain. Isn't that what you're supposed to say?"

I grinned. "Yes, it is. Except that you're the one who's really a captain."

She frowned. "Not anymore, Max. That's a long time ago now."

I nodded. "Think they'll ever come after you?"

She shook her head. "Gaddafi's got more on his mind these days than me. Or you, for that matter. Oh, we should probably keep our eyes and ears open, but I'm not really worried." She looked up at me. "Why, are you?"

I thought for a moment. If I worried about all the people in the world who might have scores to settle with me, I'd probably never leave the house. "Nah," I said finally.

"That's the spirit."

"You're starting to sound like me," I said, laughing. "Well, I've got one thing left to do. I want to call Bone. Say goodbye."

She kissed me. "Give him my love. And get back here. The river is calling."

I kissed her back, hopped off the boat, and walked up to the pedestrian bridge. I crossed over, got some change from the publican in the Green Dragon, and made the call from the red phone box on the corner.

Bone's voice was different. "What's wrong?" I said.

"There's, ah, been a development." His voice was quiet, almost hushed.

"You want to say more?" I could feel my heart start to pick up the pace. "Is it about Nadia? Or Hadley?"

"No," he said. "It's Birdwhistle. Nigel."

"What about him?"

"He's gone. Disappeared."

"What, you mean – kidnapped? Dead? Speak to me, Bone."

"No, no. Not dead. Not kidnapped. Just – gone. Run off. Scarpered, as our British friends say." A pause. "Together with the chelengk."

I waited a moment to let that sink in. "He… stole the chelengk?"

"It rather looks that way. Together with some other valuable items of jewelry from the Ottoman collection. He's just disappeared, gone into smoke. It's all anyone's talking about in college this morning. The police are going through his office now."

"Does Hadley know?"

"Yes, I called her. She's devastated; she had no idea."

I looked out of the phone box's windows at Water Street, quiet and peaceful, bathed in early morning light. Someone went by on a bicycle, milk bottles and a loaf of bread in the carrier. So completely normal, so ordinary. So uncomplicated.

After a moment, I spoke. "Well, what now?"

Bone gave an exasperated sigh. "Who on earth knows? The police are going to want to talk with Hadley, and probably, with me. They're saying that it looks like he pulled the chelengk out of the museum vault a day or so ago, and he may have skipped town over twenty-four hours ago."

"Which means he could be anywhere in the known world by now."

"Precisely."

I took a breath. "Think the cops will want to talk to me? Nadia and I were planning to start our trip this morning."

"I shouldn't think so, Max, no. In any case, you won't be hard to find if they do."

"I'll keep that in mind, thanks," I said drily.

There was silence on the line for a long moment. Then Bone spoke again. "I say, Max, would you possibly consider–"

"No," I said. "Most definitely not."

"You're absolutely sure you wouldn't–"

"I'm sure."

A long moment passed. "Yes, I rather thought so," he said at last. "Still, I had to try."

I paused. "Bone, I'm going to hang up now. Nadia and I are heading upriver. I'll be in touch."

"Smooth sailing," said Bone. There was a wistful note in his voice. "Try and stay out of trouble."

"Hah." I hung up, walked back across the bridge to the *Drôle de Tête* and climbed aboard. Nadia had changed into shorts and a long T-shirt, just the thing for a river cruise.

"How's Bone?" she asked.

I told her about Birdwhistle's disappearance, and the chelengk. As I talked, I untied our mooring ropes and gave us a gentle push away from the bank.

Her expression grew wary. "You're not thinking of—"

I raised my finger. She stopped talking. I said, in my best Arabic, "*Mish siyriki, mish muharrajini.*"

She laughed delightedly. "'*Not my circus, not my clowns?*' What on earth does *that* mean?"

I started the boat's engine. "It means no, I'm not thinking about whatever you were going to say."

I steered us in a wide circle across the Cam, got our bow pointed downstream, and opened the throttle a bit. "And now, if you'll take a seat up front and fend off the ducks, we're going to get as far away from the circus, and the clowns, as we can."

She smiled at me and blew a kiss. We moved slowly under the Green Dragon Bridge and down the river, toward the fenland and whatever lay beyond.

THE END

If you enjoyed this book, please let others know by leaving
a quick review on Amazon. Also, if you spot anything
untoward in the paperback, get in touch. We strive for the
best quality and appreciate reader feedback.

editor@thebookfolks.com

www.thebookfolks.com

Also in this series

ONE BEATS THE BUSH (Book 1)

Vietnam vet Max Donovan discovers his war-time buddy has been accused of murder. Suspecting his friend has been framed and unable to come up with the bail money, he must solve the case himself. The feathers of a rare bird were found near the crime scene, and Donovan heads into the dangerous jungles of Papua New Guinea and the shark-infested waters of the Coral Sea to discover the truth.

WITH TOOTH AND NAIL (Book 2)

When a hitman kills a policeman and makes his getaway by
stealing Max Donovan's car, the army veteran makes chase.
His quarry is a cunning and violent man heading for another
kill and won't welcome Donovan's efforts to stop him. A
thrilling game of cat and mouse in the jungle and savannah
of Senegal ensues. Only one man will come out on top.

THE SERPENT'S LAIR (Book 3)

Donovan has survived a bomb explosion in Colombo, Sri
Lanka, but is handed a powder keg in the form of a
mission to protect the author of a manuscript detailing
insurrectionist plans. He's up against powerful forces, not
least the ocean and jungle, that he'll have to strike at the
heart to subdue.

All FREE with Kindle Unlimited and available in paperback!

More fiction by the author

MURDER MOUNTAIN

A standalone action thriller

Wanted by the FBI and hiding out on a remote island in the Pacific, Peter Blake has an unwelcome visit. He's been rumbled by a man who "trades in information" and the price for not being handed over to the authorities is to use his mountaineering experience to lead a team on a dangerous mission to recover a fallen satellite. If he fails, it will cost him his life.

FREE with Kindle Unlimited and available in paperback!

Other titles of interest

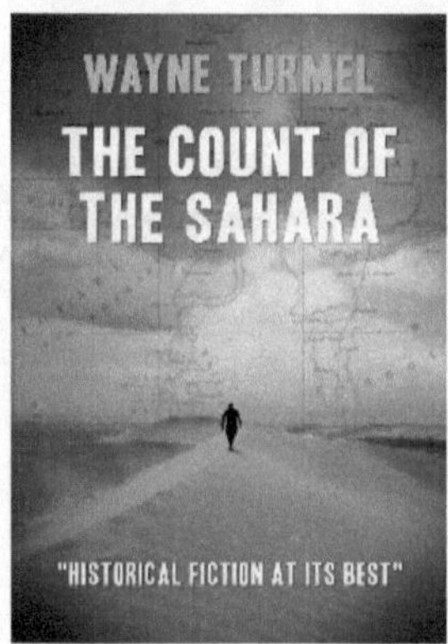

THE COUNT OF THE SAHARA
by Wayne Turmel

A young man trying to make his way in the world meets an ill-fated man quickly heading towards the end of his.

The Count of the Sahara is the story of an archaeological explorer desperately seeking fame in the harsh African desert, the men who would have him fail and a young man who sees through his faults.

FREE with Kindle Unlimited and available in paperback!

CRIMINAL JUSTICE
by Ian Robinson

An undercover cop starts walking a thin line when he infiltrates a criminal gang. He sees an opportunity to make some money and take down a pretty nasty felon, but his own boss DCI Klara Winter is on to him. Can he get out of a very sticky situation before his identity and intentions are revealed?

FREE with Kindle Unlimited and available in paperback!

Sign up to our mailing list to find out about new releases and special offers!

www.thebookfolks.com